WHEN YOU'RE SILENT

(A Finn Wright FBI Suspense Thriller—Book Six)

BLAKE PIERCE

Blake Pierce

Blake Pierce is the USA Today bestselling author of the RILEY PAGE mystery series, which includes seventeen books. Blake Pierce is also the author of the MACKENZIE WHITE mystery series, comprising fourteen books; of the AVERY BLACK mystery series, comprising six books; of the KERI LOCKE mystery series, comprising five books; of the MAKING OF RILEY PAIGE mystery series, comprising six books; of the KATE WISE mystery series, comprising seven books; of the CHLOE FINE psychological suspense mystery, comprising six books; of the JESSIE HUNT psychological suspense thriller series, comprising thirty-seven books (and counting); of the AU PAIR psychological suspense thriller series, comprising three books; of the ZOE PRIME mystery series, comprising six books; of the ADELE SHARP mystery series, comprising sixteen books, of the EUROPEAN VOYAGE cozy mystery series, comprising six books; of the LAURA FROST FBI suspense thriller, comprising eleven books; of the ELLA DARK FBI suspense thriller, comprising twenty-one books (and counting); of the A YEAR IN EUROPE cozy mystery series, comprising nine books, of the AVA GOLD mystery series, comprising six books; of the RACHEL GIFT mystery series, comprising fifteen books (and counting); of the VALERIE LAW mystery series, comprising nine books; of the PAIGE KING mystery series, comprising eight books; of the MAY MOORE mystery series, comprising eleven books; of the CORA SHIELDS mystery series, comprising eight books; of the NICKY LYONS mystery series, comprising eight books, of the CAMI LARK mystery series, comprising ten books; of the AMBER YOUNG mystery series, comprising seven books (and counting); of the DAISY FORTUNE mystery series, comprising five books; of the FIONA RED mystery series, comprising thirteen books (and counting); of the FAITH BOLD mystery series, comprising fourteen books (and counting); of the JULIETTE HART mystery series, comprising five books (and counting); of the MORGAN CROSS mystery series, comprising eleven books (and counting); of the FINN WRIGHT mystery series, comprising seven books (and counting); of the new SHEILA STONE suspense thriller series, comprising five books (and counting); and of the new RACHEL BLACKWOOD suspense thriller series, comprising five books (and counting).

An avid reader and lifelong fan of the mystery and thriller genres,

Blake loves to hear from you, so please feel free to visit www.blakepierceauthor.com to learn more and stay in touch.

Copyright © 2024 by Blake Pierce. All rights reserved. Except as permitted under the U.S. Copyright Act of 1976, no part of this publication may be reproduced, distributed or transmitted in any form or by any means, or stored in a database or retrieval system, without the prior permission of the author. This ebook is licensed for your personal enjoyment only. This ebook may not be re-sold or given away to other people. If you would like to share this book with another person, please purchase an additional copy for each recipient. If you're reading this book and did not purchase it, or it was not purchased for your use only, then please return it and purchase your own copy. Thank you for respecting the hard work of this author. This is a work of fiction. Names, characters, businesses, organizations, places, events, and incidents either are the product of the author's imagination or are used fictionally. Any resemblance to actual persons, living or dead, is entirely coincidental. Jacket image Copyright Rory Bowcott used under license from Shutterstock.com.
ISBN: 978-1-0943-8503-7

BOOKS BY BLAKE PIERCE

RACHEL BLACKWOOD SUSPENSE THRILLER
NOT THIS WAY (Book #1)
NOT THIS TIME (Book #2)
NOT THIS CLOSE (Book #3)
NOT THIS ROAD (Book #4)
NOT THIS LATE (Book #5)

SHEILA STONE SUSPENSE THRILLER
SILENT GIRL (Book #1)
SILENT TRAIL (Book #2)
SILENT NIGHT (Book #3)
SILENT HOUSE (Book #4)
SILENT SCREAM (Book #5)

FINN WRIGHT MYSTERY SERIES
WHEN YOU'RE MINE (Book #1)
WHEN YOU'RE SAFE (Book #2)
WHEN YOU'RE CLOSE (Book #3)
WHEN YOU'RE SLEEPING (Book #4)
WHEN YOU'RE SANE (Book #5)
WHEN YOU'RE SILENT (Book #6)
WHEN YOU'RE GONE (Book #7)

MORGAN CROSS MYSTERY SERIES
FOR YOU (Book #1)
FOR RAGE (Book #2)
FOR LUST (Book #3)
FOR WRATH (Book #4)
FOREVER (Book #5)
FOR US (Book #6)
FOR NOW (Book #7)
FOR ONCE (Book #8)
FOR ETERNITY (Book #9)
FORLORN (Book #10)
FOR SILENCE (Book #11)

JULIETTE HART MYSTERY SERIES
NOTHING TO FEAR (Book #1)
NOTHING THERE (Book #2)
NOTHING WATCHING (Book #3)
NOTHING HIDING (Book #4)
NOTHING LEFT (Book #5)

FAITH BOLD MYSTERY SERIES
SO LONG (Book #1)
SO COLD (Book #2)
SO SCARED (Book #3)
SO NORMAL (Book #4)
SO FAR GONE (Book #5)
SO LOST (Book #6)
SO ALONE (Book #7)
SO FORGOTTEN (Book #8)
SO INSANE (Book #9)
SO SMITTEN (Book #10)
SO SIMPLE (Book #11)
SO BROKEN (Book #12)
SO CRUEL (Book #13)
SO HAUNTED (Book #14)

FIONA RED MYSTERY SERIES
LET HER GO (Book #1)
LET HER BE (Book #2)
LET HER HOPE (Book #3)
LET HER WISH (Book #4)
LET HER LIVE (Book #5)
LET HER RUN (Book #6)
LET HER HIDE (Book #7)
LET HER BELIEVE (Book #8)
LET HER FORGET (Book #9)
LET HER TRY (Book #10)
LET HER PLAY (Book #11)
LET HER VANISH (Book #12)
LET HER FADE (Book #13)

DAISY FORTUNE MYSTERY SERIES

NEED YOU (Book #1)
CLAIM YOU (Book #2)
CRAVE YOU (Book #3)
CHOOSE YOU (Book #4)
CHASE YOU (Book #5)

AMBER YOUNG MYSTERY SERIES
ABSENT PITY (Book #1)
ABSENT REMORSE (Book #2)
ABSENT FEELING (Book #3)
ABSENT MERCY (Book #4)
ABSENT REASON (Book #5)
ABSENT SANITY (Book #6)
ABSENT LIFE (Book #7)

CAMI LARK MYSTERY SERIES
JUST ME (Book #1)
JUST OUTSIDE (Book #2)
JUST RIGHT (Book #3)
JUST FORGET (Book #4)
JUST ONCE (Book #5)
JUST HIDE (Book #6)
JUST NOW (Book #7)
JUST HOPE (Book #8)
JUST LEAVE (Book #9)
JUST TONIGHT (Book #10)

NICKY LYONS MYSTERY SERIES
ALL MINE (Book #1)
ALL HIS (Book #2)
ALL HE SEES (Book #3)
ALL ALONE (Book #4)
ALL FOR ONE (Book #5)
ALL HE TAKES (Book #6)
ALL FOR ME (Book #7)
ALL IN (Book #8)

CORA SHIELDS MYSTERY SERIES
UNDONE (Book #1)
UNWANTED (Book #2)

UNHINGED (Book #3)
UNSAID (Book #4)
UNGLUED (Book #5)
UNSTABLE (Book #6)
UNKNOWN (Book #7)
UNAWARE (Book #8)

MAY MOORE SUSPENSE THRILLER
NEVER RUN (Book #1)
NEVER TELL (Book #2)
NEVER LIVE (Book #3)
NEVER HIDE (Book #4)
NEVER FORGIVE (Book #5)
NEVER AGAIN (Book #6)
NEVER LOOK BACK (Book #7)
NEVER FORGET (Book #8)
NEVER LET GO (Book #9)
NEVER PRETEND (Book #10)
NEVER HESITATE (Book #11)

PAIGE KING MYSTERY SERIES
THE GIRL HE PINED (Book #1)
THE GIRL HE CHOSE (Book #2)
THE GIRL HE TOOK (Book #3)
THE GIRL HE WISHED (Book #4)
THE GIRL HE CROWNED (Book #5)
THE GIRL HE WATCHED (Book #6)
THE GIRL HE WANTED (Book #7)
THE GIRL HE CLAIMED (Book #8)

VALERIE LAW MYSTERY SERIES
NO MERCY (Book #1)
NO PITY (Book #2)
NO FEAR (Book #3)
NO SLEEP (Book #4)
NO QUARTER (Book #5)
NO CHANCE (Book #6)
NO REFUGE (Book #7)
NO GRACE (Book #8)
NO ESCAPE (Book #9)

RACHEL GIFT MYSTERY SERIES
HER LAST WISH (Book #1)
HER LAST CHANCE (Book #2)
HER LAST HOPE (Book #3)
HER LAST FEAR (Book #4)
HER LAST CHOICE (Book #5)
HER LAST BREATH (Book #6)
HER LAST MISTAKE (Book #7)
HER LAST DESIRE (Book #8)
HER LAST REGRET (Book #9)
HER LAST HOUR (Book #10)
HER LAST SHOT (Book #11)
HER LAST PRAYER (Book #12)
HER LAST LIE (Book #13)
HER LAST WHISPER (Book #14)
HER LAST SECRET (Book #15)

AVA GOLD MYSTERY SERIES
CITY OF PREY (Book #1)
CITY OF FEAR (Book #2)
CITY OF BONES (Book #3)
CITY OF GHOSTS (Book #4)
CITY OF DEATH (Book #5)
CITY OF VICE (Book #6)

A YEAR IN EUROPE
A MURDER IN PARIS (Book #1)
DEATH IN FLORENCE (Book #2)
VENGEANCE IN VIENNA (Book #3)
A FATALITY IN SPAIN (Book #4)

ELLA DARK FBI SUSPENSE THRILLER
GIRL, ALONE (Book #1)
GIRL, TAKEN (Book #2)
GIRL, HUNTED (Book #3)
GIRL, SILENCED (Book #4)
GIRL, VANISHED (Book 5)
GIRL ERASED (Book #6)
GIRL, FORSAKEN (Book #7)

GIRL, TRAPPED (Book #8)
GIRL, EXPENDABLE (Book #9)
GIRL, ESCAPED (Book #10)
GIRL, HIS (Book #11)
GIRL, LURED (Book #12)
GIRL, MISSING (Book #13)
GIRL, UNKNOWN (Book #14)
GIRL, DECEIVED (Book #15)
GIRL, FORLORN (Book #16)
GIRL, REMADE (Book #17)
GIRL, BETRAYED (Book #18)
GIRL, BOUND (Book #19)
GIRL, REFORMED (Book #20)
GIRL, REBORN (Book #21)

LAURA FROST FBI SUSPENSE THRILLER
ALREADY GONE (Book #1)
ALREADY SEEN (Book #2)
ALREADY TRAPPED (Book #3)
ALREADY MISSING (Book #4)
ALREADY DEAD (Book #5)
ALREADY TAKEN (Book #6)
ALREADY CHOSEN (Book #7)
ALREADY LOST (Book #8)
ALREADY HIS (Book #9)
ALREADY LURED (Book #10)
ALREADY COLD (Book #11)

EUROPEAN VOYAGE COZY MYSTERY SERIES
MURDER (AND BAKLAVA) (Book #1)
DEATH (AND APPLE STRUDEL) (Book #2)
CRIME (AND LAGER) (Book #3)
MISFORTUNE (AND GOUDA) (Book #4)
CALAMITY (AND A DANISH) (Book #5)
MAYHEM (AND HERRING) (Book #6)

ADELE SHARP MYSTERY SERIES
LEFT TO DIE (Book #1)
LEFT TO RUN (Book #2)
LEFT TO HIDE (Book #3)

LEFT TO KILL (Book #4)
LEFT TO MURDER (Book #5)
LEFT TO ENVY (Book #6)
LEFT TO LAPSE (Book #7)
LEFT TO VANISH (Book #8)
LEFT TO HUNT (Book #9)
LEFT TO FEAR (Book #10)
LEFT TO PREY (Book #11)
LEFT TO LURE (Book #12)
LEFT TO CRAVE (Book #13)
LEFT TO LOATHE (Book #14)
LEFT TO HARM (Book #15)
LEFT TO RUIN (Book #16)

THE AU PAIR SERIES
ALMOST GONE (Book#1)
ALMOST LOST (Book #2)
ALMOST DEAD (Book #3)

ZOE PRIME MYSTERY SERIES
FACE OF DEATH (Book#1)
FACE OF MURDER (Book #2)
FACE OF FEAR (Book #3)
FACE OF MADNESS (Book #4)
FACE OF FURY (Book #5)
FACE OF DARKNESS (Book #6)

A JESSIE HUNT PSYCHOLOGICAL SUSPENSE SERIES
THE PERFECT WIFE (Book #1)
THE PERFECT BLOCK (Book #2)
THE PERFECT HOUSE (Book #3)
THE PERFECT SMILE (Book #4)
THE PERFECT LIE (Book #5)
THE PERFECT LOOK (Book #6)
THE PERFECT AFFAIR (Book #7)
THE PERFECT ALIBI (Book #8)
THE PERFECT NEIGHBOR (Book #9)
THE PERFECT DISGUISE (Book #10)
THE PERFECT SECRET (Book #11)
THE PERFECT FAÇADE (Book #12)

THE PERFECT IMPRESSION (Book #13)
THE PERFECT DECEIT (Book #14)
THE PERFECT MISTRESS (Book #15)
THE PERFECT IMAGE (Book #16)
THE PERFECT VEIL (Book #17)
THE PERFECT INDISCRETION (Book #18)
THE PERFECT RUMOR (Book #19)
THE PERFECT COUPLE (Book #20)
THE PERFECT MURDER (Book #21)
THE PERFECT HUSBAND (Book #22)
THE PERFECT SCANDAL (Book #23)
THE PERFECT MASK (Book #24)
THE PERFECT RUSE (Book #25)
THE PERFECT VENEER (Book #26)
THE PERFECT PEOPLE (Book #27)
THE PERFECT WITNESS (Book #28)
THE PERFECT APPEARANCE (Book #29)
THE PERFECT TRAP (Book #30)
THE PERFECT EXPRESSION (Book #31)
THE PERFECT ACCOMPLICE (Book #32)
THE PERFECT SHOW (Book #33)
THE PERFECT POISE (Book #34)
THE PERFECT CROWD (Book #35)
THE PERFECT CRIME (Book #36)
THE PERFECT PREY (Book #37)

CHLOE FINE PSYCHOLOGICAL SUSPENSE SERIES
NEXT DOOR (Book #1)
A NEIGHBOR'S LIE (Book #2)
CUL DE SAC (Book #3)
SILENT NEIGHBOR (Book #4)
HOMECOMING (Book #5)
TINTED WINDOWS (Book #6)

KATE WISE MYSTERY SERIES
IF SHE KNEW (Book #1)
IF SHE SAW (Book #2)
IF SHE RAN (Book #3)
IF SHE HID (Book #4)
IF SHE FLED (Book #5)

IF SHE FEARED (Book #6)
IF SHE HEARD (Book #7)

THE MAKING OF RILEY PAIGE SERIES
WATCHING (Book #1)
WAITING (Book #2)
LURING (Book #3)
TAKING (Book #4)
STALKING (Book #5)
KILLING (Book #6)

RILEY PAIGE MYSTERY SERIES
ONCE GONE (Book #1)
ONCE TAKEN (Book #2)
ONCE CRAVED (Book #3)
ONCE LURED (Book #4)
ONCE HUNTED (Book #5)
ONCE PINED (Book #6)
ONCE FORSAKEN (Book #7)
ONCE COLD (Book #8)
ONCE STALKED (Book #9)
ONCE LOST (Book #10)
ONCE BURIED (Book #11)
ONCE BOUND (Book #12)
ONCE TRAPPED (Book #13)
ONCE DORMANT (Book #14)
ONCE SHUNNED (Book #15)
ONCE MISSED (Book #16)
ONCE CHOSEN (Book #17)

MACKENZIE WHITE MYSTERY SERIES
BEFORE HE KILLS (Book #1)
BEFORE HE SEES (Book #2)
BEFORE HE COVETS (Book #3)
BEFORE HE TAKES (Book #4)
BEFORE HE NEEDS (Book #5)
BEFORE HE FEELS (Book #6)
BEFORE HE SINS (Book #7)
BEFORE HE HUNTS (Book #8)
BEFORE HE PREYS (Book #9)

BEFORE HE LONGS (Book #10)
BEFORE HE LAPSES (Book #11)
BEFORE HE ENVIES (Book #12)
BEFORE HE STALKS (Book #13)
BEFORE HE HARMS (Book #14)

AVERY BLACK MYSTERY SERIES
CAUSE TO KILL (Book #1)
CAUSE TO RUN (Book #2)
CAUSE TO HIDE (Book #3)
CAUSE TO FEAR (Book #4)
CAUSE TO SAVE (Book #5)
CAUSE TO DREAD (Book #6)

KERI LOCKE MYSTERY SERIES
A TRACE OF DEATH (Book #1)
A TRACE OF MURDER (Book #2)
A TRACE OF VICE (Book #3)
A TRACE OF CRIME (Book #4)
A TRACE OF HOPE (Book #5)

PROLOGUE

Dominique Plantagenet felt divine as she glided through the opulence of the grand hall, her presence a radiant beacon that drew admiring gazes and envious whispers. Dressed in a gown of emerald silk that whispered against her skin with every step, she charmed the glittering crowd with the ease of one born to stand in the spotlight. The party, thrown by the network to celebrate the release of her latest series, was an homage to the Golden Age of Television, and Dominique was its undisputed queen.

A string quartet played melodious strains from a raised dais, their classical notes weaving between the laughter and conversations that filled the air like champagne bubbles. Servers in crisp black and white maneuvered deftly through the throng, offering delicate canapes and flutes of sparkling wine from silver trays. The clinking of glasses provided a rhythmic undertone to the festivities, punctuated by the occasional burst of genuine mirth from someone particularly taken by a jest or anecdote.

Yet, despite the allure of the celebration, a sense of confinement began to press upon Dominique's chest, the air thick with perfume and the heat of too many bodies in too small a space. Her smile remained unbroken, her laughter still rang clear, but her eyes, those windows to a soul yearning for a moment of reprieve, betrayed her longing for escape. She excused herself from a circle of producers who were hanging on her every word, feigning a need for some fresh air that no one could rightly begrudge.

The gardens of the estate stretched out before her, a sprawling testament to meticulous design and horticultural mastery. Even in the bleakest January, they were mesmerizing. Moonlight bathed the scene in ethereal silver, transforming the perfectly trimmed hedges and leafless trees into a dreamscape. Dominique took in a deep breath, the icy night air invigorating her senses, cleansing her palate of the cloying sweetness and heat of the party within.

She moved with purposeful grace along the pebbled paths that wound through a rock garden, her footsteps soft but assured. The solitude of the garden was a balm to her spirit, allowing her the luxury of introspection amidst the revelry that continued unabated behind her. It was here, beneath the watchful gaze of ancient oaks and the vigor of a biting breeze, that Dominique found the solace she sought. For a fleeting moment, she was not the star adored by millions, but simply a woman taking pleasure in the tranquility of nature.

Her thoughts meandered like the very paths she trod, touching upon memories of early auditions, long nights spent poring over scripts, and the tireless pursuit of her craft. Here, away from the limelight, Dominique could almost forget the relentless pace of her career and the ever-present expectation to dazzle and perform. Almost.

Dominique's heels clicked against the cobblestone, a staccato rhythm that accompanied the beating of her heart. The laughter and music from the party dimmed as she ventured deeper into the labyrinth of hedges and rocks, which hid sleeping bulbs waiting for the Spring. Their towering forms seemed to close in around her, whispering secrets in the rustling of hedge leaves and through bare tree branches, moving like they were conducting the night. She felt the distinct sensation of being observed, though by what or whom she could not tell. Shadows played tricks on her imagination, conjuring phantoms in the corners of her vision.

A sudden gust of wind sent a shiver down her spine. The air, previously balmy and scented with the perfume of roses and jasmine, now carried an inexplicable chill that seemed to seep through her silk dress and cling to her skin. Her breath formed a mist before her lips, and for a moment, Dominique hesitated, the sense of unease growing stronger. She wrapped her arms around herself, seeking the warmth that the night no longer offered.

Dominique pressed on, determined not to let her nerves get the better of her. But something primal and instinctive within her whispered caution, urging her to be aware of the silent threat she felt looming just beyond the veil of darkness. She knew these gardens like the lines of her favorite script, and yet tonight, each turn seemed to lead her further from safety and deeper into uncertainty.

As she rounded a bend, the crisp silhouette of a man emerged from the shadows, standing motionless as if he had been waiting for her. No words passed his lips; instead, he extended a hand, palm upturned. Resting upon his gloved fingers was a ring, its band thick and dark as the night itself, crowned with a signet that bore an emblem unknown to her. It was a grotesque thing, wrought with meticulous detail that spoke of a bygone era — an insignia that had no place in the modern world, yet there it was, as real as the dread pooling in her stomach.

Dominique's eyes flicked from the ring to the man's obscured face, searching for some hint of his intentions. But he remained as still as a statue, the only movement the occasional glint of moonlight reflecting off the metallic surface of the ring. That emblem seemed to pulse with a malevolent life of its own, its design intricate and menacing, a herald of ill tidings.

The air between them thrummed with tension, charged with unspoken threats that hung heavy as the scent of impending rain. Dominique's breath hitched in her throat, the sound deafeningly loud in the silence that enveloped them. There was no mistaking the danger this stranger presented, no denying the visceral fear that gripped her. In that eternal moment, time itself seemed to hold its breath, waiting for the inevitable to unfold in the quiet of the garden maze.

Dominique's heart raced as the ring before her seemed to pulse with a dark life of its own. The man, shrouded in shadow, remained motionless, his intentions inscrutable yet undeniably sinister. Dominique felt a scream building within her, a primal urge for survival pushing against her silent lips. But when the figure lunged forward, reality twisted cruelly—her vocal cords betrayed her, yielding nothing but a silent gasp.

Panic surged through Dominique's veins as she recoiled from the advance. Her mind, usually so adept at portraying characters who faced danger with poise, now scrambled frantically for a way out. Muscle memory from countless hours on set kicked in; she feinted to the left, hoping to slip past him, but the man anticipated her every move. He matched her step for step, his movements deliberate and terrifyingly assured.

The garden that had once been a sanctuary now felt like an elaborate trap, each manicured hedge a barrier to her escape. She darted down one path, then another, the gravel beneath her designer heels giving way to the soft earth of less-trodden ways. Her breath came in ragged bursts, fogging in the cool night air as she pushed her body to its limits.

But it was futile. The labyrinthine design of the hedges ensnared her just as effectively as any snare. With a final desperate turn, she found herself backed against the unforgiving surface of a cold stone wall. The ivy that crept over it scratched at her bare shoulders, a stark against the silk of her gown. Trapped, her gaze flickered to the man, searching for mercy where she knew none would be found.

And there it was—the last thing Dominique Plantagenet saw: the cruel glint of moonlight upon a blade. It gleamed with a malevolence that chilled her to the core, its edge sharp and unyielding as the line between life and death. No longer part of the shadows, the blade was an entity unto itself, an extension of the man's will, and the instrument of Dominique's dread realization.

Time slowed, each second stretching into eternity as the moonlight played along the weapon's steel. Dominique's eyes traced the length of the blade, from tip to hilt, as if by understanding its form, she might somehow escape its fate. Her breaths, once heaving, became shallow whispers against the weight of her terror.

In those fleeting moments, her thoughts raced back to the bright lights of the party, the laughter, and the clinking glasses, all now worlds away. How quickly the scene had turned from revelry to nightmare, the gardens from an idyllic retreat to a stage for her final act. Dominique, with her career built upon delving into others' stories, was now ensnared in a chilling narrative of her own, one with an ending she could not rewrite.

Dominique's heart pounded in her chest, a frantic drumbeat attempting to escape the confines of her body. The garden's nocturnal symphony fell silent. All that remained was her ragged breathing and the sinister whisper of leaves as the shadowy figure advanced. The cold stone pressed against her back, unyielding and as chilling as the fingers of dread that clutched her throat. Her assailant's face, a mask of malice, offered no glimpse of humanity—just a harbinger of the grim reaper come to claim another soul.

With an almost surgical precision, he struck. The sound—a horrific parody of a butcher's cleaver partitioning meat—reverberated through the quietude of the estate grounds. Dominique's eyes, wide with the incredulity of one betrayed by their own mortality, mirrored the moon above. Even as the blade sank deep, she sought to comprehend this brutal conclusion to her tale. Her mind raced, desperate for the curtain call that would end this gruesome act.

Pain erupted, a searing firebrand carving her flesh. It spread like wildfire, consuming all rational thought, leaving behind only primal fear. She gasped, a feeble attempt to draw breath, but the air became a luxury beyond reach. The world seemed to tilt, skewed on an axis of agony and terror. Yet, amidst the chaos, an odd detachment crept in—a spectator to her own demise.

The figure before her blurred, his features dissolving into the night as if he were nothing more than mist. The garden, once a sanctuary of solitude and reflection, transformed into her stage of final performance. Petals of roses scattered at her feet, a tragic audience witnessing her fall from grace. Each thorn now felt like an accusation, a reminder of vulnerability in a role she had never auditioned for.

As consciousness fled, the stark contrast between the life she lived and the death she faced struck her with poignant clarity. No encore awaited; this scene would not be repeated. Her legacy set in the echoes of a single, brutal act. And then darkness enfolded her, the last shreds of awareness slipping away like the final notes of a requiem.

Dominique Plantagenet, whose name had once glittered on marquees and whispered through the halls of television studios, had been silenced. Not with the applause she was accustomed to, but with the harsh punctuation of steel severing life. The gardens, which mere hours ago resonated with celebration, now hosted a macabre dance where the only partner was death itself.

CHAPTER ONE

Finn's muscles tensed as he faced the imposing, aged door of the cellar. He could taste the stale air that hung heavy around the large building—a remnant of its storied past. His shoulder squared against the wood, a shiver of anticipation snaking up his spine. This was it. The culmination of weeks of pursuing Max Vilne, the man who had turned Finn's life into a waking nightmare.

With a grunt of exertion and pent-up fury, Finn launched himself forward. The lock splintered under his weight; the door giving way with a protesting groan and a cloud of dust that seemed to have been lying in wait for decades. As the particles danced in the slivers of light penetrating the gloom, Finn stepped over the threshold. His heart hammered in his chest not just from the physical effort, but from the hope that he was finally closing in on Vilne—and Demi.

The room was a cavernous space filled with relics of bygone eras. Wooden crates, stacked haphazardly, bore the scars of time: faded labels, frayed ropes, and the musty scent of abandonment. His eyes darted across the shadows, searching for any sign of life, any hint of movement. But there was nothing—no Demi, no Vilne. Only silence met his ears, a silence that seemed to mock his desperation.

His gaze fell upon a piece of paper carelessly placed atop one of the crates near the center of the room. The scrawl was unmistakable—Max Vilne's taunting script. Finn's hand trembled as he reached for the note, every muscle in his body coiled tight. The words were a knife, twisting deep.

"Always one step ahead, Wright. Isn't this what you wanted? A game of wits?"

Finn crushed the note in his fist, the paper crumpling like the sound of breaking bones. His eyes burned, not with tears, but with an unquenchable fire of resolve. Max was playing with him, turning the hunt into a perverse form of entertainment.

And then Finn's breath hitched. There, placed with deliberate care on a rickety wooden chair, was a shoe—a dainty thing, incongruous in this place of decay. Demi's shoe. The sight of it, so small and vulnerable, was a visceral blow to Finn's gut.

The shoe was pristine, almost gleaming against the dust-covered floor, as if it were an exhibit rather than a forgotten item. It was a message, a statement from Vilne. He might as well have been standing there, smirking at Finn with that ice-cold gaze of his. Finn was sure he had had him this time, certain Max was there in that cellar.

Finn crouched beside the shoe, a surge of memories flooding through him—the shape of Demi's foot sliding into it, the laughter they shared on evenings out when the world felt kinder. Now, it was a symbol of her peril, a beacon of urgency that propelled Finn forward. His hands clenched into fists, the note still wrinkled within his grasp.

"Damn you, Vilne," he muttered under his breath. He stood up, setting his jaw. The chase wasn't over; it was merely entering its next harrowing phase. Finn knew he couldn't afford the luxury of grief or fear—not yet. There would be time for that later, after he saved Demi, after he ended this once and for all.

He pocketed the solitary shoe, a tangible piece of Demi to keep him anchored to the reality of his mission. The cellar, with its stagnant air and oppressive silence, was just another riddle in Max Vilne's twisted game, but Finn Wright was no stranger to puzzles. With renewed determination, he prepared to delve deeper into the labyrinth, knowing that each step took him closer to the woman he'd failed once, but vowed never to fail again.

Finn's pulse thudded in his ears, a rhythm that matched the ticking clock of Demi's fate. He surveyed the dank cellar once more, the shadows seeming to mock him with their secrets. The scent of dust and old wood was thick, but underneath it all lingered the faintest trace of Demi's perfume, a whisper of jasmine that cut through the darkness like a knife's edge.

The sound of hurried footsteps broke the silence, and Amelia Winters burst into the room, her chest rising and falling rapidly from exertion. Her green eyes darted across the crates, taking in the scene with the precision of a hawk. She caught Finn's gaze, her expression a mix of frustration and concern.

"Where is she, Finn?" Amelia's voice was sharp, every word edged with a shared urgency.

"I thought we were on his tail," Finn replied, his voice low and tense. "Vilne was here. I'm certain of it." His hand went to his pocket, feeling the shape of Demi's shoe through the fabric—an anchor in this storm of chaos.

Amelia moved closer, her eyes never leaving his. "He's playing with us, isn't he? But how does he stay one step ahead?"

"Because he enjoys the game," Finn said, bitterness lacing his words. "Max Vilne doesn't just want to win; he wants to see us lose."

"Then let's disappoint him." Amelia stepped back, her eyes scanning the room anew, searching for something they might have missed. "We've got eyes on this place. Surveillance should have picked up where he took her."

"Should have," Finn echoed, a muscle in his jaw twitching. "But Vilne knows our moves before we make them. He's always been good at anticipation."

"Let's get upstairs. We can check the security feeds, see exactly where he exited the building with Demi." Amelia's voice was steady now, her initial rush of adrenaline giving way to the calculated calm of an experienced investigator.

"Right," Finn agreed, pushing past the hollow feeling in his stomach. He followed Amelia out of the oppressive cellar, each step heavy with the weight of responsibility. He couldn't shake the image of Demi's shoe on the chair, a taunt designed to unravel him. Max Vilne wanted a reaction, but Finn would give him nothing. Instead, he would be the relentless force that finally put an end to Vilne's sadistic spree.

Finn's gaze darted around the cellar. The shadows cast by the scant light seemed to mock his desperation. The room was a tableau of abandonment; old crates huddled against the walls like silent sentinels of forgotten wares. A shiver of urgency ran through him as his eyes caught an anomaly on the floor, a trail that disrupted the thick dust—a tangible sign of struggle. Finn approached a particularly large crate, its wood bloated with age; it looked out of place somehow. His hands, driven by instinct honed from years in the field, reached out and he shoved the crate aside.

The sound of wood scraping against concrete reverberated through the quiet like a thunderclap, setting his nerves on edge. Beneath where the crate had stood was a hatch, metal edges eaten away by rust, a relic hidden beneath layers of time. He could feel Amelia's presence behind him, her breaths measured but quick. "That looks like part of an old service tunnel network," she observed, her voice low but carrying easily in the confined space. "From the Victorian era, I'd wager. They run like veins beneath London."

Finn didn't respond, his focus narrowing to the task at hand. Crouching, he felt along the hatch's edge for a grip. His fingertips found purchase on a ring pull, iron cold and unyielding. With a grunt of exertion, he yanked upward. The hatch resisted, before yielding with a groan of neglected hinges, revealing a gaping maw that led into darkness below.

"Ready?" he asked, not waiting for confirmation as he swung his legs into the void, feeling a rush of cooler air from the tunnel greet him. The descent was short, his boots connecting solidly with the damp earth below. He extended a hand upwards, supporting Amelia as she followed suit, her lithe form descending gracefully into the cramped quarters of the tunnel.

They stood side by side in the pitch blackness, the clamor of the outside world muffled by layers of earth and stone. The darkness was total, oppressive, as if it sought to swallow them whole. Finn could hear Amelia's steady breathing, a comforting counterpoint to the hammering of his own heart. His fingers brushed against the rough texture of the tunnel wall, tracing the damp bricks laid centuries ago, each one a silent witness to history—and now, to their urgent pursuit.

"Stay close," he whispered, his voice barely above the sound of water trickling somewhere in the unseen distance. The need to find Demi, to ensure her safety, tightened his chest like a vice. Max Vilne had taken more than enough from him, from all those who crossed the killer's path. Finn vowed silently that this chase would end differently.

Finn's hand hovered in the void, fumbling for a light switch that didn't exist. He cursed under his breath, the pitch-black tunnel pressing against him with a weight that felt almost physical. His sense of sight stripped away, every other sensation seemed amplified—the cool, musty air brushing against his skin, the distant drip of water echoing from the depths, the soft scuff of Amelia's boots on the earthen floor.

"Here," Amelia's voice cut through the darkness, a small click followed by a narrow beam of light piercing the shadows. The flashlight in her hand was a slender lifeline in the oppressive dark. Finn blinked against the sudden brightness, chastising himself inwardly for his lack of foresight.

"Left mine back in the car," he muttered, his words an admittance of uncharacteristic negligence.

"Thought you were a scout when you were a kid? 'Be prepared', isn't that what they say?" There was a hint of teasing in Amelia's tone, but her eyes remained fixed ahead, the light revealing the contours of the tunnel—a rib cage of arches and pipework overhead, like the skeletal remains of some ancient leviathan.

"We also learned never to lift people up, not kick them down," Finn replied, a wry smile flickering across his face before determination settled back onto his features like a familiar mask. He stepped forward, his eyes adjusting to rely on the slim beacon Amelia provided. Every fiber of his being was tuned to the task at hand—finding Demi, alive and unharmed, the hopeful refrain playing on loop in his mind.

The two investigators moved cautiously, the beam of the flashlight casting long, dancing shadows as it swept over the walls. They proceeded in a tense silence, their senses straining for any sign, any clue that might lead them to Demi. And then, there it was—a glint of moisture on the ground caught in the artificial light.

"Stop," Finn said abruptly, holding out an arm to halt Amelia's advance. He crouched down, the muscles in his legs taut as he inspected the wet footprints and the accompanying drag marks that scarred the dirt floor. There was no mistaking the pattern—the staggered imprints of a man's heavy boots and the erratic trail of something—or someone; being pulled along.

"Vilne," Finn growled, the name tasting like bile on his tongue. The realization hit him with the force of a blow. Max had been here, had dragged Demi through this very tunnel. The evidence was fresh, the earth still damp beneath his fingertips. It was a silent testament to the struggle that must have played out in the darkness.

"Looks recent," Amelia noted, her voice steady, but Finn could hear the underlying edge of concern.

"Too recent." The words were barely a whisper, a reflection of the cold dread that settled in Finn's stomach. Max Vilne was close, perhaps closer than they imagined. The game of cat-and-mouse was reaching its critical point, and Finn felt the familiar burn of adrenaline fueling his resolve. He would not let this monster slip through his fingers again—not with Demi's life hanging in the balance.

With a nod to Amelia, Finn rose to his feet, his jaw set in firm lines. The chase was on, and he would follow the trail wherever it led. It was more than just a mission; it was a promise, a debt owed to the past and to the woman who had once held his heart. He would find her or die trying.

Finn's pulse hammered in his ears, a rhythm that matched the urgency of their pursuit. The flashlight's beam danced over the slick walls of the tunnel, casting shadows that seemed to writhe in anticipation of what lay ahead. He could feel Amelia's presence beside him, her breaths coming fast but measured, a testament to her training and resolve.

"Be careful," she warned, her voice barely rising above the sound of their footsteps echoing off the stone. "This could be exactly what he wants us to do—walk right into a trap."

He shot her a glance, his blue eyes glinting with an intensity that reflected the gravity of their situation. "There's no time for caution, Amelia," Finn countered, his tone laced with desperation. "Every second we hesitate, Demi's chances get slimmer."

Without waiting for a response, he hastened his pace, his boots sliding on the damp ground as he navigated through the tight space. Amelia kept up, her own determination matching his stride for stride. The darkness seemed to close in around them, a suffocating blanket that threatened to smother all hope. But Finn wouldn't allow it; he couldn't. This was more than a search; it was a race against the ticking clock of a killer's twisted timeline.

Their breaths came out in puffs of white, merging with the cold air of the underground passage. The tunnel stretched on a relentless path that seemed to mock their efforts with its never-ending twists and turns. Finn's mind raced, thoughts colliding with each other—the possibility of losing Demi, the haunting echoes of past failures, and the burning need for justice that had become his life's fuel.

And then, without warning, he saw it—a splash of crimson against the earthen floor. His heart lurched, the sight of the blood sending a jolt of fear through him so potent it was almost physical. It was fresh, too fresh, and it painted a story more harrowing than any words could convey. His gaze followed the trail, and there, just meters away, stood an open door.

The thunderous sound that reached his ears was incongruent with the silence they had been enveloped in just moments before. It was rhythmic and heavy, like machinery or... or something worse. His throat tightened at the thought, the image of Demi lying lifeless on the other side flashing before his eyes.

"Amelia—" he started, but the urgency clawing at his insides left no room for discussion. With a surge of adrenaline, Finn bounded towards the door, leaving unfinished warnings and strategies behind. There was only one thing that mattered now: Demi.

As he neared the threshold, his hand reaching out to push the door wide, the world seemed to hold its breath. Finn stepped through, into the unknown.

CHAPTER TWO

The stale air of the London Underground wrapped around Finn Wright like a suffocating blanket as he and Inspector Amelia Winters emerged from the shadows into the dimly lit tunnel. His boots scuffed against the concrete, the sound echoing off the walls with a hollow persistence that matched the pounding in his chest. The fluorescent lights flickered sporadically overhead, casting an otherworldly glow on the labyrinthine network of tunnels that snaked beneath the city's pulsing heart.

Finn's senses were on high alert, his eyes scanning the depths of the tunnel for any sign of movement. Despite the chill of the subterranean passage, sweat beaded on his brow, a mixture of anticipation and the remnants of fear. Here, in the bowels of London, every shadow seemed like it could conceal Max Vilne's hulking, vengeful outline.

A glint of metal caught his eye from down the tracks, and Finn instinctively reached back to ensure Amelia was close. She was there, her presence a silent reassurance. They moved forward cautiously, their combined experience keeping them vigilant yet ready to act at a moment's notice.

And then they saw them. Not thirty yards ahead, where the tunnel curved gently out of sight, Max Vilne's gaunt figure was illuminated by the harsh lighting. He was half-dragging, half-choking, a woman whose desperate gasps for air sang a discordant melody with the distant rumble of an approaching train. Demi.

"Amelia," Finn breathed, tension coiling like a spring in his gut. His former fiancee's face was contorted in pain and terror, her elegant features marred by the brutal grip of Max's hand around her slender throat. Every protective fiber within him screamed to sprint forward, but years of training held him back. A direct approach would risk Demi's life even more.

Max's head snapped up, his dead eyes locking onto Finn's with a predatory intensity. There was no mistaking the malicious satisfaction that twisted his lips. Demi's eyes were wide, pleading, silently begging for rescue that Finn wasn't sure he could provide fast enough.

"Stay behind me," Finn murmured to Amelia, though he knew she was already calculating the best course of action. Together, they advanced, careful to avoid the telltale third rail that ran parallel to the tracks — a silent, deadly barrier between them and Max's menacing form.

As they closed the gap, Finn kept his gaze fixed on Max, trying to read the intentions of a man whose intellect was rivaled only by his capacity for cruelty. The atmosphere grew heavier with each step, the tension between predator and prey crackling in the air like static before a storm. Finn's mind raced, searching for an opening, a weakness, anything he could use to save Demi without triggering Max's violent impulses.

"Vilne!" Finn called out, his voice steady despite the tempest inside him. Max's response would decide the fates of all four individuals on this desolate stretch of the Underground, and Finn braced himself for the confrontation that would follow.

The chill of the London Underground seeped into Finn's bones as he and Amelia navigated the dimly lit tunnel, their steps echoing off the walls in a haunting cadence. The air was thick with the scent of metal and stale electricity, a constant reminder of the city that pulsed above them.

"Careful," Amelia's voice came through sharp and clear, slicing through the oppressive silence. "Remember, the rails are live. Touch one, and it's over."

Finn nodded, his eyes never leaving the scene unfolding before him. Max had positioned himself on the far side of the electrified rail, Demi's slender form wracked with sobs, her breaths coming in short, panicked gasps. The steely grip Max maintained around her throat was a silent threat, an unspoken promise of violence that hung in the damp air between them.

"Max!" Finn called out again, his voice reverberating off the curved walls. The evil in Max's eyes grinned back at him with a snide arrogance that sent a surge of anger coursing through Finn's veins.

"Ah, Finn, always the hero," Max taunted, his words dripping with disdain as he tightened his hold on Demi, eliciting another whimper from her lips. "But what can you do? Step over the line, and you fry. Stay there, and she dies. Quite the dilemma, isn't it? Don't you love the drama of it all?"

The fluorescent lights flickered overhead, casting erratic shadows across Max's face, giving him an almost demonic appearance. Finn's hands clenched into fists at his sides, every muscle coiled and ready to spring into action.

"Let her go, Max," Finn said, his voice a low growl of barely contained fury. "This is between you and me."

"Is it?" Max's laugh echoed mockingly around them. "You put me in prison to rot, Finn. Now I will eat away at your life like a cancer."

Tears streamed down Demi's cheeks as she struggled to draw breath, her eyes locked on Finn's in a silent plea for salvation. Finn felt a familiar ache in his chest, the memory of their broken relationship mingling with the desperation to save her now.

"Max, think about this," Finn tried to reason. Every instinct telling him that engaging Max in a battle of wits was a precarious path. "What do you gain from hurting her?"

"Gain?" Max's voice was light, almost playful, but the undercurrent of malice was unmistakable. "Oh, Finn, this isn't about gain. It's about sending a message. And the message is clear: no one ruins my plans and walks away unscathed."

Finn's jaw tightened as he took in the sight of Demi, the woman he had once planned to spend his life with, now a pawn in a madman's game. He could see the terror in her eyes, feel the weight of responsibility pressing down on him. He had to end this, but how?

"Think of your legacy, Max," Finn urged, trying a different angle. "You're better than this. You don't have to be remembered as a monster."

"Legacy?" Max scoffed, his grip never wavering. "My dear Finn, we're all monsters here. Some of us just hide it better than others."

Finn's focus didn't waver, his gaze fixed on Max, searching for any sign of remorse or humanity. But all he saw was the facade of a deranged killer, one who reveled in the power he wielded and the chaos he could cause. The challenge was clear; Finn would have to tread carefully, using every ounce of his skill to navigate this deadly chessboard.

The sound of the oncoming train reverberated through the tunnel, a deep and relentless rumble that seemed to shake the very air around Finn. He could feel its approach in his bones, a primal warning of the massive force bearing down upon them. The dim lighting cast an eerie glow on the soot-streaked walls, the shadows dancing wildly as the light flickered with the rhythmic thudding.

"Max!" Finn's voice cut through the noise, urgent but controlled. "This doesn't end well for anyone if you don't let her go."

Max's eyes, dark pits in the gloom, remained fixed on Finn, unblinking and devoid of empathy. The grip he had on Demi's throat was cruel, a vise of malice and control. She gasped for breath, her struggles to weaken against his iron hold.

"Come now, Finn," Max taunted, "You know this is just the final act. The crescendo of our little drama. You can't honestly believe I would simply walk away."

Finn ignored the sting of frustration and the churning dread in his gut. He knew the psychological games Max played all too well; they were a weapon he wielded with the same precision as a surgeon's scalpel. But Finn also knew that any sign of weakness would only embolden Max further.

"Listen to the train, Max. It's the sound of what's coming. You think you've thought of everything, but there's always an endgame. And yours is here, in these tunnels."

As if on cue, the front lights of the train pierced the darkness, casting a glaring spotlight that heralded its unstoppable advance. The ground vibrated more violently now, the rails singing with impending arrival.

"Your endgame perhaps," Max sneered, "but not mine."

Before Finn could respond, movement flickered at the periphery of his vision. On a nearby platform, silhouetted figures emerged from the shadows—police officers in tactical gear, each one poised and ready for action. Their presence was a silent testament to the closing net, the culmination of Finn's meticulous planning.

"Max, look around you!" Finn's voice rose above the growing clamor. "There's nowhere left to go. It's over."

Max glanced sideways, taking in the sight of the authorities with a dispassionate gaze. For a moment, Finn saw something flicker in those cold eyes—a recognition of the odds, perhaps, or the acknowledgment of a cornered animal.

"Over?" Max's lips curled into a mirthless smile. "We've only just begun."

But Finn knew better. He saw the imperceptible shift in Max's stance, the readiness to flee or fight that all predators possessed. Even as the train bore down upon them, hurtling through the tunnel like a metallic beast, Finn knew the encounter was far from concluded. Max Vilne was a master of escape, and as the police closed in, Finn braced himself for the chaos that was sure to follow.

The laughter erupted from Max's throat, a sound so vile and discordant that it seemed to merge with the screech of metal on metal as the train hurtled closer. Finn's muscles coiled like springs, every sinew straining to launch forward.

"Max!" he bellowed. But his plea was drowned out by the cacophony of the approaching train and the echo of Max's malevolence bouncing off the grimy tunnel walls.

With a swift, brutal motion, Max hurled Demi toward the unforgiving steel tracks. Time fractured, distorting into a viscous slow-motion nightmare. Demi's eyes—wide with terror—locked onto Finn's for a fleeting instant that promised an eternity of regret.

"NO!" Finn's cry tore from his chest, a raw explosion of anguish. He lunged, but the distance between them yawned like a chasm. His fingertips grazed nothing but the dank air of the London Underground.

Then Amelia, finding a closer angle, leaped into the fray, a blur of determination and courage. Her body cut through the space between Demi and death, her hand snatching a fistful of Demi's coat just as the girl's limbs flailed over the electrified rail.

With Herculean effort, Amelia hauled Demi back from the precipice, the pair of them tumbling away from the tracks in a tangle of limbs mere moments before the train thundered past. Its wheels screamed a metallic wail that seemed to resonate with Finn's pounding heart.

As the last car blurred by, there stood Max on the opposite side, untouched by the chaos he had conjured. His grin sliced through the lingering dust motes suspended in the air, a Cheshire cat's smile promising more madness to come. There was no triumph in Finn's chest, only the icy grip of dread, knowing that evil incarnate had once again slipped through the fingers of justice.

Max's silhouette flickered, a ghostly mirage against the receding lights of the train. Then, just like smoke drawn into the ether, he was gone. The void where he had stood was now filled with the echoes of his departing laughter, a haunting reminder of the monster who walked among them.

Amelia's breaths came hard and fast, her chest rising and falling with the tempo of survival. She cradled Demi, whose sobs mingled with the fading rumble of the train. For a heartbeat, Finn felt guilt in his bones; the woman he loved consoling the woman to whom he had once been engaged.

But there was no time for such reflections. As the adrenaline ebbed, reality set in like cold steel in Finn's veins. Max Vilne had vanished into the labyrinthine bowels of the city, leaving behind only the sinister promise that this game of cat and mouse was far from over.

"Amelia?" he asked softly.

Amelia nodded. "I'm okay, just cracked my shoulder and back a little, I think."

Finn touched her hand for a moment and she drew it away under the gaze of Demi.

The screech of the train faded into a distant growl, leaving behind an eerie silence that enveloped the London Underground's grimy tunnel. Finn Wright's heart was pounding in his chest, a relentless drumbeat that matched the throbbing pain coursing through his clenched fists. His gaze fixed on Demi, her face streaked with tears and the grime of the track bed, her chest heaving with each terrified breath.

"Hey, hey, look at me," Finn murmured, his voice a soothing balm against the raw edge of panic. He reached out and drew her close, enfolding her in a protective embrace. The warmth of her body, trembling against his, reignited a fierce protectiveness within him. "You're safe now, Demi. You're safe."

He felt her nod, her sobs ebbing as she clung to him, her fingers digging into the fabric of his jacket as if it were a lifeline. Around them, the underground seemed to hold its breath, the darkness oppressive, the walls oozing with the residue of fear and desperation. But here, in the narrow circle of Finn's arms, there was a sanctuary, however fleeting.

"Let's get you out of here," Finn said, his voice steady despite the storm of emotions raging inside him. He helped Demi to her feet, supporting her weight as they began to navigate out of the tunnel. Each step was a defiance, a silent rebuke to the chaos Max Vilne had sought to unleash.

"What did he do to you all this time?" Finn asked, waiting nervously for the answer.

"Nothing," she said. "He didn't want me 'spoiled' before my time, apparently. He fed me, didn't talk to me much, and that was it. The only thing is this." She pulled back the sleeve of her top and revealed a gash in her arm. "I got that when he was dragging me through the tunnels.

"We'll get that looked at," Finn said. "And a therapist might be..."

"I can do that when I get home," Demi said quietly.

The path forward was lit by the intermittent lights that dotted the tunnel, casting elongated shadows that danced macabrely on the curved walls. Twisted metal and shattered concrete bore testament to the violence of recent events, a brutal landscape forged from terror. Yet Finn guided Demi through this post-apocalyptic scene with unwavering resolve, his every sense alert for further danger.

As they approached the mouth of the tunnel, the dim light of the platform filtered in, a promise of safety after the abyss. Finn's eyes met Amelia's, her expression a complex tapestry of relief and concern. Without words, she turned and led the way up the steps to the bustling city above, where life moved on, ignorant of the horror that had unfolded beneath its streets.

Emerging into the night air, Finn blinked against the harsh glare of emergency vehicle lights that painted the scene in stark contrasts of blue and red. Paramedics converged upon them, a whirlwind of efficiency and urgency. They gently ushered Demi onto a waiting gurney, their trained hands moving deftly to assess her injuries.

"Take care of her," Finn implored, his voice almost lost amidst the cacophony of sirens and voices.

Demi looked up from the gurney and held out her hand. Finn took it.

"You're not coming, are you?" she said.

Finn felt his eyes well up with tears. "Vilne is still out there. We can talk about it later, Demi."

"No," she said. "When you've been through something like this, you know life is short and you want to get started on the next chapter as soon as possible. I..."

"Demi, try to rest..."

"Finn," she said through weary eyes. "I came to the UK to persuade you to come home. But you're never coming home, are you? At least, not with me?"

"I don't know where my home is anymore," Finn said softly. "I know it's in the US, but once, it was with us, wherever we would be."

"How did we get so broken?" she said through tears.

"Maybe we weren't broken," Finn added. "Maybe we just didn't fit to begin with. I thought it was the idea of you having an affair that broke us, but it wasn't. I had been too distant from you for too long. That's on me."

"Can't we fix it?" she sobbed.

Finn shook his head. "I love you, Demi. I always will. But sometimes you need more than even that to build a life together. I think you know deep down, we don't have the legs. If it wasn't a year ago that we split up, it would be now, or in a year? Hell, it could have been after we had kids, but one way or the other, we wouldn't have worked. I'm so, so sorry."

Demi covered her mouth with her hands as tears streamed down her cheeks.

Then something surprised Finn. She wiped the tears away and nodded, then said: "I think you're right. I want the Finn, who is works a normal job and comes home each night without the weight of the world on his shoulders. I want his main concern to be what we watch on TV, not untangling a case."

Demi looked at Finn and smiled, kindness in her eyes.

"But then I'd be turning you into someone else," she said. "Seeing you and Amelia chase down Max Vilne, I don't think I can be part of that world. I don't want to wait up each night wondering if I'm going to get a call that you've been hurt or worse."

She squeezed Finn's hand. "I think I'm ready to go home and find out what's next for me."

Finn raised Demi's hand and kissed it. "I hope you find happiness, Demi. You deserve it. And if you're ever in trouble..."

"I know you'll come running," she said, letting go. "Goodbye, Finn Wright."

Finn watched as the ambulance crew attended to Demi, but she seemed to be okay without any visible injuries other than the cut on her arm. The doors closed and Finn felt a mix of relief and pain in his chest, but before he could think through his feelings, he turned and saw a second ambulance; a mirror image of the one that was taking Demi away. All but for the occupant.

He watched, a silent sentinel, as Amelia was lifted into the back of it. She had risked everything to save Demi, her bravery a beacon in the consuming darkness. Even now, as she lay on the stretcher, her determination was palpable—a force not easily extinguished.

"Amelia!" Finn called out, taking a step towards the ambulance as the doors swung open. She turned her head slightly, her eyes locking with his for a charged moment.

"Are you okay?" he asked, running over to her side.

"I'm fine, Finn," she said. She pointed to the two paramedics attending to her. "I just like watching men fuss over me."

"That's why I don't do it," Finn smiled. "But then, that's probably why my love life is the way it is."

Amelia locked eyes with him for a moment. It was as if she were about to say something, to address the closeness that had grown between them, but then her expression changed as though she felt the very talk of it would ruin them.

"No sign of Vilne?" Amelia asked.

"No," said Finn. "Not yet."

"We were so close," Amelia said with a clenched fist, padding her knee. "Can I get up now?" she asked one of the paramedics.

"It looks like you hurt your head and..."

"I'm fine," she said, wincing and stepping off the gurney. "Thank you."

"You should rest," Finn added.

"Every inch of those tunnels will be scoured for Max Vilne," she said, her voice steady despite the fatigue that etched lines into her face. "We'll flush him out."

Finn shook his head, knowing all too well the mind they were up against. "Vilne's not some rat in a sewer," he replied, his gaze fixed on the entrance to the underground station nearby. "He'll have planned this out meticulously. There will be an escape route we haven't found, hidden exits scattered like breadcrumbs only he can see. London has so many abandoned tunnels, if knows of them, he'll use them."

Amelia's eyes held a spark of defiance, but Finn saw the concern there too. "But what he didn't plan was you and me," she countered, her tone softer now.

Finn felt the tightness in his chest ease slightly at her words. "Amelia, your bravery today..." He trailed off, unable to fully articulate his gratitude, the enormity of her actions. "I owe you more than I can ever repay."

The moment hung between them, charged with the unspoken bond of two people who had faced death together and come out the other side. But it was a fleeting connection, soon overshadowed by the gravity of their situation.

"What now?" Amelia asked, breaking the silence as she wrapped her arms around herself, warding off the chill of the winter night.

Finn glanced over at Demi, who stood a few paces away, her face ghostly pale in the half-light. "Demi needs to go home," he said softly. "Away from all this madness, back to safety. I'll speak with my contacts at the Bureau and see if I can get her protected until we catch Vilne."

"And you?" Amelia's question was tentative, probing the wound that was Finn's past.

He let out a long breath, his shoulders tensing. "No, our paths diverged a long time ago." His voice was flat, carrying the weight of a failed relationship, the loss of what could have been. "That chapter has closed"

Turning back to Amelia, Finn met her gaze squarely. "But you... Vilne will see you as the one who took his prize now. He already had you as a possible target because you're close to me. It's possible you're going to be his number one target now. He wants to torture me."

The air seemed to grow colder with his words, the threat against Amelia tangible and immediate. Finn's resolve hardened; he would not let Vilne's vendetta claim anyone else, especially not someone who had shown such courage.

"You need to stay vigilant, Amelia, please," he warned, the urgency clear in his tone. "Max Vilne will want revenge for what you did today."

CHAPTER THREE

Finn Wright's fists were a blur as they hammered against the heavy bag with a rhythmic thud that echoed through the cavernous space of the dilapidated London gym. Each impact sent a jolt up his arm, reverberating in his shoulders and down his spine. The musty scent of sweat and old leather was pungent in the air, mixing with the metallic tang of rust from the aging equipment that surrounded him.

The gym was an island of grit amidst the sprawling city, its walls adorned with peeling posters of boxing legends, the floor littered with chalk dust and discarded wraps. It was here in this temple of controlled violence that Finn sought refuge, a place where he could channel the roiling storm within him into each disciplined strike.

Christmas had come and gone with little fanfare, the festive lights throughout the city doing nothing to pierce the shadow cast by Max Vilne's absence. Somewhere out there, the cunning predator remained at large, his whereabouts as much a mystery as the outcome of Finn's impending court date. That day loomed over Finn like a guillotine, ready to sever his ties with the FBI or absolve him of the unintended consequences of a year-old hostage rescue gone awry. The anticipation gnawed at him, but here, amidst the echoes of punches and the grunts of effort, he found temporary solace.

His breaths came in ragged gasps, steaming in the frigid air as he pushed his body to its limits. Every strike against the bag was a silent declaration—a refusal to be broken by the weight of his past transgressions and the bureaucratic limbo that shackled him. He imagined the bag as his own personal crucible, each punch forging him anew, stronger and more resilient.

But even the pounding rhythm of his training couldn't fully silence the ghosts that haunted him. Each time his gloves made contact, snapshots of past cases flickered behind his eyes—shadowy figures, victims' cries, and the ever-present specter of Max Vilne, taunting him from the darkness.

It had been quite a year living in England. After proving his worth solving a high-profile crime in an unofficial capacity, he had been hired as a consulting detective for the Home Office. A special team, consisting of himself, Amelia, and Rob, using Hertfordshire Constabulary as their base of operations, had been used to tackle several major murders the government felt needed a less orthodox approach. Finn and his two friends had already seen much of the UK, and yet there was so much more to explore. Finn just wished he could do that without the thorn of Max Vilne in his mind.

The shrill ring of his phone shattered his focus. Finn's hand instinctively reached for the device, the sweat from his brow dripping onto the screen as he brought it into view. "Amelia" lit up the display in stark, digital letters—a beacon of the present cutting through the fog of his troubled thoughts.

He hesitated for a fraction of a second, knowing that answering the call would wrench him from the sanctuary of his routine. But Amelia wasn't just any caller; she was his partner, the one who stood by him when the world seemed intent on tearing him down. With her keen insight and unwavering dedication, she had proven herself indispensable as a colleague, but it was the swirling feelings, which Finn had developed for her, that made him somewhat uncertain for what the future held for them.

Finn peeled off his gloves, the Velcro tearing loudly in the quiet aftermath of his halted workout. His chest heaved as he tried to steady his breathing, preparing himself for whatever urgency Amelia's call might bring. Whatever it was, he knew it meant stepping back into the fray, back into the labyrinthine world of crime and punishment.

As he pressed the phone to his ear, his heart settled into a wary rhythm. The chase, it seemed, was far from over.

Finn pressed the phone against his ear, the muffled sounds of the gym receding as Amelia's voice pierced through, sharp and laced with urgency. The familiarity of her tone was a stark contrast to the cold, hard resolve he had been cultivating with each punch thrown into the leathery embrace of the training bag.

"Amelia," he began, his words punctuated by the rhythmic gasps of breath he fought to control. "Did you have a good Christmas?" He pressed on despite the tightness in his chest, an unspoken concern threading through the simplicity of the question.

There was a pause, the briefest of hesitations, before she responded. "It was nice, Finn," she said, her voice softer now, touched by a hint of something that sounded like regret. "But I was worried about you being alone. You should've come with us." Her sincerity hung between them, a bridge over the distance their professional boundaries usually imposed.

"Would've loved to," Finn replied, allowing a wry smile to tease at the corners of his mouth, "but then I'd have had to bring Rob along for the ride." A small laugh escaped him, the sound foreign in the stark confines of the gym. It was a feeble attempt to lighten the mood, but the underlying tension remained, taut and unyielding.

The line crackled with silence, and Finn could almost picture Amelia rolling her eyes on the other end. He didn't need to see her face to know that her next words would steer them back into familiar territory—the kind that came with case files and crime scenes.

"Is this about a new case?" he asked, bracing himself against the inevitable pull back into the world he was trying to keep at bay. His hands clenched reflexively, knuckles white even as he consciously loosened his grip on the phone.

"Yes," Amelia confirmed, and the weight of the word was almost palpable. "A woman named Dominique Plantagenet has been murdered. The murder—it's...it bears an uncanny resemblance to another recent death, Rebecca Hanover's case."

The names were unknown to Finn's mind, a blip on the radar of his thoughts. They held no personal significance for him, as he had never known Rebecca Hanover or Dominique Plantagenet. His focus remained unwavering, fixed solely on the task at hand. But he knew, like all of his cases, he would become deeply familiar with them and care about bringing them justice.

"Tell me everything," he said finally.

Amelia's voice crackled with a hint of frustration as she replied, "I don't have all the details yet, Finn. But I do know that Rob has been gathering information at headquarters. He'll send us more on the specifics en route." Her words hung in the air, leaving Finn with a sense of anticipation and an underlying unease. The thought of returning to the confines of the Hertfordshire Constabulary made him both excited and uneasy. He was enthused by the opportunity to be on a case again, but he worried that it would be at a cost—taking his eyes off Max Vilne and where he might be.

With a deep breath, Finn let the cacophony of past cases fill his mind—the images, the sounds, the gut-wrenching losses. They were all part of who he was, part of what drove him. He couldn't turn away now, not when this new case beckoned. The chase was everything. He exhaled slowly, the determination seeping back into his bones like warmth from a long-forgotten fire.

"Amelia," he uttered, his voice barely above a whisper, yet carrying the steel of resolved conviction. "I'm in."

"Are you sure, Finn?" she asked. "I know how occupied you've been looking for any glimpse of Vilne."

"I'm sure."

"Having your attention in two places," Amelia said, "can also divide your results."

"Amelia," Finn said, more forcefully this time. "I can do this."

The decision hung in the air between them, a pivotal moment where past collided with the present, where the specter of former glories and failures lent weight to his choice. But Finn Wright was no stranger to risk; it was an old companion, one that had walked beside him through countless darkened doorways and whispered promises of redemption.

He could almost taste the danger, the tantalizing edge of consequence that bordered every decision in this line of work. It was a flavor he knew well, one that had soured in his mouth more times than he cared to admit. Yet here he was, ready to dance with fate once more, to step back into the world of crime solving where the stakes were life itself.

"Okay, Finn," she said. "The crime scene is an hour out from here."

"I'll pick you up," he offered.

"Okay, but no terrible jokes on the drive," she said. "Otherwise, there'll be a third murder victim."

"See you soon," Finn said with a laugh.

He ended the call, the silence of the gym settling around him like a cloak. He could sense the curiosity of the other patrons, their gazes lingering just a little too long, but he paid them no heed. His world had narrowed to the task ahead—to the challenge that awaited him beyond the grime-streaked walls of this place of sweat and exertion.

As he gathered his things, his movements deliberate and precise, he felt the familiar surge of adrenaline begin to course through his veins. The thrill of the chase, the intricate dance of wits and wills—it was all coming back to him. For better or worse, Finn Wright was about to dive back into the depths to navigate the murky waters of murder and malice.

CHAPTER FOUR

Finn maneuvered the unmarked police vehicle through the serpentine bends of the coastal road, its tires crunching over a mixture of gravel and frost. Amelia Winters watched as the bleak January landscape unfolded beside them—an expanse where the North Sea met the East Coast of England in a frigid marriage. The sea churned, steel-colored waves topped with froth, colliding with the rocky shore in a relentless assault. Salt-laden gusts swept inland, carrying with them the whispers of ancient shipwrecks and maritime secrets. Skeletal trees bent away from the ocean's breath, and the sky was a canvas of oppressive gray, as if it mourned the sun it had lost.

The desolation of the coast mirrored Finn's recent demeanor—distant, cold, and enigmatic. Amelia found solace in his silent company but couldn't help but feel bewildered by the chasm that had formed between them. Only weeks ago, they had brushed shoulders with death, their lives hanging by a thread as they pursued a killer through treacherous waters. It was then, with adrenaline still saturating his voice, that Finn confessed his love for her. But those words now felt like echoes in an empty hall, the memory tinged with the aftertaste of unspoken regrets.

Amelia's thoughts oscillated between moments of danger and tenderness, their partnership an intricate dance around the flames of intimacy. She wondered if Finn's reluctance stemmed from something she had inadvertently done or said. Or perhaps it was the weight of his past—a failed relationship, a suspension dangling over him like Damocles' sword, and the specter of civil court proceedings—that kept him at arm's length. His eyes, usually so revealing, were now shuttered windows behind which she could only guess at the turmoil.

Questions bubbled within her, seeking an outlet, yet she hesitated to voice them. They traveled together, two kindred spirits bound by duty and shadowed by memories, each step forward mired in uncertainty. As Finn steered the car through another curve, the skeletal branches reached towards them like bony fingers, scraping against the backdrop of a somber sky. A silence hung between them, thick as the coastal fog that sometimes blanketed these shores—and just as impenetrable.

The relentless January wind clawed at the coastline, tearing through the barren fields and gnarled trees that dotted the rural landscape. Swells of gray ocean rose and fell like the ragged breaths of the earth itself, their crashes against the cliffs a natural percussion that underscored the isolation of the East Coast of England this time of year. Finn's hands were steady on the wheel as he navigated the narrow road, the car a lone sentinel passing through the desolate expanse.

"Know anything about the place where this all went down?" Finn's voice broke the silence, his gaze briefly flicking to Amelia before returning to the road.

Amelia shifted in her seat, her eyes drawn to the stark contrast of the dark water churning beside the frosted land. "It's a mansion just outside Thornheart," she replied, noting the slight lift of Finn's eyebrow at the name. "Sounds befitting of a murder mystery, doesn't it?"

"Thornheart," Finn repeated, an amused smirk tugging at his lips. "Sounds like the setting of every Gothic novel ever written. Sometimes I think you're all making fun of me with these place names."

"Quite the contrary," Amelia mused, folding her arms across her chest. "It's got history. The village is known for a Saxon knight who supposedly fended off a Viking invasion almost single-handedly Local legend has it that his spirit still watches over Thornheart."

A chuckle escaped Finn as he envisioned such a scene—the clash of steel and the cries of warriors long gone. "I hope the villagers are more welcoming than their ancestral guardian," he said, the corners of his eyes crinkling with mirth.

"Speaking of Vikings," Amelia quipped, casting a sidelong glance at Finn, "you do have that Scandinavian look about you. Better hope they don't harbor any grudges."

"Ah, but I come bearing the gift of New World charm," Finn retorted. "That comes in handy against swords and pointy sticks."

The laughter between them was a fleeting reprieve, a momentary respite from the gravity of their profession and the complexity of their feelings. Yet beneath the banter, there was an acknowledgment—an unvoiced recognition of the bond that had been forged in the crucible of danger and the shared pursuit of criminals. It was a camaraderie that danced precariously on the edge of something deeper, something neither of them had yet found the courage to explore fully.

The road ahead curved gently, leading them further into the heart of an enigma that would test their resolve. And as they drew closer to

Thornheart, the very air seemed charged with the whispers of secrets waiting to be unearthed, each turn bringing them one step nearer to the truth that lay shrouded within the walls of the ominous mansion.

The countryside unfurled around them like a brooding tapestry, its colors muted under the overcast January sky. The road snaked between two monolithic hills that rose like ancient sentinels on either side. Amelia's eyes traced their craggy faces, half-expecting to see the echoes of old legends carved into the stone. The East Coast of England never failed to remind her of the country's enduring history—a past steeped in blood and bravery.

As they descended into the valley, the quaint image of Thornheart village emerged, nestled within the arms of the landscape as if cradled by the very hands of time. Beyond the clustered roofs, an imposing structure commanded attention, its grandeur undiminished by the distance. The mansion—where death had most recently left its indelible mark—loomed like a silent titan, windows gazing out over the village with an almost sentient watchfulness.

Amelia could sense the mansion's presence pressing against the car windows, its dark silhouette dominating the surrounding buildings and etching itself into her thoughts. The vehicle hummed beneath her, steady and reliable, much like Finn's unwavering focus whenever they approached the heart of an investigation. Yet today, a different kind of apprehension stirred within her.

"Beautiful and haunting," Amelia murmured, her voice barely above the thrum of the engine. "A dangerous combination. I used to dream of places like this when I was little, being a detective and solving cases. But instead of it being a childhood adventure, it's always been more complicated. Some places feel like they were born to remain a mystery."

"Or perhaps this is where mysteries go to die," Finn replied, his gaze briefly meeting hers before returning to the road. "You know, like an old folks home for mysteries. I hear the staff aren't very welcoming there, but the soup is a real treat."

"Do you ever take anything seriously?" Amelia asked with a smile.

"Some things, Amelia."

She knew he meant something by that. He always did when he used her first name.

The silence stretched between them, laden with words that hung unsaid. Amelia's mind wandered back to that harrowing day when they had both nearly drowned on a case, water closing in, breaths coming short, and Finn's voice breaking through the fear—words uttered in the rawness of near-death that had not been spoken of since.

She had hoped to speak with him about it at Christmas. But when he turned down her invitation to Christmas dinner with her family, she wondered if he now regretted saying it. Amelia had waited long enough.

"About that day—the day you said—" she began, her pulse quickening as she finally broached the subject that had haunted their every interaction since.

Finn's grip on the steering wheel tightened imperceptibly, his jaw clenching for a moment before he exhaled slowly. "I'm sorry if that made you uncomfortable, Amelia," he said, his voice steady but threaded with something she couldn't quite name.

"Uncomfortable isn't the word I'd use," Amelia responded, turning to face him fully. Her heart felt like it was being pulled taut, the words she needed to say piling up behind her lips. "It's the silence that followed. That's what's uncomfortable."

He glanced at her, his blue eyes reflecting a storm of emotions that seemed to clash with his controlled demeanor. It was there, in the briefest flicker of vulnerability, that she saw the weight he carried—the unresolved past that shadowed his present. He had been through so much in the last year: the court case, suspension from the FBI, losing his fiance, relocating to a new country, facing a serial killer who always seemed to be one step ahead; the list went on. Amelia wondered if bringing up the fact that Finn had told her he loved her might get lost in the whirlpool of all those pressures.

"Sometimes, silence says more than we intend," Finn muttered, almost to himself. The mansion was drawing closer now, the details of its ornate architecture becoming clearer. But for Amelia, the greater clarity lay in the admission hanging unspoken in the air, and the realization that the barriers between them were not just of Finn's making.

Amelia stopped herself from saying more for a moment, though she wanted to resolved things one way or the other. She had to think about the best way to approach things with him.

As they parked by the mansion, a heavy stillness settled upon them. They stepped out into the biting January air, the mansion standing silent on the precipice of revelation, as silent as the questions that remained unanswered between them.

Amelia's gaze followed the sweep of Finn's arm as he turned off the ignition, the car's engine falling silent as though it too held its breath against the oncoming revelation. The mansion loomed ahead, its grim facade a testament to histories untold and secrets well kept. The January sky cast a dull gray pallor over the landscape, and the sea churned restlessly in the distance, its waves a steady murmur against the rocky coast.

"Back when Max took Demi," Finn began, his voice a low rumble that seemed to resonate with the cold air around them, "I felt like my world had tilted on its axis." He paused, his hands resting on the steering wheel as if they might still steer him clear of the truth he was about to reveal. "The moment I got the call, every feeling I had for you became a betrayal. A betrayal of her. I felt terrible guilt for thinking about you while Demi was in danger."

Amelia watched him closely, her keen eyes searching his face for the shadows of guilt that often played upon his features. It was a rare thing to see Finn Wright unguarded, his emotions bleeding into the space between them.

"Have you ever cut a deal with the powers above? God, maybe... It was as if by admitting I cared for you, I'd somehow put Demi directly in harm's way," he continued, his voice tinged with embarrassment. "As though my feelings could twist fate. It's superstitious, I know... foolish even. But I felt like if I wished for you, somehow she would get hurt by Vilne."

There it was, the revelation she hadn't expected—a vulnerability laid bare beneath the steely resolve of the man she had come to know not just as a partner but as something more. She felt the weight of his confession settle in her chest, a strange mix of relief and sadness.

"Superstition has a way of making us believe we have control in situations where we have none," Amelia said softly, reaching out to place a gentle hand on his. She wanted to offer comfort, to bridge the gap that had formed between them, filled with unsaid words and unacknowledged feelings.

She shifted her gaze to the mansion as they stepped out of the vehicle, the gravel crunching beneath their feet. Its presence was imposing, each window appearing as an eye holding vigil over Thornheart. As they moved towards the entrance, Amelia's thoughts drifted to Finn, seeing him not just as her stoic partner but as a man wrestling with his own demons.

"Maybe we should talk about it later," Amelia suggested, her voice carrying through the chill air. Yet, even as she spoke, she recognized her own reticence, the lingering grief that clung to her like a second skin since her fiance's death.

Finn nodded, his expression unreadable, but made no move to speak further on the matter. It was as if the house itself demanded their attention, the murder within its walls a siren call they couldn't ignore.

With a final look at the foreboding structure before them, they stepped towards the building, leaving their personal crossroads untraveled for the time being.

CHAPTER FIVE

The grandeur of Thornheart Manor loomed ominously as the slate January sky above it whispered the threat of a storm. Finn Wright's hand gripped the steering wheel, navigating the sleek car over the gravel driveway that crunched like bone fragments beneath the tires.

Finn and Amelia cautiously made their way up the winding path that led to Thornheart Manor. The imposing Victorian mansion stood tall against the darkening sky, its weathered stone facade exuding an air of mystery and intrigue. The scent of damp earth and decaying leaves hung heavy in the air, adding to the eerie atmosphere that surrounded the grand estate.

As they stepped onto the creaking wooden porch, Finn couldn't help but notice the intricate details carved into every inch of the ornate double doors. The once vibrant paint had faded over time, leaving behind a ghostly reminder of its former glory. He reached out to grasp the tarnished brass doorknob, feeling a chill run down his spine as he turned it.

The moment they crossed the threshold, Finn felt an unsettling presence wash over him. The grand foyer stretched out before them, with a sweeping staircase leading up to a gallery adorned with portraits of long-dead ancestors. Dust particles danced in the dim light that filtered through stained glass windows, casting eerie shadows on the delicate Persian rug beneath their feet.

Amelia's voice broke through Finn's reverie as she whispered, her words barely audible in the oppressive silence of Thornheart Manor. "This place gives me chills," she admitted, her eyes scanning their surroundings with what looked like a mix of curiosity and trepidation.

Finn nodded silently in agreement, his gaze drawn to a massive stone fireplace that dominated one wall of the lobby, its flames dancing high yet contained.

Constable Jones, a young and eager officer known to them, approached Finn and Amelia with a sense of urgency. His uniform was crisp, his badge gleaming under the dim light of Thornheart Manor. "Detectives Wright and Winters," he greeted them with a nod, his voice hushed as if afraid to disturb the heavy silence that hung in the air. "I've been assigned to assist you in navigating the crime scene."

Finn acknowledged Constable Jones with a curt nod, appreciating the officer's dedication despite his evident nerves. "Lead the way, my man," he instructed, his tone as jovial as possible given the circumstances.

The constable hesitated for a moment before gesturing towards a set of ornate double doors at the end of the grand foyer. "This way," he said softly, his voice barely audible above the crackling fire.

As they followed Constable Jones through the doors, Finn couldn't help but notice how their surroundings shifted from opulence to decay. The once polished wooden floors gave way to worn carpeting that seemed to absorb their footsteps, muffling any sound they made. The walls were adorned with faded tapestries depicting scenes from forgotten eras, their colors muted by time.

This place is a facade, he thought.

They arrived at a closed door guarded by two uniformed officers who nodded respectfully at Finn and Amelia as they approached an opened the door.

As they crossed the threshold marked by fluttering police tape, the silence bore down on them in opposition to the opulence that surrounded them. The murder scene lay ahead, meticulously cordoned off, yet nothing could restrain the cold presence of death that saturated the air. Finn's gaze fell upon Dominique's body; her pale features were set in an expression of shock and agony. The stillness around them felt like a heavy cloak, and he knew this case would peel back layers far beyond what the eye could see.

"I'll be at the lobby if you require me," Jones said, looking ill.

"No worries," Finn answered with a kind smile. He knew how sick a scene like that could make you, and he felt no ill will to any police officers who didn't have the stomach for a murder investigation.

"Notice the pose," Finns said, firmly.

Amelia nodded. "Knees bent, hands outstretched, palms up... Looks like the killer posed her that way."

"I wonder if it has a religious connotation," Finn mused. "The way her body is, it almost reminds me of crucifixion."

"I saw her in the West End once doing a play... I thought she seemed immortal. Didn't stand a chance, here, poor woman," Amelia murmured next to him, her voice betraying a hint of sorrow for the fallen star of Thornheart Manor.

"Looks that way," Finn replied, his eyes never leaving the corpse as he knelt beside it. His fingers hovered close, careful not to contaminate the scene, as he traced the air above her twisted form.

A shiver ran through him, not from the creeping chill but from the realization of what lay before him. The method of murder was theatrical, calculated. It spoke volumes of the killer's intentions and possibly their identity. Finn's mind, a catalog of crime scenes past, thought that there was something familiar about the kill and the position of the body, though he couldn't quite put his finger on it just yet.

"There's soil on her arm," Finn said. "She wasn't murdered here. She was moved indoors. We should have forensics check the grounds for any sign of blood."

"Agreed," Amelia said, watching closely.

"Winters, look at this," he then said, his voice low and steady. "The wounds to the side of the body, the positioning—it's not random either. I can't tell for certain, but even the stab wounds look staged somehow. There's something false about this all, like the stage has been set for maximum effect." He could almost hear the echoes of applause from Dominique's recent performance, where she had brought history to life on stage. But now, it seemed history had been reenacted in her death.

Thornheart Manor, with its stone gargoyles peering down from the eaves, became an even more sinister backdrop for the investigation. Finn wondered if the murderer had chosen this place, this method, to send a message. As he stood and stepped back from the body, Finn felt the weight of the challenge before them. They were not only hunting for a killer but deciphering the narrative of a murderer who had turned death into a spectacle.

"Execution-style," Amelia noted, her analytical mind already piecing together the profiles and motives. "If this was staged, the body moved after the kill, it's too specific. She was an actress, after all."

"Exactly," Finn agreed, his jaw tightening. The killer was taunting them, hiding behind the curtain of history. Yet every act leaves a trace, and Finn Wright was determined to uncover it. A chill ran through the room as if a ghost walked by.

"Art imitating life or vice versa," Finn murmured, more to himself than to Amelia, who was meticulously examining the body's position.

Finn's mind churned with the grim tableau before him; Dominique's body lay still and pale, her last moment an expression of unspeakable horror frozen in time. Finn's eyes, however, were drawn not to the body but to the artifacts left behind—a message from the killer. There was something beside her.

The note was aged, its edges fraying and the ink faded to a dusky brown. The words were English, but from another era. Its placement was conspicuous, just inches from Dominique's outstretched hand as if she had been reaching for it. Stooping down, Finn used a gloved finger to hold down one corner of the paper, which the ghostly chill threatened to steal away. He read the older English script, the words cryptic yet laced with arrogance.

"Thou art slain... no medicine in the world can do thee good," he recited softly. The verse was from Shakespeare, 'Richard III', a play steeped in treachery and death, but just as he was about to tell Amelia this, she interrupted.

"Richard the third," she said, calmly, smiling with a raised eyebrow. "You didn't think a good English girl had never studied Shakespeare, Finn?"

Amelia's mind as well as her beauty excited him, even when close to such hostile crimes. His lips formed a thin line as he stood back up, feeling the tendrils of a theory taking root. The killer had not only reenacted a historical execution but left them a literary breadcrumb. This murderer wanted their deeds to be seen, understood, and marveled at—as if murder were a form of perverse artistry.

"Showboating," he muttered, his gaze sweeping the floor for more clues. That was when he saw it.

"Doesn't it look like Dominique's hand is almost pointing?" Finn said.

"Come to think of it, her index finger..." Amelia kneeled down on the ground and followed the line from the dead woman's hand. With gloved hands, she pulled something out from beneath an antique sofa, stood up and put it in Finn's hand.

And there it was, gleaming dully against the blue latex of his glove—a small metal disc imprinted with a symbol. A signet ring's emblem, unmistakably deliberate in its placement by the killer. Finn crouched once more, eyes narrowing as he inspected the sigil—an intricate crest that spoke of lineage and legacy. It was familiar in a way that gnawed at him, a piece of a puzzle that he couldn't quite place.

"Amelia," he called without looking up, "take a look at this."

She moved closer, peering over his shoulder at the emblem. Her breath caught slightly, a reaction not lost on Finn. He knew that she, too, understood the weight of their discovery.

"It looks like an old coat of arms," Amelia said. "Wealthy families all have them, and they would once wear signet rings like that to showcase the influence of their family lineage."

"Someone's playing a game with us," Finn said, his voice low and steady. "This was too easy to find. The killer has staged this, I'm certain of it."

"Then the killer wanted us to find this," Amelia replied, determination etching her features. "That's a dangerous mindset. Perhaps he wants us to stop him."

"Maybe, or he's like Vilne and likes to toy with the people chasing him." Finn nodded as he thought through it, the urgency of the hunt surging within him. They were against a foe who reveled in the theatrics of their crimes, and every clue was another step towards unmasking them. In the embrace of Thornheart Manor, with the hills looming like silent sentinels outside, Finn felt the inexorable pull of the chase. The killer had left a deliberate trail, but the reason behind that remained a mystery.

Finn stood up, the cold air of Thornheart sending a shiver down his spine despite the adrenaline that coursed through his veins.

"Carefully collect these," Finn instructed a nearby forensics member, his tone leaving no room for doubt as to the gravity of the task. He pointed to the old note and the emblem, their presence at the scene a macabre punctuation to Dominique's final act. "We need everything these can tell us. Cross-reference the emblem with any archives on British royalty—this killer wants us to follow their historical breadcrumbs."

The forensic scientist, clad in sterile white that contrasted starkly with the dark stone of the courtyard, nodded solemnly. They began the meticulous process of collecting the evidence, each item encased within a clear plastic bag, sealed against contamination. Finn's gaze remained fixed on the scientist's careful movements, ensuring the integrity of what could be the key to unlocking the murderer's identity.

Once the evidence was secured, Finn turned his attention back to the crime scene, his eyes scanning every inch of the space with methodical precision. Dominique's body lay in repose upon the ground, her pale skin almost blending with the snow that surrounded her. Her position was unnatural, limbs splayed in a silent testament to the violence of her last moments. Finn crouched, studying the way her fingers were curled, the angle of her head, the pattern of blood that had seeped into the frosty earth beneath her—the tableau before him a grotesque still life.

Amelia, who had been conferring with another officer, caught Finn's eye and gave a slight nod.

Finn straightened, his mind racing as he committed the scene to memory. There was something here, amid the chaos and the carnage, something crucial that he was on the cusp of understanding. Behind the facade of this winter crime lay a message written in blood and history, and he would decipher it.

Finn's gaze swept over the crime scene, the low winter sun casting elongated shadows across Thornheart Manor's frostbitten grounds and through the window. The cold bit into his skin even while inside, but it was the sight before him that sent a deeper chill through his spine.

What am I missing? he thought.

Then, he saw something else. Finn moved quickly and started to take his shoes off.

"Finn, have you finally lost your mind?" Amelia asked.

"Hold these," he said to a constable standing nearby.

Finn then stepped up onto an old armchair, took out a flashlight from his pocket, and then looked down at Dominique's body. He moved the light around.

"It's hard to see, but it's there!" he said, excitedly.

His eyes, sharp and unyielding, picked up on an anomaly—a constellation of minuscule particles near the emblem that had been deliberately placed in line with Dominique's finger. They glinted, almost blending in with the lush carpet that cradled them. Not dust—too reflective. Not glass—too irregular. He crouched for a closer examination, noting their crystalline structure. Salt? No, something else.

"Amelia," he called without looking up, trusting she would hear the urgency threaded in his voice. She was there within moments, her presence a silent question.

"Take a look at this," Finn said, moving closer and gesturing towards the discovery with a gloved hand. Amelia leaned in, her brow furrowing as she too recognized the oddity of the find.

"Looks like tiny fragments of something," she said. "We'll need these sampled. The question is, are they important or just pieces of dirt?"

"Nothing about this crime is accidental," Finn instructed, his tone leaving no room for delay. She nodded, signaling to the forensic team who converged with tweezers and evidence bags, treating the tiny particles with the reverence due to potential keys to a murderer's mind.

Finn took off his gloves and put them in his pocket.

The task was completed with efficiency born of practiced hands under Finn and Amelia's watchful eyes. As the forensic scientist sealed the bag, he stood, his thoughts racing. These particles were left for a reason. A piece of the puzzle that didn't fit yet, but when it did, it would illuminate corners of darkness that the killer inhabited.

As the last of the evidence was secured, and the team began to disperse, Finn felt the stirrings of a familiar restlessness in his gut. It was more than the biting air around him or the isolation of Thornheart nestled between looming peaks—it was the acute awareness that there was always another madman willing to kill. Sometimes it felt like the chase was never ending.

"Plantagenet..." Finn whispered. "That's an old royal name, isn't it?"

"Yes," Amelia said. "And with the coat of arms, we have to consider the fact that there may be a royal connection here."

"We'd have to see if the other victim is connected to royalty somehow," Finn mused.

"The other victim's second name is Hanover," Amelia explained. "I know the Hanovers have been members of the royal family before, but there are plenty who just share the name. It could be a coincidence."

"I have a feeling none of this is going to be by chance," Finn replied, gravely.

"We should head out," Amelia said.

"To Garden City?" Finn asked, confused. "That's an hour away."

"No," Amelia answered. "There's a town not far from here. They have a pathologist and a small forensics lab."

"Excellent," Finn said. "Then, I need to eat."

"You can think with your stomach at a time like this?" Amelia asked.

"What can I say," he said. "I still have to feed."

"You sound like a cow," Amelia laughed.

One of the nearby officers smirked and then looked at the ground.

"You want me to starve," he said. "I know it."

"Come on," Amelia said, pointing to the doorway. "We'll grab something suitably American on the way."

"You know how to make a guy feel at home, Winters."

After walking through the hallways of Thornheart, they were soon back outside into the increasing cold of the January day.

With a final glance at the manor, Finn turned on his heel, every step back towards the car propelled by the beat of necessity. Amelia fell into stride beside him, her gaze meeting his with a shared intensity. They needed to unravel the killer's message, decode the significance of the unexpected particles, and predict where this morbid fascination with the past would lead next.

Their breaths misted in the air, visible evidence of life in a place touched by death.

CHAPTER SIX

The chill of early morning had not yet lifted when Finn and Amelia arrived in Hangton, a quaint town that seemed to have been plucked from an earlier era and dropped into the modern world. The stone buildings stood resilient against time, their weathered surfaces speaking of centuries past. Finn's piercing gaze swept over the small police building they approached, its facade a testament to bygone craftsmanship.

With the bagged evidence secure under his arm, Finn led the way, Amelia close behind. The door creaked on its ancient hinges as they entered, the sound echoing through the empty hallway. Their footsteps resonated against the stone floor, a rhythmical clatter that disturbed the silence. Finn felt the weight of the evidence in his hands; it was tangible proof, yet it whispered mysteries unsolved.

"That hot dog was not good," Finn said. "It was decidedly un-American."

"You know, Finn," Amelia said with a playful glint in her eyes, "if this detective thing doesn't work out for you, you could always pursue a career as a food critic."

Finn chuckled, his footsteps echoing through the empty hallway. "Well, I do have an impeccable palate. Maybe I'll start rating crime scenes based on their snack options."

Amelia grinned. "I can see it now: 'Thornheart Manor gets three stars for its finger sandwiches and excellent choice of murder weapons.'"

They traversed the corridor, the air growing dense with the mustiness of aged paper and furniture polish. The forensics lab, tucked away at the end of the hallway, was a tiny room that could have been mistaken for a broom closet had it not been for the elaborate setup within. Finn's eyes skimmed over the neat arrangement of forensic tools and chemicals that lined the shelves—order amidst chaos.

Dr. Carter was a man so engrossed in his work that their entrance barely registered. Bent over his microscope, he was surrounded by slides and petri dishes, his concentration palpable. The atmosphere was tense but thrumming with intellectual energy, a silent storm brewing in the confines of the forensic battlefield.

"Dr. Carter," Finn began, his voice slicing through the stillness, "I'm Finn Wright, a consulting detective with the Home Office, and this is Inspector Amelia Winters. We're here regarding the Plantagenet case."

The doctor straightened, pushing his glasses up the bridge of his nose with a practiced motion. He turned to face them, his expression one of mild interest that failed to mask the keen edge of his intellect. The lines etched into his face hinted at a mind that rarely rested, always in pursuit of truth hidden within microscopic worlds.

"What do you have for me?" he said, stretching out his hand.

Without a word, Finn handed over the sealed evidence bags containing the old note and emblem, then another with the fragments. They were relics from another time, out-of-place amid the high-tech instruments, yet Finn knew that they were keys to unlocking the present-day horror that had befallen Dominique Plantagenet.

"Found these at the crime scene," Finn added, watching as Dr. Carter accepted the bags with a nod. His fingers were precise and steady, betraying years of experience handling the delicate and the damning.

As the doctor prepared to examine the artifacts under his microscope, Finn stepped back, giving him space while remaining close enough to observe. The tension in the room shifted, anticipation hanging heavy in the air like a curtain of fog. He just hoped that Dr. Carter could find something useful for them.

"These fragments look interesting," the doctor said.

Dr. Carter's eyes never left the eyepiece of the microscope, his gaze as fixed and intense as a hawk preying on its quarry. Finn stood nearby, his own eyes riveted not on the evidence itself, but on the soft glow emanating from beneath the doctor's lens, illuminating centuries-old secrets. He felt Amelia's presence beside him, her quiet anticipation a mirror to his own.

"Ah," Dr. Carter muttered, almost to himself. He then scrutinized the note and the fragments once again before standing up and saying: "Iron gall ink. No doubt about it."

Finn leaned in slightly, his focus sharpening on the old note that lay beneath the scrutiny of Dr. Carter's microscope. Iron gall—an ancient formula whose resilience against time made it both a historian's boon and a forensic challenge.

"Commonplace during the Tudor period," Dr. Carter continued, adjusting the focus with a practiced hand. "Used for its durability. But this... this has been well-preserved. Remarkable, really. That's what your fragments are, as well."

"Is there any chance this was written recently on ancient paper? Could it help us date the note?" Finn's voice was steady, betraying none of the urgency that pumped through his veins.

"Potentially," Dr. Carter replied without looking up. "But iron gall can be replicated even now by those with the right knowledge. It might tell us more about the person who wrote it than when it was written. But you would have to have an intimate love for scholarly works to do so."

Finn absorbed this, the gears in his mind turning. The profile of their suspect was coming into sharper relief—someone with an affinity for the archaic, a knowledge of history, perhaps even academic. His thoughts were interrupted by Dr. Carter straightening up, pushing back from the scope.

"I'll need more time for a comprehensive report," he said, locking eyes with Finn. "There are layers here, nuances that require careful analysis."

"Understood," Finn nodded, his resolve solidifying. There were other avenues to explore while they waited.

A knock came at the door and in stepped the fresh faced Constable Jones again.

"Are you following us?" Finn asked.

"Eh... Pardon, Sir? No. I... I work out of here and thought you could do with a place to carry out your work, too," Jones said, his face red.

"Don't listen to him," Amelia said. "You're doing fine work, Jones." She turned to Dr. Carter. "Keep us posted, Dr. Carter, and thank you for your efforts."

Finn enjoyed making fun of people in a harmless way, and while Amelia did the same, Finn admired the way she always, in the end, built people up. There was enough tearing down of people to fill the Grand Canyon in the world.

With a gesture from Constable Jones, they stepped out of the lab and into the maze of stone corridors once more, moving towards a small, sparsely furnished office that had been set aside for their use. Constable Jones unlocked the door and flicked on the light, revealing a simple desk and two chairs bathed in the sterile fluorescence.

"Your workspace is in here. If you need anything else, please let me know," Jones said, gesturing inside before taking his leave.

"Looks like the kid has done us a solid," Finn said, pointing to the files sitting on their desks, and a makeshift evidence white board that had been wheeled in.

"Yeah," Amelia said, agreeing. "And there are files here for both the Dominique Plantagenet murder and the Rebecca Hanover case. Should help us compare the two a little more to see if there is indeed a connection."

The files marked 'Hanover, R' were waiting for them, thick with the weight of unanswered questions. Finn took a seat, the chair groaning under his frame as he reached for the first of the reports. As Amelia pulled the second chair closer, Finn felt a familiar thrill—to have Amelia by his side, his equal at every turn, sometimes, his superior. He could smell her perfume and tried not to get lost in it.

"Let's take a look at Rebecca's case," Amelia said, opening up some files.

They began to sift through the pages, reports first. Each line was a potential thread, each statement a possible lead. Then came the crime scene photographs—stark, gruesome testimony of Rebecca Hanover's final moments. Finn's eyes traced over each image, cataloging the details, the positioning of the body, the absence of personal effects.

"Positioned the same way as Dominique Plantagenet. It's almost certainly deliberate," he said, pointing to the knees brought up slightly to the side. "And look at the wrist, the palm outstretched. It's so familiar again."

Amelia passed him a witness statement, her finger tapping a particularly intriguing passage. He read it, his brows knitting together. There was a pattern emerging, something that tugged at the edges of his understanding, a whisper of connection that teased at the periphery of his consciousness. He filed it away mentally, another piece in the ever-growing jigsaw puzzle that was Rebecca Hanover's murder.

"Take a look at this," Amelia murmured, sliding another photograph across the desk. It showed an item found at the scene, something so ordinary yet so out of place that it sent a shiver down Finn's spine. An antique fountain pen, the tip dipped in Rebecca Hanover's blood.

"Another piece of dramatic flair. Was there a stab mark from the pen?" Finn asked Amelia.

"No," she said. "But it was definitely Rebecca's blood, not the killer's."

"So, we have an actress dead, and this pen..." Finn said. "Could the killer have something to do with writing, maybe?"

"Like a playwright?" Amelia asked.

"Yeah," he said. "You know, I used to write short stories and had a couple published in a small magazine back home."

"Really?" Amelia asked. "You are full of surprises... Wait, it wasn't erotica, was it?"

"Hardly," Finn said. He held in the desire to tell her that it was about his childhood in Florida, how hard he had lived there, growing up in a town that only saw him as a troublemaker. "But I do remember feeling a little bitter every time I got a rejection from a magazine. Some writers can be pretty bitter."

"Enough to kill..." Amelia echoed.

They then continued and worked in near silence, the only sounds the rustle of paper and the occasional muted clink of Amelia's ring against her mug. Together, they delved into the life and death of Rebecca Hanover, seeking the invisible strands that connected her fate to Dominique Plantagenet's. And somewhere in the depths of those files, Finn sensed the truth lurking, waiting for the keen edge of his intellect to cut it free.

Amidst the sea of documents and photographs that lay scattered across the desk like leaves in autumn, his eyes were drawn to a faded playbill, corners worn and ink smudged by time. The bold type announced a school production of "Mary Stuart" with a flourish that belied the tragedy it foretold.

"Amelia, look at this," Finn said, voice low but urgent, pointing to a newspaper article under the mess. The air in the cramped office felt heavier as Amelia leaned over, her presence a calming force in the maelstrom of their investigation. It was a school theater program of some sort that brought in professionals to help train the students in case they later wanted to apply for a career in the dramatic arts. Looks like it was taken very seriously by all involved. A bit of PR for the school and the area."

"Rebecca Hanover... she directed a play," she observed, pointing to the fine print where Rebecca's name was listed as the director. "Mary Stuart is about Mary, Queen of Scots, isn't it?"

"Exactly," he replied. "And Dominique played in Richard III just before her death. Historical figures, both dethroned, both betrayed." Finn's mind raced, drawing lines between points of data that seemed disparate but now shimmered with potential relevance. This couldn't be coincidence. It was too specific, too strange. The thematic echo reverberated through the musty air of the office, mingling with the scent of old paper and the faint hint of stale coffee.

"Two women linked by more than just their untimely deaths," Amelia added, her tone suggesting she, too, could sense the undercurrents pulling them towards something deeper.

"Roles that speak of power struggles, of being cast down..." Finn murmured, half to himself. His mind was a whirlpool, thoughts and theories swirling with dizzying speed. The pieces of the puzzle were aligning in his head, forming a picture that was still incomplete, but every bit as unsettling as he feared.

"Is it the plays, the roles, or the history they represent?" Amelia pondered aloud, tapping a pen against the edge of the desk. Her analytical gaze met Finn's, a silent exchange of ideas and questions passing between them.

"Or all of it?" Finn suggested. "A murderer with a penchant for drama—or history. Or both." He couldn't shake the feeling that they were on the cusp of a breakthrough, that the shadows were parting ever so slightly to reveal the outline of their quarry.

"Let's see what else we can find," Amelia said, determination lining her features as she turned back to the files.

Finn nodded, his focus narrowing as he sifted through the avalanche of information. Each document, each statement was another step down a path that seemed to spiral into darkness. He knew the danger of tunnel vision, the risk of seeing patterns where none existed. But his gut—a visceral, almost primal instinct honed by years on the field—whispered that they were on to something.

His hands paused on an interview transcript, words leaping out at him: "According to cast members, Rebecca was obsessed with getting the history right, insisted on authenticity." It was a small detail, innocuous to an untrained eye, but to Finn, it was a beacon. Authenticity—the thread that wove through both cases, binding them together with a sinew of purpose.

"History might not repeat itself, but it certainly rhymes," Finn muttered, feeling the chill of revelation crawl up his spine. They were delving into a narrative penned by a killer, one who drew from the past to script the present, and it was up to them to write the final act, hopefully not with a fountain pen dipped in blood.

Finn's mind returned to the note as something else jumped out at him.

"Amelia," he called softly. "I think the killer left those fragments deliberately, like a grim calling card. He wants us to know that he is a stickler for detail and authenticity."

Amelia nodded.

"And look what I found," Finn grinned.

She was at his side in an instant, her curiosity piqued by the tone of his voice—a timbre reserved for moments when a piece of the puzzle clicked into place.

"The note and the fragments," he said, "Wouldn't a historian have access to that sort of thing? I mean old materials."

"It's possible," Amelia ventured, brows knitting together as she leaned in closer. "Certainly someone with interest in that area would be more likely to have access to ancient parchment and ink."

"Yeah," Finn confirmed, his mind already racing ahead. "So look at this..."

Finn held up a piece of paper with known associates of Rebecca Hanover. This man here, he seems like someone with a penchant for antiquities, particularly those with a literary slant."

"Professor Harold Hemingway," Amelia replied, looking at the paper. "This report says that in the days leading up to Rebecca Hanover's death, she consulted with him for research about a play."

"An expert on Tudor manuscripts, Old English, and antiques," Finn added, the edges of the scene before him sharpening with acute clarity. Hemingway's connection to royal emblems and ancient notes was more than just academic—it was personal, intimate. "Given that he works near here, it's more than possible that Dominique Plantagenet could have also consulted him while preparing for a role. She could have asked him details about how people lived in antiquity to make her performance more authentic."

"If so, it could be a coincidence," Amelia countered, though her voice carried a note of skepticism. She was playing devil's advocate, as was her wont, challenging Finn to cement his theory with hard facts. "I mean, an actress and a director probably moved in similar circles when they lived out here on the coast."

"Coincidences are the alibis of the unimaginative," Finn quipped, echoing a sentiment he'd read somewhere long ago. But he knew better than to rely solely on gut feelings and conjecture.

"You really, really want to sound like a Victorian detective, don't you?" Amelia smiled.

"Maybe I've been reading too much Sherlock Holmes," he said. "Though I think I'd look good with a pipe, don't you?"

Amelia seemed to ignore the joke. "We should speak with this professor and find out if he has a connection to both victims. It's the only thread we have between the cases, other than both working in theater and the staging of the bodies."

"Then, let's get to it," he said before feigning an English accent and holding an imaginary pipe to his mouth. "The game is on!"

"With care," Amelia warned, her hand brushing against his for a moment—a fleeting touch that grounded him. "He's well-respected by the looks of this, connected no doubt considering his place of work. Accusations could backfire on us if we're not certain."

"You're no fun," Finn sighed, still using his terrible approximation of an English detective's accent from the Victorian era. "I promise to behave myself."

"Sounds like a plan," Amelia agreed, laughing. "We won't get Dr. Carter's lab results for a while, so we should head out in the meantime."

The blade of suspicion pointed unwaveringly toward Professor Hemingway. All that was left now was to look him in the eye and question him.

"And we should do it fast," Amelia said. "I have a horrible feeling that if we waste any time, more bodies will hit the floor."

"Fast, I can do," Finn said, standing up and rushing out of the door alongside his partner.

CHAPTER SEVEN

The engine of the unmarked police car roared like a caged beast straining against its confines as Finn Wright pressed his foot mercilessly onto the accelerator. Beside him, Amelia Winters gripped the dashboard with white-knuckled hands, her eyes fixed on the blur of scenery whipping past the window.

"I know I said fast," Amelia said with a jolt, "but I didn't mean warp speed."

"I'm driving incredibly safely," Finn replied.

"Last time you said that," she groaned, "you ended up in a ditch submerged in water and I had to save you."

"As I remember it," Finn grinned, knowing he was near to their destination, "we saved each other."

"Finn..." Amelia said, her voice changing as the world whizzed by outside.

"Why do I get the feeling you're about to pry?" Finn smiled.

"No... I... You haven't mentioned your court case for a while, and I was wondering if..."

"It had been resolved?" Finn sighed. "Sadly not."

"I still can't believe they are trying to blame you for what happened to the hotel," Amelia said, shaking her head.

"It was over a year ago now," Finn answered, somberly. "But there are some at the FBI who have it in for me. They never liked me taking the initiative, especially when I was chasing Max Vilne. They thought I was reckless going in alone and facing him, but the hostage would have died, otherwise."

Finn slowed the car as they moved off a main road and passed a green sign for the university. As the car slowed, he turned and smiled at Amelia before returning his eyes to the road ahead.

"If they find me culpable for the fire damage during Vilne's original arrest back home," Finn said. "Then I'll be out of a job and financially ruined. So you might have to put up with me permanently..."

"That wouldn't be so bad," Amelia answered. "When will you know?"

"Weeks now, I think," he said. "But since Vilne escaped, I wanted to bring him in before that happened. Now, he's still out there, and we're on another case."

"Every case is important..."

Finn didn't say anything, but he knew she was right.

Oldbridge University loomed ahead, an institution steeped in history and academic prowess, now tainted by the sinister shadow of murder. As Finn swerved into the university grounds, his mind raced with the possibilities that lay within these ivy-clad walls. The ancient parchment pieces and the suspect's possible connection to both victims were their only leads, pointing them unerringly towards Prof. Harold Hemingway—a man whose knowledge of such artifacts would have been enough to explain the antique pen, signet ring, and parchment at the death scenes.

"Left here," Amelia instructed, her voice cutting through Finn's concentration as he navigated the serpentine roads that snaked through the campus. "Did they make this place a maze so that people couldn't run out on their classes so easily?"

Every second mattered, and yet the university seemed to conspire against them, its layout a puzzle that added precious time onto their journey.

The antiquated stone buildings of Oldbridge rose around them like silent sentinels of a bygone era, their facades etched with the wisdom and wear of centuries. Finn couldn't help but feel the weight of all those years in the atmosphere of the place, a stark reminder of how small a piece they were in the grand tapestry of history. Yet, it was in this place of learning where evil had threaded its way, and it was here that they would hope to confront it.

"Over there, Hemingway's office is in the North Wing," Amelia said, pointing towards a particularly imposing structure that seemed to watch over the others with an air of austere authority.

Finn swung the car into a parking space with a precision born of years spent in high-pressure situations.

"I think I brought up my lunch," Amelia said. "Next time, I'll drive."

"I got us here in one piece, didn't I?" Finn replied.

"Barely," she quipped.

"Did you almost lose your false teeth?"

"Pretty sure you're older than me, Cowboy," retorted Amelia.

"So this is the place?" Finn asked, gesturing to several large, Elizabethan looking buildings.

"I believe so."

Finn took another look at the campus. "Looks classy. You better let me take the lead."

Amelia let out a snort as she involuntarily laughed hard.

Finn found it adorable. "If you are going to snort, please don't do it in front of the academics."

"Come on, you," Amelia said.

They exited quickly, their feet sounding on white gravel as they made their way to the entrance of one of the buildings. The hallowed halls of academia were quiet, the usual thrum of student life absent under the cloak of investigation.

"I guess it's pretty dead around here on a Saturday," Finn observed.

Finn and Amelia stepped through the heavy wooden doors of the Elizabethan building, their footsteps echoing in the empty corridor. The dim lighting cast long shadows on the walls, adding to the eerie atmosphere that seemed to permeate the entire campus.

"The case file said his office is on the ground floor here," Amelia said.

"Feels like we've stepped back in time," Finn muttered, his eyes scanning the rows of closed office doors lining both sides of the hallway.

Each door bore a small brass plaque with a name and title, indicating the occupant within. Amelia nodded in agreement, her gaze focused on a particularly ornate door at the far end of the corridor.

"That must be Hemingway's office," she said, pointing towards it.

They approached the heavy oak door marked with a brass plaque engraved with Hemingway's name.

"Cordial or intrusive?" Finn whispered.

"Let's try intrusive for a change," Amelia answered.

Finn's hand hovered over the handle.

"Ready?" Amelia asked, her voice steady, but Finn could see the anticipation in her eyes.

"Always," he replied, his grip tightening. With a deep breath, he pushed the door open and stepped into the unknown.

Finn stepped across the threshold, the scent of old leather and parchment letting him know that this was a sanctuary for the intellectually devout. More than that, it also let him know they were on the right track.

The office of Prof. Harold Hemingway was less a room and more a monument to the past, with historical artifacts lining the walls like sentinels. Among them were ancient manuscripts encased in glass and relics Finn could only guess at their origins. The air was thick with the musk of time-worn books on linguistics, which filled towering shelves to the brim.

Amelia brushed her fingers across a globe antiquated by centuries, its surface a tapestry of explorations long concluded. At the center of this academic treasure trove sat Hemingway himself, hunched over his desk littered with parchments so similar to those found at the crime scene that Finn's pulse quickened.

"Professor Hemingway?" Finn's voice cut through the stillness, causing the elderly man to look up with a start. His hair was a wild mane of white, his clothes a disarray of academia—tweed jacket with elbow patches worn thin, bow tie askew. He peered at them through round spectacles, magnifying wary eyes.

He glared at them for a moment and then almost grunted. "I know you two, I've seen your cases in the Times. Finn Wright, isn't it and Amelia Winters?"

Finn usually liked when people recognized them, he had grown accustomed to that. But when a suspect knew more about them than they did of him, that provided a distinct disadvantage.

"Detective Wright, Miss Winters," he reiterated with a cautious nod, as if acknowledging players in a chess game he had been anticipating.

"We'd like to discuss your research, particularly your work with antique documents," Amelia said, unfurling photos of the fragments recovered from Dominique's murder scene.

Hemingway's gaze flitted to the images before returning to his visitors, his composure seemingly unruffled. "Fascinating, isn't it? The way history leaves its mark," he mused, too casually for Finn's taste.

"Your expertise could help us understand how these came to be found where they were," Finn pressed, watching the professor closely. "The fragments were found at a murder scene. The woman in question is Dominique Plantagenet. She was killed last night."

Hemingway raised an Eyebrow.

"Do you know her?" Amelia now asked.

"I know of her," he said. "A splendid Shakespearean actress. A real loss to the stage. I am sorry to hear this."

"Have you ever consulted with her over one of her roles?" Amelia continued.

"Not that I'm aware of," the old man answered with a wry grin. "You seem to be addressing me as some sort of suspect, correct?"

"We're just following inquiries," Amelia offered. "But you did consult for Rebecca Hanover?"

"Ah!," Hemingway replied, pushing back his chair with a creak that seemed to echo off the dense bookshelves. Standing, he appeared even frailer than Finn had anticipated; the stoop in his posture spoke of many years bent over scholarly pursuits. Yet there was something about the way his eyes darted, a tension in his shoulders that belied his composed exterior. "Now, this makes sense. You think the two murders are related? No?"

"You did consult with Rebecca, helping her research a play?" Finn prodded.

"Yes, but I have consulted on many subjects," the old man grumbled. He waved his hand away as though batting a fly. "I am, for want of a better term, a polymath. I have extensive knowledge of a variety of historical periods and subjects from physics, to sociology, even cryptography, but as you can see, I'm a stuffy old academic. I'm hardly fit for a murder, never mind two."

"If I dig," Finn said quietly. "You're telling me I won't find any likewise connection to Dominique Plantagenet."

"Those who dig," the man said, glaring at Finn, "will shape the soil into that which they look for, understand?"

"Rebecca. Hanover." Amelia said pointedly.

"I've no idea how any of my work could relate to your investigation," Hemingway continued, shuffling papers into a semblance of order on his cluttered desk. "I'm just a historian. Occasionally, those in the theater and television world ask me to run my eye over a script or two for historical accuracy, and I'm glad to. But that is it. I assure you."

"Speaking of assurances, where were you last night when Dominique Plantagenet was murdered?" Finn asked, his tone even but firm.

"Here," the professor answered too quickly, "working on my latest paper on Anglo-Saxon runes."

"Anyone who can confirm that, Professor?" Amelia chimed in, skeptical.

"Mrs. Penrose, the night custodian. She saw me when she locked up," the professor retorted, an edge of panic creeping into his voice despite the confident words.

"Thank you, we'll verify that," Finn said, exchanging a glance with Amelia.

Finn's patience was waning as the minutes ticked by, the room feeling smaller, more confined. It was the same sensation that gnawed at his stomach during undercover stings—waiting for the moment when everything could unravel. The musty scent of aging paper and leather-bound tomes seemed to thicken the surrounding air. Prof. Hemingway's office, a cave of academia, was a stark contrast to the sterile interrogation rooms Finn was accustomed to.

Finn saw a bead of sweat on the old man's brow. He was sure the man was holding something back.

"Professor," Finn asked. "How would you like to join us down at the police station for a little chat?" His voice betrayed none of the urgency he felt pulsing beneath his calm demeanor.

"Of course, I understand," Hemingway replied, his tone oddly high-pitched. The old man's hand quivered as he reached for the phone, fingers tapping in a number with surprising speed. The harsh sound of the dial tone cut through the silence before being replaced by the muffled buzz of an answered call.

"Mrs. Penrose? Yes, it's Harold. Could you send security to my office?" Hemingway's eyes flickered toward Finn and Amelia, and the trace of panic they had sensed earlier now flared into something more akin to fear. "I do not seek trouble. Just a precaution, you understand. I want witnesses here."

The tension in the room ratcheted up another notch. Finn could feel Amelia's eyes on him, her own senses picking up the shift in atmosphere. The professor was hiding something; his voice had the brittle quality of glass on the verge of shattering. Finn's mind raced through the possibilities, each more damning than the last. What was Hemingway afraid of? Or rather, who? The problem was, Finn knew they didn't have enough to force the man into an interview room.

He wanted to change tact.

"Professor, if you come..." Finn said, stepping forward.

Before Finn could speak further, Hemingway stood abruptly, his arm sweeping across the desk in a broad, erratic arc. A precarious stack of books teetered and toppled, raining down upon Finn's foot with the force of an unexpected blow.

"Damn!" Finn grunted, pain jolting up his leg. He stumbled back, knocking into a shelf lined with delicate artifacts that clattered ominously but held their ground.

"I won't be handled by the likes of you," the Professor shouted.

Amelia's laughter broke through the tension like a crack of lightning, sharp and unexpected. She quickly covered her mouth with her hand, but her eyes danced with irrepressible mirth. "You okay there, tough guy?" she teased, the corners of her eyes crinkling.

"Fine," Finn gritted out, though his foot pulsed with every heartbeat. The absurdity of being taken down by ancient literature wasn't lost on him, and despite the throbbing in his toe, a reluctant smile tugged at his lips.

"We weren't going to force you, Professor," Amelia said, reassuringly.

The door to the office burst open and one uniformed security guard and a man wearing a tweed suit rushed in, their faces painted with concern. "Everything alright, Professor?" the suited man asked, scanning the room, his hand resting on the baton at his belt.

"Fine, fine, Hastings," Hemingway assured them, waving a dismissive hand. "This is my assistant, and I'm sure he'd be glad to show you out."

"What is the meaning of all this?" Hastings said. "The Professor is not a well man."

"Hastings!" Hemingway snapped. "I'm sure they do not need to know of my medical woes."

"Sorry, Sir," Hastings replied.

"Besides," Hemingway said with an impish grin. "It was just a little accident."

"Accident? The old man is deadly with a book," Finn said, straightening up and giving the guards a nod of appreciation. "I wouldn't like to be stuck in a library with him."

"I'm sure you'll live," the professor said.

"I could have you charged with assaulting an officer of the law," Finn said, still hobbling.

"As I understand it," the professor said, smiling. "You're not an officer of the law, at least not in these lands. Besides, it was an accident."

"If you've quite finished..." Hasting said. "I'll show you out."

Amelia stepped forward and handed the professor a card. "If there's anything else you think of, please contact us."

The professor nodded.

But as they were about to leave, Finn turned and asked: "When you've been asked to consult on a project, are you ever asked to look over props like old knives, that sort of thing?"

The old man's face went pale. "Please, I have work to do."

Finn nodded knowingly, and they left.

As they exited the cluttered office, Finn couldn't shake the feeling that they were missing a vital piece of the puzzle. Hemingway's call to campus security, his sudden movement—it was all too rash, too ill-tempered for what should have been a simple conversation.

"Please forgive the Professor," Hasting said, walking alongside them.

"When you say he isn't well..." Amelia started.

"A bad heart," Hasting said, mournfully. "We don't know how long he has. Could be two years, could be two months. I've been brought in to assist him as long as he wants as his archivist, but he has been a bit erratic lately..."

"Okay," Finn said, shaking Hastings' hand. "You've got your work cut out for you, my man. See you."

They walked over the threshold and back into the cold air.

"I don't like this," Finn said to Amelia once they were out of earshot. "Something doesn't add up here with Hemingway. If he's sick, could he be settling scores before he goes?"

Amelia nodded, her face set in a determined line. "Agreed. Let's see what Mrs. Penrose has to say about our professor's alibi."

Finn leaned against the cool metal of their unmarked car, his gaze lingering on the stone facade of Oldbridge University's oldest building, where the shadows played tricks on the eyes and every corner seemed to whisper secrets. The campus was quiet now, the usual hustle of academic life having ebbed away into the encroaching dusk. He rubbed at his chin, feeling the stubble that bristled there, as he dissected their encounter with Hemingway.

"His hands," Finn murmured, almost to himself, "They were trembling when he picked up that book—the one that ended up on my foot." His voice held a hint of frustration, the pieces of the puzzle not quite aligning in his mind.

Amelia, who had been flipping through her notes, looked up. "Parkinson's, maybe? He fits his profile—elderly, academic..." She trailed off, her thoughts mirroring his own. "But his frailty doesn't fit the killer's MO. Quick, precise, strong enough to overpower both victims much younger than him."

"Exactly." Finn pushed off from the car and began to pace, each step measured and deliberate. "The evidence we have is compelling. The parchment particles, his expertise in linguistics, his access to the props..." He stopped, running a hand through his hair. "But we saw him move in that office, Winters, there's no way he has the physicality required for the crimes."

"Could be a red herring," Amelia suggested, closing her notebook with a snap. "Someone planting evidence to throw us off scent. We've seen it before, especially with high-functioning psychopaths."

"Or an accomplice." Finn's jaw clenched at the thought. Someone else out there, pulling strings, using Hemingway's knowledge for their own dark purposes. It was a chilling prospect, but it would explain the inconsistencies.

"Or that." Amelia conceded, her eyes reflecting the dying light as she regarded him. "So what's your gut telling you? Other than needing to eat more bad hot dogs?"

Finn stopped his pacing and stood still, letting the weight of the question settle on his shoulders. His gut had never led him astray before, even when logic seemed to contradict it. He closed his eyes briefly, allowing the events of the day to replay in his mind, seeking the elusive thread of truth amidst the tangled web of facts and observations.

He opened his eyes, meeting Amelia's questioning gaze with a resolute stare. "Hemingway isn't our killer, but let's get a constable to verify his alibi with Mrs Penrose. I still feel like Hemingway could be involved, even if more indirectly."

Amelia raised an eyebrow, the surprise evident on her face. "Despite everything pointing to him? That's a bold statement, Finn."

"Too bold, too obvious," he said, certainty lacing his words. "It's the subtleties that tell the true story, not the glaring neon signs. And Hemingway... he's just another piece of the backdrop."

"Alright then," Amelia replied, a spark of admiration in her tone for his instinctual read on the situation. "But it doesn't leave us with much to follow. We need another lead."

Finn's lips curved in a grim smile. "We go back to the beginning. Re-examine the evidence, look for the connection we're missing. And we keep a close eye on Hemingway, just in case we're wrong."

"Back to square one." Amelia nodded, her determination matching his. "Feels like a rubbish version of Snakes and Ladders."

"We're going to have to talk about your jokes, Winters," Finn said. "They aren't up to standards at the moment."

Amelia walked to the car door and opened it. "You must be rubbing off on me."

"Where to?" Finn asked. "Back to the station?"

"No," Amelia answered as the clouds rushed in above them. "We should speak to the next of kin. Perhaps they'll no something... Anything."

CHAPTER EIGHT

Finn was still mesmerized by the English countryside, even after living there for nearly a year. As they drove, the sun hung low in the sky, despite it only being afternoon, a weary sentinel on its ceaseless march toward early dusk, as Finn Wright guided the unmarked police car through winding country lanes. The farther they drove from the clamor of London, the more the landscape seemed born from another era. Fields stretched out like yellow green seas, weary grass hoping for Spring, resisting winter's hold.

Beside him, Amelia sat with her gaze fixed on the file spread open on her lap. Her brow was furrowed, a testament to the weight of the case that had brought them to this corner of England. The car's engine hummed a steady rhythm, punctuated by the occasional crunch of gravel beneath tires.

They arrived at an old rectory nestled within a copse of ancient oaks, their gnarled limbs reaching for the faded azure above. As Finn parked the car, he couldn't help but feel the gravity of history pressing down upon them. The rectory, with its ivy-clad walls and Gothic windows, held the somber majesty of a forgotten time.

"Looks like something out of a Brontë novel," Amelia mused, her voice pulling Finn back to the present.

"Let's hope our visit here is less Wuthering Heights and more Agatha Christie," Finn replied, offering her a brief smile that didn't quite reach his eyes.

"You are full of surprises, Finn," Amelia said.

"I read," he said.

"Books with pictures don't count."

"I told you," he offered. "I even write short stories. Did you forget my literary prowess?"

"It must have got lost in amongst all of that charm," she said with a smile. Finn felt like she meant it, and that stirred something deep inside of him.

They approached the rectory and Finn knocked an old blackened knocker against the aged oak of the front door.

They were greeted at the door by a housekeeper whose stoic manner belied a watchful eye.

"I'm Inspector Winters," Amelia said. "This is Finn Wright, a consulting detective with the Home Office. We're here to speak with Lady Plantagenet about the untimely death of her niece."

"Oh, it's terrible news," the housekeeper said. "I know her ladyship is very pleased you are both on the case." She looked around and then whispered: "But she can be a little harsh at first, please bare with her."

"I'll use my New World charms," Finn said, smiling.

The housekeeper blushed and then said "follow me, please."

She led them through a narrow hallway lined with ancestral portraits—silent sentinels keeping vigil over the home. Their gazes seemed to follow Finn and Amelia, adding to the weight of scrutiny they already felt from the living.

Lady Agatha Plantagenet received them in a drawing-room where time stood still. Heavy drapes framed tall windows, filtering the light to cast a golden hue across the furniture. Family portraits, ensconced in gilded frames, adorned the walls—each face painted with the stern countenance of nobility.

"Detective Wright, Inspector Winters," Lady Agatha began, her voice the rustle of dry leaves. "Your presence here is both unexpected and unsettling."

Finn took note of her poise, the way she held herself with the bearing of one who had weathered many storms. Her eyes, the color of faded denim, held a depth of sorrow that spoke of recent grief.

"Apologies for the intrusion, Lady Agatha," Finn said, his tone respectful. "We're investigating circumstances around your niece's death and believe you might be able to help us understand some things."

"Please, have a seat." Lady Agatha gestured to a set of wing back chairs before settling into her own. Finn noted the delicate tremble of her hand, the only betrayal of her composed exterior.

"Thank you," Amelia said, accepting the invitation. Finn remained standing, preferring to keep the vantage point.

"Your niece, Dominique—did she ever mention anything about feeling under threat?" Finn asked.

"She mentioned receiving anonymous calls before her death," Lady Agatha said.

"Can you tell us anything about that?" Finn inquired, getting straight to the point.

Lady Agatha's gaze drifted to the window, as if the answer lay beyond the glass, in the encroaching night. "Yes," she confirmed, her voice a whisper. "She was frightened. Said she felt eyes upon her at all times, as though she was being watched by someone with malevolent intent."

"Did she have any idea who could be responsible?" Amelia asked gently.

"None," Lady Agatha replied after a long pause. "But I could hear it in her voice—the fear was real. And I must say, I always thought this would come from being in the theater. I always said she didn't have the fortitude to put up with being in the public eye. Stalkers are always a danger when you are as famous as my niece. I would have hired her a bodyguard, but she always said no."

Finn nodded slowly, processing the information. He could feel the day's light dimming around them, much like their chances of finding the killer before another life was taken.

The shadows of the room seemed to stretch and congeal as the day's light waned, casting an aged patina over the family portraits that watched from the walls. The air was heavy with whispers of the past, and Finn felt its weight as he scrutinized Lady Agatha, whose somber eyes held centuries of lineage. She reached beneath the mahogany coffee table, withdrawing a parcel wrapped in brown paper, aged like the leaves of an old manuscript.

"Before Dominique... passed," Lady Agatha said, her voice trailing off as she carefully placed the package on the table, "she received this."

Amelia leaned forward, the fabric of her blouse catching the last rays filtering through the window, creating a soft glow around her. But Finn's attention remained fixed on the package, a sense of foreboding tightening his chest. He stepped closer, his hands resisting the impulse to reach out and tear away the paper himself.

Agatha's fingers worked slowly, deliberately, peeling back the layers to reveal a leather-bound script, its corners worn, its spine cracked with age. Emblazoned on the cover was the title 'Richard III,' the name etched as though by a quill from another era.

"An odd gift for Dominique," Finn murmured, his gaze locked onto the script.

"Indeed," Agatha replied, opening the cover. There, nestled between the pages, lay a note, the parchment yellowed and curling at the edges.

"This is an older form of English," Amelia breathed, recognition flickering across her face. "Older than the previous note. Harder to make out and understand."

Finn didn't need to understand it to know its origin; the looping script was unmistakable. His memory flashed back to the crime scene—Dominique's lifeless hand, the paper clutched within. The note they'd found may have been written in an older form of English, but it bore the same archaic handwriting.

Lady Agatha's hand trembled visibly as she held up the note for them to see. Her eyes, once steely with aristocratic resolve, now brimmed with unspoken dread. The familiar scrawl seemed to mock them from the page, speaking of secrets long buried, of vendettas nursed through generations.

"Does this mean something to you, Lady Agatha?" Finn asked, his voice steady despite the pulse quickening at his temple.

"More than I wish it did," she whispered, the glint of ancestral jewelry at her throat dulling as if in sympathy with her growing unease. "It's Old English. In modern English it would say something akin to: The curtain shall fall soon enough."

Finn took the note, his fingers brushing against Agatha's. The contact sent a jolt through him, a current that spoke of fear and dark histories intertwined. The script was a specter, conjuring images of hooded figures and whispered plots carried through time by some malevolent force that refused to relinquish its grasp.

"Another piece connected to acting," Amelia said quietly, her analytical mind seemingly piecing together the implications.

"All of this seems to be connected to Richard III as a play," Finn's response was cryptic even to his ears. Yet he could not shake the feeling that they were being drawn deeper into a maze constructed long before their own lifetimes had begun. The note in his hand was a guidepost, one that pointed down a path shrouded in menace and mystery.

As he folded the note, tucking it carefully into his pocket, Finn knew that their investigation had just taken a turn into the obscure corridors of history. They were no longer merely hunting a murderer; they were excavating the secrets of the dead, hoping to find answers among the echoes of silent screams and ancient bloodlines.

"Why did he use an older form of English?" Finn mused out loud.

"Because he's trying to show how smart he is," Amelia answered.

"Maybe," Finn sighed. "Or maybe he just wants to be dramatic."

"I think he varies things," Amelia answered. "He's doing that deliberately to put us off."

Finn's attention was now caught by rows upon rows of nearby books. "That's some collection."

"My late husband's."

Finn's eyes roamed over the high shelves and dark wood paneling of Lady Agatha's library. The scent of old leather and the faint mustiness of paper filled his nostrils as he searched for something, anything, that might serve as a clue. He half hoped to stumble upon a family secret that would point to the killer, like the old horror stories from the 20s he often read as a kid. Amelia was similarly engaged, her gaze sharp as she perused the book titles and examined ornate objects with care.

But there was nothing to be found.

"If that's all," Lady Agatha said, looking tired. "I would like some privacy now."

"Let's wrap it up," Finn said, scanning the last shelf before him. His hand lingered on the spine of a book about the Wars of the Roses, feeling the grooves of the embossed fabric. He withdrew it, flipped through the pages out of habit, and then replaced it with a sense of finality. They had exhausted their search within the dim confines of the rectory and come up empty-handed.

"Thank you for your time, Lady Agatha," Amelia said.

"I'll show you out myself," the elderly lady smiled, wearily.

Leaving the library behind, they traversed the creaking hallways one last time. Finn noted the portraits lining the walls, their solemn faces watching over them in silent judgment. There was a whisper of the past here that clung to the air like cobwebs; it was tangible yet elusive, hiding its secrets well.

"Thank you for your hospitality, Lady Agatha," Finn said as they reached the front door. Her nod was brief, a mere dip of her chin, as if she too were weighed down by the knowledge that their visit had stirred more shadows than light.

"Take care," Amelia added, offering a small smile that seemed out of place in the gloom of the hallway. Lady Agatha's hand lifted in farewell, the jewels at her throat catching the waning daylight as the door closed behind the detectives.

***

The drive back to Hertfordshire HQ was quiet, the weight of unanswered questions filling the car like a third passenger. Finn gripped the steering wheel, knuckles white, while Amelia sat beside him, her fingers tapping against the open case file in her lap. The script from Dominique's package lay atop the other papers, its edges curling slightly.

"Anything from Agatha's reactions strike you as off?" Finn asked, breaking the silence. His gaze remained fixed on the road ahead, leaving the periphery of his vision to capture Amelia's response.

"Other than her obvious dismay at that note? Not overtly," Amelia considered, biting her lip thoughtfully. "But there was a hesitance when we mentioned the anonymous calls. As if she knew more than what she let on."

"Could be family secrets," Finn mused, adjusting his rear-view mirror. "Plantagenets have skeletons aplenty in their closets, no doubt. But none that seem to want to dance with us."

"Or we're not playing the right tune," Amelia countered, leaning back against the headrest. "Dominique's fears, the play script, the note... It's all connected somehow. I just can't shake the feeling that we're missing a crucial piece."

"Or someone's deliberately misplacing it for us," Finn said, his tone grim. "Max Vilne wouldn't hesitate to make this as convoluted as possible if he were the puppet master."

"He's nothing to do with this, Finn," Amelia said, gently patting his arm. "We need to stay focused on the case at hand." Amelia's determination was palpable, her eyes reflecting the streetlights as dusk settled around them.

"Agreed," Finn replied, feeling the familiar stir of resolve within him. "I'll spend some time looking over Richard the Third. I've read it before, but there seems to be some connection. We might get lucky with something the killer has used from it."

Finn pressed the accelerator, urging the car through the snarl of London traffic with a deftness born of years on these streets. The day's fading light cast long shadows across the dashboard, mirroring the darkening of his thoughts. They had combed Lady Agatha's home with precision, turning over memories and minutiae alike, yet each clue seemed to only burrow deeper into obscurity.

"Crossroads," he muttered under his breath, eyes scanning the horizon where city met sky—a junction of ends and beginnings.

"Sorry?" Amelia glanced over, her profile outlined against the backdrop of the passing cityscape.

"Nothing," Finn shook his head slightly. "Just thinking aloud." He could feel the weight of the case like a lead vest—every detail they unearthed was heavy with significance, yet slippery as an eel when it came to tangible leads.

"Are you sure?"

"I can't remember the last time in my life when I didn't feel at a crossroads," he answered. "And I'm worried I always take the wrong turn."

"No, you don't," she said with a smile. "We've got five hard cases under our belts. You've proven yourself time and time again. And your personal life... Think of it as an opportunity opening up rather than a door closing."

"Is there an opportunity?" Finn asked.

"Maybe," Amelia answered. "I think we should call it a day and get some rest. Hopefully the night will be a peaceful one.

Finn knew that it would not be.

They then sat in silence for the rest of the drive until they reached Great Amwell, where Finn bid Amelia goodnight and retired within, hoping that things would be clearer in the morning. But the night would not let him go so easily.

CHAPTER NINE

The London night embraced him like an accomplice, its shadows draping around his form with a familiarity that felt almost affectionate. He stood motionless, a specter blending into the darkened alleyway, his eyes intently fixed on the soft glow emanating from a third-floor window of the apartment building across the street. The gentle murmur of city life—the distant honk of taxis, the muffled laughter of passersby—played like background music to the scene unfolding before him.

Inside that warmly lit room, Jillian Bruce drew her bow across the strings of her violin, the notes soaring, dancing through the air with a grace that belied the heaviness in his chest. Unaware of his watchful gaze, she moved through her nightly routine, her silhouette casting an elegant shadow against the curtains which fluttered ever so slightly with each breath of the night wind.

The killer had to see her. Carefully, methodically, the killer climbed up the side of the building, moving up several pipes that clung to the outside. Finally, the killer stopped, able to look inside.

On the wall opposite was a large portrait, and killer grinned at it, menacingly. It was the legendary King of Scotland, Robert the Bruce. A king whose lineage was the reason the killer was there in the first place.

Jillian, with her lithe fingers and the crown of auburn hair cascading over the delicate arch of her shoulders, was more than just another inhabitant of this sprawling city. She was a direct descendant of Robert the Bruce, her lineage woven into the very fabric of Scotland's tumultuous history. And now, she unknowingly played for an audience of one—a man whose appreciation for her talents was dwarfed only by the darkness in his soul.

As the melody swelled, her movements became more fervent, more impassioned, as though the music itself were a living entity within her. He watched intently, every note etched into his memory, every shift of her body cataloged for later reflection. This was no mere observation; it was a study, a dedication to detail that would serve a purpose far beyond tonight's voyeuristic pursuit.

In the quiet comfort of the London night, the killer found solace. It was not the solace of peace or contentment, but one of anticipation—a prelude to the chaos he was destined to unleash. The city's ambient glow cast a pale silver light across the alley, giving the contours of his face a spectral quality as he peered up at her window. His presence was as intangible as the mist that sometimes crept along the Thames in the early hours of dawn, yet it was there, persistent and waiting.

There was beauty in the unseen, in the moments that lay dormant between the heartbeats of the city. As he stood watching Jillian Bruce, oblivious in her artistic solitude, he savored the stillness before the storm, the silent overture to a symphony of dread.

He could have stayed all night, hidden in the shadows, absorbing the sight of Jillian lost in her craft—but his purpose required discipline, and his time here neared its end. His heart thrummed in a rhythm that competed with the distant, muffled sounds of car engines and sporadic laughter from passersby enjoying the London nightlife. The pulse was not born of fear or cold; it was excitement that coursed through his veins as he watched her—a performer for an audience of one.

The killer knew the time had come. His hands searched for a small diamond-tipped tool in his pockets. Pulling it out, he moved to another window of the apartment along a ledge, and carefully cut into the glass, creating a hole big enough to undo the latch.

Then, he was inside, but he moved silently, clinging to the shadows like a ninja of old. There, he waited and watched.

Jillian Bruce moved within her apartment with an unconscious grace, her silhouette casting long, elegant shadows on the walls as she swayed gently to music only she could hear. Her arms rose and fell, harmonious and fluid, commanding the bow and strings with a natural ease that left him spellbound. There was something innately captivating about her, perhaps a vestige of her noble lineage, and it drew him in, igniting a perverse sense of attraction that twisted within him like a dark vine seeking sunlight.

He observed, patient as a sculptor chiseling at marble, noting each subtlety: the way her hair tumbled over her shoulders as she tilted her head, the slight furrow of concentration between her brows, the rise and fall of her chest with each breath drawn into her lungs. It was intimate, this silent study of her, and yet so detached—fitting for one who saw people not as souls but as pawns in a grander design.

It wasn't just her movements that held his attention. His eyes, sharp and discerning even in the low light, caught sight of the partially opened window at the back of Jillian's apartment. A slender gap inviting the night air to caress the interior, whispering secrets that only he would understand. No doubt she relished the feeling of the cool breeze against her skin after the heat generated by hours of practice, the fresh air mingling with the scent of wood and rosin.

Jillian Bruce, a talented violinist, unwitting participant in this morbid dance, remained blissfully ignorant of the fate that he had crafted for her—a fate now symbolically resting in his hands. The lineage she bore proudly in her name had drawn him to her, a moth to the flame, and he could not resist the allure of adding her to his collection of silenced histories.

The killer's grip tightened around the small, diamond-tipped tool hidden within his palm. His heart pounded with a mixture of excitement and dread as he approached Jillian Bruce from behind, his footsteps silent against the plush carpet. Her music continued to fill the room, masking any sound of his presence. With each step closer, he could feel the weight of history pressing down upon him, urging him to fulfill his twisted destiny.

As Jillian reached the crescendo of her performance, her body swaying with an ethereal grace, the killer seized his moment. In one swift motion, he lunged forward and covered her mouth with a gloved hand, muffling her startled gasp. He stabbed again and again, relentlessly. Panic flashed in her eyes as she struggled against his iron grip, but it was futile. He had already planned every move meticulously. With a surge of strength fueled by his warped conviction, he forced her limp body onto the floor, smothering any remnants of life that remained within her.

As he gazed upon the emblem in his hand, which he dropped to the floor next to her dead hand, a shiver of satisfaction ran down his spine. It was as if the very legacy of Robert the Bruce was sanctioning his act, compelling him to continue on this path of dark homage. He relished the feeling, allowing it to wash over him like a dark tide.

The emblem was more than a mere signature—it was an announcement, a declaration that another chapter of history was about to be closed by his hand. He imagined the headlines, the frantic scramble of investigators trying to piece together the puzzle he so artfully designed, always remaining one step ahead. For now, though, the emblem was his alone to admire.

In the solitude of the night, with London's endless labyrinth sprawled out before him, he felt like a king overlooking his domain.

But unlike the monarchs of old, his rule would be whispered in hushed tones, his reign marked by the chilling legacy he left behind—one that Finn Wright, no matter how determined, would struggle to decipher.

    He looked down at his hands, the dim light of a nearby lamp casting them in a pale glow. It was time to retreat, to vanish before any trace of his presence could be discovered. And the city welcomed him back into its embrace.

CHAPTER TEN

Despite the morning sun, the steering wheel felt cold under Finn Wright's grip as he navigated the unassuming streets of a silent suburban neighborhood. The houses, lined up like aging sentries, bore witness to the lives unfolding within their walls. One such dwelling, a modest two-story with peeling white paint and a shingle roof in need of repair, held secrets that Finn was determined to uncover. It was the home of the first victim, Rebecca Hanover.

Sleep hadn't come easy the night before, but it rarely did for Finn when his mind was on a case.

"Number forty-two," Amelia Winters stated from the passenger seat, her finger pointing to the house that seemed to shrink away from their scrutiny, as if it could recede into the shadows of its own dark history. She consulted her notes briefly, then slid them into her satchel without another word, her face set in a stoic mask that Finn had come to recognize as her armor against the emotional toll of their grim work.

Finn parked the car, the engine's hum dying into silence as he turned the key. He stepped out onto the curb, feeling the weight of the winter air press against him, thick with the coming rain and laden with an ominous whisper that seemed to emanate from the house itself. Amelia joined him, her gaze sweeping the street before returning to the task at hand.

"Let's see what Rebecca's ghost has to say," Finn murmured, more to himself than to Amelia. He led the way up the cracked walkway, his hand resting on the service pistol concealed beneath his jacket. Not that he expected trouble in broad daylight, but old habits died hard, and he had long since learned to trust the prickling sensation on the back of his neck—the silent alarm bell that seldom lied.

The front door of Rebecca Hanover's former home offered no resistance as Finn turned the key provided by the local police. It swung open with a muted creak, revealing a narrow hallway coated with the dust of abandonment. Sunlight filtered through dirty windows, casting angular patterns across the floorboards and illuminating particles of dust that floated lazily in the still air.

Stepping inside, Finn allowed the door to close behind them with a soft click. The sound seemed too loud in the hush of the house, a violation of the sanctity of the crime scene that stood preserved in time. He drew in a breath, tasting the mustiness of disuse, and felt an involuntary shiver snake down his spine—an echo of the horror that had once unfolded within these walls.

"Feels like walking into a crypt," Amelia murmured, her voice low and reverent.

"We all live in crypts of our own making," Finn replied, his eyes scanning the entrance for any sign that might connect this place to the murder of Dominique Plantagenet. But everything lay untouched, frozen in time as a place of everyday life violently interrupted. Finn wondered if the lack of any sign of a struggle or break-in might mean that Rebecca knew the killer, trusting him until it was too late.

He could almost sense Rebecca's presence here, a lingering imprint of fear and surprise forever etched into the atmosphere. This was where she had lived; this was where her story had ended. Finn led the way, his footsteps deliberate and cautious as he navigated the narrow hallway of Rebecca Hanover's former home. He observed the walls, touched by the faintest hints of yellowing wallpaper that had peeled at the edges like old scabs. The stale air was heavy, carrying a silence that seemed to pulse with unanswered questions. Amelia followed close behind, her presence a steady reassurance amidst the gloom.

Finn's eyes darted from one corner of the hallway to the other, his senses heightened by the eerie stillness that enveloped them. A bead of sweat trickled down his temple, and he discreetly wiped it away with the back of his hand. He couldn't shake off the feeling that they were being watched.

"You know, Amelia, I've always wanted to meet a friendly ghost. Maybe one will pay us a visit."

Amelia chuckled softly, her eyes scanning their surroundings. "Well, if one does, let's hope it doesn't have any unfinished business to attend to."

As Finn took another cautious step forward, his foot collided with an old wooden chair leg that had been carelessly left in the hallway. The chair teetered precariously for a moment before crashing onto the floor with an echoing thud.

Startled by the sudden noise, Finn jumped back instinctively and let out an embarrassed yelp. "Whoops! Just testing my reflexes."

Amelia burst into laughter at Finn's reaction, unable to contain herself any longer. "Smooth move, fearless detective." Finn feigned bravery as he straightened his posture and adjusted his jacket.

"Just making sure you're on your toes too, Inspector Winters."

Amelia raised an eyebrow playfully and crossed her arms over her chest. "Oh please, Finn. I'm always on my toes."

The levity was momentary as a gloom descended once more upon the place.

"Check the baseboards, corners," Finn instructed tersely, voice barely above a whisper, "Any sign of forced entry, any disturbance."

Their eyes combed the environment, searching for the subtle deviations that might connect this scene to Dominique's—a thread to follow in the labyrinthine weave of their case. As they moved, each step felt like a descent further into the psyche of the individual who'd shattered the sanctity of these walls. Finn's jaw clenched; the methodical undoing of lives was an act he could never reconcile with, much less understand.

In the living room, the furniture lay draped in ghostly white cloths, undisturbed since the investigation had concluded. The couch's outline beneath its shroud was soft, unassuming, belying the violence that had once breached its confines. It was all too easy to picture the killer here, moving with cold precision through the space.

"Nothing out of place," Amelia noted, echoing his own observations. Her tone carried the weight of frustration, a reflection of their shared need to find something—anything—that would guide them toward a lead.

"Let's see where she was found," Finn said, leading the way to the back of the house. His mind was a taut wire, every sense sharpened on the edge of anticipation.

The room was modest, the bed made with a meticulousness that spoke of Rebecca's character, the tidiness that marked her life now a silent exhibit of her end. Finn approached the bed, squaring his shoulders as if bracing against an unseen adversary. Here, amid the stillness, the lack of struggle was palpable—the scene was entirely devoid of the chaos that typically accompanied violence.

"Like Dominique," he murmured, more to himself than Amelia. "No signs of resistance. It suggests surprise...trust, maybe?"

"Someone she knew... Or someone light on their feet," Finn mused.

Amelia drew closer, her gaze lingering on the pillowcase, smooth except for the hollow where Rebecca's head had rested that last time.

"Both victims caught off guard," she mused, "and both times, no one heard a thing. Professional, efficient."

Finn nodded, absorbing the room's details—the placement of a bedside photograph, the angle of the open window's curtains fluttering softly in the gentle breeze. It was a freeze-frame of normalcy, disrupted only by the memory of what had transpired. Finn's hands itched for his notepad, the compulsion to document each minute observation a well-honed instinct.

"A hitman?" he finally said, his voice a low rumble of disquiet. "Every move calculated and swift. Could someone like Professor Hemingway have hired a pro? Feel like I'm chasing shadows."

"Shadows can still lead us to light," Amelia countered, her optimism undiminished.

"Let's hope so," Finn conceded, feeling the weight of the case pressing down upon him. But it was that very pressure that honed his resolve. This killer had taken too much, hidden too well. It was time for the shadows to give up their secrets.

Finn ran a hand along the dust-free mantle, his fingertips skimming over the assortment of framed photographs—smiling faces frozen in happier times. The air hung heavy with silence, as if the house itself held its breath, guarding secrets of the past. Sunlight filtered through gauzy curtains, casting a warm glow that seemed at odds with the chill settling in his bones.

"Look at this," Amelia called softly from across the room.

He joined her by the bookcase, where novels and knick-knacks lined the shelves in meticulous order. She pointed to a row of hardcovers, their spines aligned with military precision. "Even the books... It's like someone came through here with a ruler."

"Rebecca may have had an obsessive attention to detail," Finn mused, eyes narrowing as he scanned the titles—an eclectic mix that spoke of broad interests or perhaps a mind in search of distraction. It was a stark contrast to the chaos that death usually left behind; there was no toppling stack of papers, no overturned lamp to mark a struggle. Even in the presence of such order, however, there was an undeniable void—a life interrupted.

"Or a deliberate attempt to leave no trace," Amelia offered. Her voice was steady, but Finn could detect the underlying strain. They were both feeling the tug of frustration, the nagging sense of being perpetually one step behind a ghost.

"Let's move on to the bedroom," Finn suggested, leading the way down the hallway. His shoes made soft impressions on the plush carpet, the sound somehow intrusive in the homelike quiet.

The bedroom door creaked open to reveal a sanctuary that appeared untouched by time or tragedy. The bed was made up neatly, the comforter's edges crisp and smooth. A dresser stood against the opposite wall, its surface clear except for a solitary jewelry box and a ceramic figurine of a dancer, mid-pirouette.

"God, it's like she just stepped out," Amelia whispered, echoing Finn's thoughts.

He circled the room slowly, taking in every inch—the slight fading of the wallpaper where picture frames had once hung, the faint scent of perfume that lingered in the air. There was a precision to everything, an eerie exactness that left the impression of life paused rather than stolen.

"I can't help the feeling that the killer hung around..." Finn's voice trailed off. He thought of Dominique's body, the same hollow vibe of a staged set waiting for actors who would never return.

"Do you really think the killer would hang around to... Tidy?" Amelia asked.

"I know it sounds weird," he said. "But think about it, maybe the killer had so much disdain for his victims, that he hate to cleanse their environment, too. This wouldn't be the first case where that sort of thing has happened. Like a post-death ritual."

"I don't see much else here that we can get at," Amelia pointed out.

It was then that something caught Finn's eye, something that would have been overlooked by most detectives. He walked over to a small shelf where several pictures sat. Various family and friends stood in the photos, smiling without a care in the world.

"Why are two photo frames faced down?" Finn asked.

He reached out and lifted one. In it, Rebecca stood in front of a sprawling mansion on a summer's day. Net to her were an older couple.

"Her parents, I'd imagine," Amelia said, looking at the photograph in Finn's hands.

"What makes you assume that?" Finn asked.

"The matching wedding rings," she said. "And you can see the family resemblance with Rebecca. I wonder if the killer turned the photo downward out of guilt so that the parents couldn't see him."

"I'm not sure our killer has any remorse," Finn added. He reached out to lift the other photograph. On it was the same mansion from a different angle, this time a young girl about 8 years old in a summer's dress was holding a daffodil in her hands in front of it.

"I don't think Rebecca had any siblings," Amelia mused out loud.

"It's not the family's gaze he's turning down," Finn said, gruffly. "It's the house. Where is this?"

Amelia answered straight away. "It's the Hanover family estate. I'm sure I've seen pictures of it before."

"Is it far?" Finn asked.

"No," came the answer.

"The killer had a connection to that place," he said. "Why else turn its gaze away? I think we need to head there and see what we can uncover."

Amelia nodded and looked around. "This place gives me the creeps, anyway."

***

The gravel crunched under the tires of their unmarked car, a gritty sound that felt like crushed snow. Finn's grip on the steering wheel was firm, his knuckles whitening as they approached the Hanover family estate. A wrought-iron gate parted before them, revealing a world of manicured lawns and hushed opulence.

Amelia's gaze swept over the expansive grounds, her sharp eyes assessing, cataloging. She turned to Finn with an unreadable expression. "Quite the contrast from the city's clutter."

"Money buys space and silence," Finn replied, his voice low. The estate spread before them like a carefully curated exhibit, each tree and shrub placed with intention.

They parked beside a fountain, its water murmuring secrets to the surrounding statues. As they exited the vehicle, Finn took in the stately home that loomed before them—a testament to old wealth and enduring legacies. He could almost feel the weight of tradition pressing against him, a tangible reminder of the lives shaped within these walls.

"The office called ahead. Mr. and Mrs. Hanover are expecting us," Amelia said, leading the way up the steps. Her confidence was a beacon he found himself drawn to, especially now, when every lead seemed to slip through their fingers like smoke.

The door opened before they could knock, and a woman stood there, her age etched into the lines of her face. Her eyes were clouded with grief but carried an unmistakable strength. Beside her, a man, stooped with sorrow yet fortified by resolve, extended his hand to Finn.

"Detective Wright, Inspector Winters. We are the Hanovers... Rebecca's parents. Please come in," he said, voice brittle like autumn leaves.

"Thank you for seeing us at such short notice," Finn said, crossing the threshold. The interior of the house was another realm altogether. Every surface spoke of care and attention, each artifact a whisper from the past.

"Can we offer you tea or coffee?" Mrs. Hanover asked, her politeness a veneer over her pain.

"Nothing for us, thank you," Amelia replied gently. "We won't take much of your time."

They settled into a sitting room where the air seemed thick with memories. Finn could almost hear the echo of laughter that once filled the room, now stifled by tragedy. Rebecca's parents sat across from them, hands clasped together like a lifeline. Finn thought of Rebecca as a girl in that summer's dress, not a care in the world. He hated how cruel the world could be.

"Tell us about Rebecca," Amelia prompted softly, her notebook open but her eyes fixed on the couple, inviting trust.

Mrs. Hanover inhaled sharply, steeling herself. "Our daughter was vibrant, full of life. She loved the theater, always involved in some production or other." Her voice wavered, "She had such dreams..."

"Did she have many friends from the theater?" Finn inquired, leaning forward. His mind raced—Rebecca's passion for the stage mirrored Dominique's. Was it merely a coincidence?

"Many," Mr. Hanover confirmed, his voice rough. "But after she... passed, few have been in touch. It's a transient world, the theater."

Finn noted the subtle shift in the man's tone, a shadow of disapproval perhaps. He filed it away mentally; every nuance mattered.

"Was there anyone special in her life? Someone she might have confided in about any troubles in her life?" Amelia asked.

"Rebecca was private about her relationships," Mrs. Hanover said, and Finn detected a flicker of something akin to reluctance. "She didn't bring friends home often."

"I was a bit like that when I was younger," Finn offered a sympathetic nod. He observed the couple, their shared grief creating an impenetrable bond. Yet, there was more to unravel here—layers of a life cut short, pieces of a puzzle that refused to fit neatly together.

"Anything you can remember could be crucial," Amelia added, her voice soft but insistent.

Mr. Hanover's gaze met Finn's squarely. "We want justice for our daughter, Detective. We'll help in any way we can."

"Thank you," Finn said, feeling expectation settle on his shoulders. "So there were no arguments or problems with anyone in the run-up to her death?"

"No," Mr Hanover replied. "Our daughter didn't get into that sort of thing."

"And what about boyfriends or anything like that?" asked Amelia.

Mr Hanover sighed. "Rebecca didn't have a boyfriend."

"Well..." Mrs Hanover said. "There was a nasty piece of work she saw for a time. James Blackwood is his name."

Finn looked at Amelia knowingly and then said: "What made him nasty, exactly?"

"He tried to take our Rebecca away," Mr Hanover said, abruptly.

"Like kidnap?" asked Amelia.

"It might as well have been," Mr Hanover replied. "The boy persuaded her that she had to give up her birthright. That she needed to fight against the 'elites' of English society."

"Birth right?" Finn asked. "Wait. Your second name is Hanover. I take it that's not a coincidence?"

"No," Mrs Hanover replied. "We're technically royalty. Charles here is 23rd in line."

"Oh," Finn nodded. "That's amazing."

Amelia gave Finn a look that he knew well—it was a silent sign that they were on the right track. Another death, another distant royal wiped out.

Amelia leaned forward, her eyes fixed on the grieving parents. "Can you tell us when exactly Rebecca and James Blackwood split up? How long before her death?"

Mr. Hanover sighed heavily, his voice tinged with sorrow. "It was only a few weeks prior," he replied, his gaze distant as he recalled the painful memory. "Rebecca came back to the estate one evening, visibly upset. She told us that she had ended things with James because he had become too radical for her tastes." Mrs. Hanover nodded in agreement, tears welling in her eyes. "She said that James was consumed by his beliefs and wanted to fight against what he called the scum of English society. It frightened her, and she didn't want any part of it."

Finn's mind raced as he processed this new piece of information. James Blackwood's radical views certainly could have been motivation enough to kill off a couple of high society flyers. Could there be a connection between James and the murders? He made a mental note to dig deeper into James Blackwood's background.

"Did Rebecca mention anything specific about why she broke up with him?" Amelia asked gently, her pen poised above her notebook.

Mr. Hanover shook his head sadly. "She didn't go into much detail, but she did say that James became increasingly obsessed with his cause and started talking about taking drastic actions to achieve it."

Amelia scribbled down notes while Finn remained in his thoughts.

Finn couldn't shake the royal family hypothesis. He was more certain than ever that this was what was motivating the killer, but was there something else behind the murders, too? Something deeper?

"Did Rebecca ever express any fears or concerns about James?" Finn asked cautiously.

Mrs. Hanover hesitated for a moment before answering, her voice trembling slightly. "She never explicitly mentioned being afraid of him, but there were times when she seemed... unsettled. Like something was bothering her."

Finn's intuition prickled at the mention of Rebecca's unease. He couldn't help but wonder if she had caught a glimpse of James' darker side, the side that could potentially lead him down a path of violence.

"Do you happen to have his address?" Finn asked.

"Of course," Mr Hanover said, taking out a small notebook from his inside pocket, jotting down a few words, and then handing the paper to Finn.

"Thank you for sharing this information with us," Amelia said, her voice filled with empathy. "We will look into James Blackwood and his possible connection to Rebecca's murder."

Mr. Hanover nodded, his eyes filled with a mix of gratitude and desperation. "Please find whoever did this to our daughter. We need justice for Rebecca."

Finn felt the weight of their expectations resting heavily upon him as he met Mr. Hanover's gaze. "We will do everything in our power to bring the killer to justice," he promised, his voice steady.

The Hanovers showed Finn and Amelia to the door, and then Finn stood next to the unmarked police car, in thought.

"Pound for your thoughts?" Amelia asked.

"Isn't it a penny?" Finn asked, bemused.

"Not these days with the exchange rate," Amelia laughed.

"We need to question this James Blackwood person," Finn suggested.

"Yeah," Amelia answered. "But you seem a little more perturbed than just that?"

"I was just thinking back to our previous case and the activists surrounding Richmond Castle," he said. "We know firsthand how dangerous someone with the wrong cause can be."

"Agreed," Amelia replied, opening the door to her car. "We'll keep our eyes out for trouble. I just hope this time we don't end up in a watery ditch."

CHAPTER ELEVEN

The gravel crunched under the tires of their unmarked car, a soundtrack to the unease churning in Finn's gut as they approached Blackwood's home. The evening was drawing in, and soon it would be dark. The building loomed ahead, its weathered facade and overgrown garden mirroring the decay that seemed to cling to James Blackwood's reputation. Finn's hand rested on the door handle, feeling the cold metal against his palm—a grounding sensation against the buzz of his instincts.

"Looks homely," Amelia remarked sarcastically, her voice low but steady as she scanned the structure with a detective's practiced eye.

"If by homely, you mean a bomb site," Finn replied, pushing open the car door. The air was heavy with the scent of damp earth and something else, something that reminded him of old pages. He stepped out, his boots sinking slightly into the soft ground as he closed the door with a soft thunk behind him.

Together, they navigated the path to the front door, sidestepping a rusted bicycle and an assortment of garden tools left carelessly on the lawn. As they reached the porch, the wind picked at the loose shingles above them, echoing the restlessness stirring within Finn. This place was a physical echo of Blackwood—the man's essence permeated through the rotting wood and shattered windows.

Amelia rang the bell, the sound hollow in the silence that followed. Finn watched her, appreciating her calm demeanor despite the setting. She met his gaze briefly, a silent exchange before the door creaked open.

James Blackwood stood in the doorway, a figure of suspicion cloaked in his twenties. His sharp features seemed chiseled with defiance, framed by a tangle of dark hair that fell unkempt over his brooding eyes. There was an air of intensity about him, as if every word spoken was carefully chosen to convey a hidden agenda. Dressed in worn jeans and a faded black t-shirt that bore the emblem of a clenched fist, he exuded an aura of rebellion that clashed with the quaint surroundings of his neglected home. His gaze lingered on Finn and

Amelia with a mix of challenge and calculation, hinting at depths darker than the shadows that danced behind him.

"Mr. Blackwood?" Amelia inquired.

Mr. Blackwood hesitated at the threshold, his eyes darting between Finn and Amelia with a guarded wariness. "I can smell a pig from a mile away. What do you want? I don't think this is a good time," he said, his voice tight with anger.

Amelia's gaze remained steady, her tone firm yet composed. "We have some questions regarding a matter of importance, Mr. Blackwood. The murder of Rebecca Hanover. It would be in your best interest to cooperate."

Blackwood's jaw clenched, his reluctance palpable as he shifted on his feet. "No. I don't want to talk about it or her. You can't just let you barge in like this," he stammered, a flicker of defiance in his eyes.

Amelia took a step forward, her presence commanding yet reassuring. "We understand your concerns, Mr. Blackwood. However, if you choose not to assist us voluntarily, we will return with a warrant and the necessary backup to conduct our search," she stated evenly.

Finn observed the subtle play of emotions on Blackwood's face—a fleeting struggle between defiance and apprehension. The mention of a warrant seemed to tip the scales as unease clouded Blackwood's features.

"This is for the best, James," Amelia said, gently this time. "Five minutes and we will be out of here. Make it easy on yourself."

"Or we'll make it hard," Finn said in an authoritative voice. He knew Amelia was playing 'good cop', it was only fitting that he took the other role.

"I... I don't want any trouble. But you'll need to be quick," Blackwood finally relented, his voice strained. "Fine, come in."

As Finn followed Amelia inside, there was an unspoken tension hanging in the air—an undercurrent of suspicion and unease that lingered within the walls of Blackwood's home. The faint scent of stale air mingled with something more acrid as they ventured further into the shadowed interior.

Finn's gaze swept over the dimly lit hallway as he followed Amelia into James Blackwood's home. Blackwood was a collector, a man buried in books like Professor Hemingway. But books with a different bent.

Instead of historical artifacts and tattered manuscripts on British royalty, his eyes landed on cluttered shelves adorned with books on anti-establishment politics and manifestos. The titles screamed rebellion, their covers bearing bold slogans and provocative imagery that mirrored Blackwood's own defiant stance against the establishment. Finn couldn't help but notice the same simmering discontent that lurked beneath the surface of Blackwood's demeanor. Each book was a manifesto in itself, a silent proclamation of dissent that painted a vivid picture of Blackwood's ideological leanings. Finn realized that this was a confrontation with someone whose beliefs ran deep and dangerous. But were those convictions enough to fuel murder itself?

Finn watched as Amelia's gaze swept over the room before settling on Blackwood, who stood rigidly before them. "Thank you for your cooperation, Mr. Blackwood," she said calmly, her words carrying an unspoken warning beneath their polite veneer.

Blackwood nodded tersely, an uneasy tension threading through the silence that enveloped them like a shroud.

"Well?" Blackwood said, turning to face them, his voice carrying an edge that matched the atmosphere of his abode. "What do you want to know? Whether I killed Rebecca?"

Finn's gaze didn't waver from the items scattered around them. It was as if they had walked into the mind of the killer, seeing first-hand the obsessive disdain for the crown. Each pamphlet, each vitriolic article felt like a clue, but also a distraction. There was too much here, too many pieces that fit the profile, yet nothing that directly tied Blackwood to the murders.

"Something like that," Finn said, keeping his tone neutral, before pointing at the scattered books and pamphlets. "Quite the collection," Finn finally said.

"Knowledge is power," Blackwood replied cryptically, though the words felt hollow in the dense air of the room.

"Know thy enemy?" Finn said rhetorically.

As Finn looked at Blackwood, his thoughts circled back to Rebecca Hanover's signet ring—the royal crest that had been so incongruous in her modest home. Here, amidst Blackwood's vehement rejection of monarchy, such an item would be an anomaly, a piece out of place in his carefully curated display of dissent.

Finn knew these were only threads. He needed more if his suspicions were to prove correct. He eyed Blackwood, whose posture was rigid, his eyes a flickering dance of defiance and annoyance. The man's voice cut through the silence, sharp as a blade.

"I've told you before—I had nothing to do with either death." His words clashed with the radical literature that wallpapered the room, their every syllable tinged with the fervor of his beliefs.

"Either?" Amelia said with a raised eyebrow. "So, you are aware..."

"I keep tabs on local law enforcement," he grimaced. "Someone has to. I know Dominique Plantagenet was killed recently as well. Then you come knocking on my door because I'm an anti-establishment campaigner. Well, let me tell you, I had nothing to do with either. That Dominique lady probably got what was coming to her. But Rebecca... She meant something to me."

"It's not hard to connect your motive," Finn began, holding the man's gaze, "your house screams 'elites must die'." He gestured to the walls, where pamphlets and posters screamed for the end of monarchy.

"Beliefs aren't crimes," Blackwood countered, his chin lifting in challenge. "And I assure you, Detective, I'm not foolish enough to turn my convictions into murder. I might be an anarchist, but that doesn't mean I think murder is fine."

"Nonetheless," Amelia chimed in, her tone level but firm, "we need something concrete. Where were you on the 6th of January, the night Rebecca Hanover was killed?"

"I... I can't remember."

Finn could see that he was lying.

"Can't or won't?" Finn asked. "You know, sometimes a murderer feels guilt and they don't want to be reminded of their terrible crime."

"You lot are full of it!" James said, angrily. "I don't kill. That's one thing I don't do."

"Ah," Finn said with a grin. "But there is something you do that's a crime. So, could it be that you were doing something you shouldn't have been on the night Rebecca Hanover was killed, and that's why you refuse to tell us?"

James Blackwood's lips formed a tight line, his eyes evasive as Finn pressed for his whereabouts on the night of Rebecca Hanover's murder. The room felt suffocating, heavy with unspoken accusations that lingered between them like a tangible barrier. James' reluctance to cooperate only fueled Finn's suspicions further, each refusal a piece of the puzzle that seemed to fit too perfectly. Finn's gaze sharpened as he observed James closely, noting the subtle shifts in his demeanor—the nervous flicker in his eyes, the tightening of his jaw. It was the telltale signs of someone hiding more than just their alibi. The pieces began to fall into place in Finn's mind like a sinister jigsaw puzzle. "Okay! I was at a protest. That's all," he said through gritted teeth.

"And what exactly were you protesting?" Amelia asked.

"King George IV..." He said. "There's a statue of him in Bingham Town. We want it gone. Imperialist nonsense!"

"Was it peaceful?" Amelia asked.

James' eyes darted around, clearly looking for something to cling his hopes onto. "You weren't just at a protest, were you?" Finn's voice was calm but edged with steely determination. "You were doing somewhere else that night, weren't you? Committing a crime." A shadow passed over James' face, a fleeting moment of vulnerability before it hardened into defiance once more. "I don't know what you're talking about," he retorted, though the tremor in his voice betrayed his unease.

Finn leaned in closer, his tone lowering to a dangerous whisper. "Don't play games with us, Mr. Blackwood. Perverting the course of justice is a serious offense. You either start talking now, or we take you in for obstructing this investigation."

The weight of Finn's words hung heavy in the air, casting a pall over the room as James grappled with the ultimatum laid before him.

Amelia swiftly pulled out her phone, fingers flying across the screen as she searched for information on that fateful night. Her brows furrowed slightly before she looked up at James with an inscrutable expression.

"There were reports of vandalism at a statue of King George that same night," she stated evenly, her gaze piercing through James' facade. James scoffed dismissively. "You can't prove I did anything to that statue or that I saw anything. But I was with other people there for much of the night." Amelia arched an eyebrow before replying coolly, "We'll see about that. Get your witnesses ready to back up your story."

"How many witnesses?" Finn asked, wondering if it was all a ruse.

"Three, at least," he said. "Tommy Gillis, Mercy Willis, and Jack Millis."

Finn burst out laughing. "Gillis, Willis, and Millis? What are they a brass trio?"

"Don't laugh at me!" James said, loudly. "That's their names. They all live in a squat together in 18 Darington Lane in Bingham."

"We'll check that," Amelia said, noting it down. Finn was still laughing at the rhyming names and she nudged him in the ribs.

Finn wiped his brow and tried his best to keep a straight face.

"Let's talk about the night Dominique was killed—two nights ago." Finn said, eyeing Blackwood keenly as the man cleaned the black residue from his hands. "Where were you?"

"Here," Blackwood replied, meeting Finn's gaze squarely. "Alone, unfortunately, which I realize isn't ideal for my situation. But I spent the evening working on a draft for a speech."

"Can anyone corroborate that?" Amelia asked.

"Only my computer," Blackwood said, nodding toward an ancient desktop that hummed in the corner, its screen a dull glow amidst the clutter. "I sent emails late into the night. Timestamps will prove it."

"Emails alone aren't airtight," Finn mused aloud. "But they're a start."

"Check them, then," Blackwood urged, an edge of frustration creeping into his voice. "You'll see I'm telling the truth."

Finn wasn't certain, but it felt like the alibi would hold. They would need to verify it, though.

"Right," Finn finally conceded, nodding slowly. "We'll look into it."

He could feel Amelia's eyes on him, her own cogs turning. They both knew an alibi could be fabricated, but Blackwood's demeanor suggested a man confident in his innocence—or at least in his ability to persuade others of it. The line between the two was razor-thin, and it was Finn's job to determine on which side Blackwood truly stood.

Amelia's gaze bore into James Blackwood as she broached the delicate subject, her voice steady and probing.

"Mr. Blackwood, can you tell us about your relationship with Rebecca Hanover?"

A flicker of emotion crossed James' face before he composed himself. "Rebecca... she was everything to me," he began, his tone softening with a hint of regret. "We were together until a few weeks before her death."

Finn, observing closely, interjected with a direct question. "Why did you split up then?"

James hesitated for a moment, the weight of his answer evident in his eyes. "She couldn't leave her family behind for my cause," he admitted, a tinge of sorrow coloring his words. Finn's voice held an edge as he probed further.

"Were you more interested in the publicity of convincing a Hanover to forsake their royal ties or did you genuinely care for Rebecca?" The question seemed to strike a chord within James as he looked down briefly before meeting Finn's gaze resolutely.

"I cared for her deeply," he replied somberly, the sincerity in his voice palpable. Amelia then took the lead in questioning once more.

"Did you know of anyone who might have wanted to harm Rebecca?"

James shook his head slowly. "No, I can't think of anyone who would do such a thing to her." His brows furrowed slightly before adding, "But I wouldn't put it past some high society members to go to extremes if they felt threatened by Rebecca abandoning her royal lineage."

"That's a stretch," Finn said. "She's not a high-profile royal. It wouldn't bring the scandal you'd think if the 24th in line to the throne decided to turn against it."

The room fell into a contemplative silence as James' words lingered in the air like an unspoken accusation against those who held power and privilege. Finn noted the genuine concern etched on James' face, a stark contrast to the defiance he had shown moments earlier. As Amelia made notes of their conversation, Finn couldn't shake off the sense that beneath James Blackwood's fervent beliefs lay a heart burdened by loss and regret, tangled in a web of convictions and emotions that ran deeper than mere activism.

Amelia gave Finn a look of closure before turning to James.

"Thank you for your time, Mr. Blackwood," Amelia said, her voice cutting through the quiet. Her professionalism was impeccable, but Finn caught the slight furrow of her brow which betrayed her uncertainty as well.

"No doubt you'll fake some rotten charge," Blackwood replied, his hands clasped behind his back. "Those in power are all the same."

Finn watched him closely, noticing the subtle clench of Blackwood's jaw, the way his eyes darted towards the door as if longing for their departure. He could almost hear the unspoken thoughts that must be racing through Blackwood's mind, wondering if they believed his alibi, questioning what their next move would be.

"Your beliefs," Finn started, gesturing around the room, "they put you in a... particular light given the nature of these crimes."

"Beliefs are not evidence, Detective Wright," Blackwood retorted sharply. "And I have no love for violence. My fight is with words, not bloodshed."

"Words can inspire actions in others," Finn pointed out, his voice steady.

"Then find someone who has acted on them," Blackwood shot back, his tone bordering on defiance.

Amelia gathered her notes, giving Finn a look that signaled it was time to leave. As they moved toward the door, Finn took one last sweeping glance at the room—a visual echo of Blackwood's conviction against the throne.

He turned to James as he was leaving. "James, I'm not the biggest fan of aristocracy. But don't let your beliefs poison you. I'll be back if your alibi doesn't check out. Mark my words."

They stepped outside into the afternoon light, which did little to dispel the shadows that lingered in Finn's mind. Blackwood's alibi might hold water, yet everything else about him seemed to fit the profile they had built for the killer. But there was nothing concrete to tie him to the murders... Yet.

Finn felt the cold breeze brush against his face as he and Amelia made their way to their car. The visit to Blackwood's house had left him with more questions than answers. His instincts, honed by years of navigating the treacherous waters of criminal minds, whispered that there was more to uncover about James Blackwood.

"His alibi for Rebecca could be solid," Amelia mused as she slid into the passenger seat.

"But not Dominique. Seems being the operative word," Finn replied, his gaze fixed on the rear-view mirror, reflecting the decrepit facade of Blackwood's home.

"Are you suggesting we don't take him at his word?" Amelia asked, a sense of playfulness in her voice.

"That guy is trouble," Finn said, starting the engine.

"He might be, but let's not assume guilt just yet. But we should check the alibi ASAP," Amelia suggested, hope threading through her words.

"Right. And check the CCTV footage too around this area and at that statue. It's a long shot, but maybe it caught something that goes against Blackwood's claims."

"Let's hope for his sake that Blackwood's just a loudmouthed activist with an unfortunate hobby," Amelia murmured as they buckled up. Her voice held an edge of doubt, mirroring Finn's own thoughts.

"Hope, but don't bet on it," Finn said, putting the car into first and getting them moving.

"Can we get a constable to check the alibis? I think I might need some time to think the case over at the cottage," Finn said. "Get a little perspective on things. We don't have any fresh leads anyway... Would you mind?"

"No," Amelia said. "If that's what you want. I'm going to work late, so if you can drop me off at HQ on the way, I'd appreciate it."

Finn let out a laugh. "If you think that sort of emotional blackmail is going to work... You'd be right... I'll come with you and we can go over things for a few hours. Then, I'm hitting the hay."

"You just can't get away from me that easily," Amelia smiled.

Finn wished she knew how much of a blessing that truly was.

The car rolled away from Blackwood's home, leaving behind a scene etched with questions and the lingering unease that came with unfinished business.

CHAPTER TWELVE

Finn's hand pushed open the door of his cottage with a fatigue that seemed to creak on its hinges. Three hours of combing through records and making inquiries had taken its toll.

The stale air of disuse greeted him, mingling with the scent of old books and wood polish—a familiar aroma that was both comforting and suffocating in its encapsulation of solitude. He stepped inside, the click of the door shutting behind him resonating like a period at the end of another long, fruitless day. The cottage in Amwell Village, a haven provided by his friend Rob, now felt empty somehow.

Finn felt a deep unease settle into his bones. He longed to come home to a family, to a woman he loved. But all of that seemed so distant now, a twinkling possibility, dipping below the horizon.

For a short time, Demi had been there. But now she was back in the US under the careful eye of Finn's friends in the FBI for her own protection, Finn could feel the loneliness sitting on his shoulder like an imp clawing its way into his mind.

He shrugged off his jacket, the fabric whispering against the quiet backdrop of the cottage. It landed over the back of a chair, joining the silent company of shadows that stretched from the corners of the room. A sigh escaped him, one that seemed to carry the burdens of a man who had seen too much, yet could not unsee the horrors that clawed at the edge of his consciousness. His gaze drifted momentarily to the mantelpiece where a single photograph stood—a picture of him, Amelia, and Rob on a rare day of respite, smiling, haunted by the irony that even their brightest days were colored by the dark strokes of crime-solving.

Finn knew now that his friends were all he had. If he was forced to return to the US and restart his FBI career, he knew he could be losing the only anchor in his personal life.

A small room he thought of as a study beckoned him—a siren calling to a sailor weary of navigating the treacherous waters of human malice. As Finn crossed the threshold, he was enveloped by the chaos of his profession. Case files stacked precariously on every surface spoke of a mind ceaselessly at work; each dossier a story, a life interrupted by violence. In the center of the clutter stood an oversized cork board that dominated the wall, a tapestry woven with the threads of ongoing inquiries. Red yarn zigzagged across the pins and notes, making connections where there seemed to be none, mapping out the labyrinthine path of a killer's mind.

These were the tracks of Max Vilne's maneuvers, but now that he had disappeared, it was time to use the board for the Hanover and Plantagenet murders.

He approached the board with a reverence reserved for altars, for this was his shrine to the chase, his relentless pursuit crystallized in photos, maps, and scribbled deductions. Here, amidst the sea of information, was the visual echo of his thoughts—his theories, hunches, and dead ends. The dim light from his desk lamp cast an amber glow, throwing his shadow against the board as if he were both guardian and part of the mysteries pinned there.

With a practiced motion, Finn set about updating the board with the new case, fingers deftly adding and rearranging pieces of the puzzle, copies from Wellhaven Station and Hertfordshire Constabulary aligning them with new insights gathered throughout the day. Each shift of paper, each new pin pushed into the cork, was an act of defiance against the enigma that loomed before him. And as he worked, the silence of the cottage wrapped around him, punctuated only by the soft rustle of paper and the ticking of the clock—an ominous metronome counting down the moments until the killer would strike again.

For a moment, dread washed over him. The thought of being old and still chasing shadows, with no one to love or to love him by his side—that was terrifying. Would he always devote himself to detective work, at the cost of his personal life?

Finn's fingers hovered momentarily over the files, his breath shallow in the stillness of his study. The scent of aged paper and ink filled the air—a familiar combination that usually comforted him, but tonight it felt like an oppressive fog. He exhaled slowly, grounding himself in the task at hand, and placed the manila folders side by side on the desk's worn mahogany surface.

Victim #1: Rebecca Hanover. Victim #2: Dominique Plantagenet. The names alone were enough to conjure images of regal lineages and forgotten histories, but it was the similarities in their deaths that gnawed at Finn's mind. Both women were found with an eerie serenity painted on their faces as though they had been laid to rest rather than brutally stolen from life. That was how they had been staged. The killer wanted them to be seen like that.

Finn opened the first file, a photo of Rebecca spilling out onto the desk. Her eyes seemed to hold a secret that now lay beyond Finn's reach. Next, he unfolded Dominique's file, her image a haunting echo of Rebecca's—both shared the same poised elegance, a trait that had perhaps marked them for death.

The room was quiet except for the occasional crackle of the fire that struggled against the chill seeping through the cottage walls. Finn reached for the stack of photos of personal items collected from the crime scenes, tangible fragments of lives cut short. Among the possessions—a locket, a playbill, a dried rose—was a photograph that brought Finn to a sharp halt.

It was a picture from a local newspaper where Dominique Plantagenet had been visiting a school production of a Shakespearean play a few years previous. She was standing with the cast, and there it was beneath the picture: Rebecca Hanover's name. She was one of the teenagers in the production.

Finn leaned back in his chair, the leather creaking under the shift of his weight. How had they missed this? It wasn't just two victims linked by similar circumstances—they knew each other. They shared a moment, secrets perhaps... possibly even the knowledge that someone they knew was capable of murder.

A chill slithered down his spine as he considered the implications. If the killer knew of their connection, was it a message? A vendetta against a hidden sin perceived through a twisted lens? Or was it something more insidious, a murder spree intricately tied to the very threads of their existence?

Finn Wright stood before the cork board, it surface a maze of evidence. The edges of photographs curled slightly, as if recoiling from their neighbors: the scrawled notes, the maps with red pins like drops of blood marking the events of terror. He pinned up the photos of Rebecca Hanover and Dominique Plantagenet with meticulous care, the pushpins piercing the board with soft thuds. The images were stark, capturing moments of life now violently severed.

Beneath each photograph, he laid out the details of their lives and deaths. The royal lineage was there, an ancient echo resonating through their existence, painting targets on their backs. The method of murder—a calculated brutality that spoke of intimate rage—was outlined next. And now, this newly discovered acquaintance, revealed in a candid shot of the two women.

With coffee cup in hand, the bitter liquid long since grown cold, Finn leaned back into his chair. His eyes danced over every detail, every line in their biographies, every witness statement. He absorbed the cadence of their lives—their routines, their passions, and ultimately, their fears. Hours ticked by, unnoticed, as he immersed himself further into the investigation, the sense of urgency within him building to an almost unbearable pitch.

Finn's eyes flickered beneath heavy lids, struggling to maintain their vigil over the sea of papers that now ebbed and flowed across his desk. The clock perched on the mantelpiece chimed a somber tune, marking the passage into a new day, its hands cresting past midnight. Finn's study, once a sanctuary of solitude and contemplation, had morphed into a battleground where shadows cast by the moonlight through the windowpane grappled with the dim glow of his desk lamp.

With each tick of the clock, the room seemed to grow denser, the air thick with the unsaid and the unknown. His mind, a relentless detective in its own right, scoured for patterns within the chaos of information—a killer's twisted breadcrumb trail. He wrestled with motives shrouded in darkness, each theory he conjured up more menacing than the last. Why these victims? Was it their connection to royalty, or was there something deeper, something personal that bound them to their fates?

It was as if the cerebral cogs were grinding against the weight of his exhaustion, yet the urgency of the hunt kept them turning, kept him from surrendering to the siren call of sleep. He could feel the answers simmering just below the surface, elusive phantoms darting through the murky depths of his consciousness. The specter of the killer loomed large, a riddle wrapped in enigma, clad in the cloak of night.

The thoughts swirled in Finn's head, a maelstrom of possibilities and dead ends. He leaned back, dragging his hand down his face, feeling the stubble that prickled there—a tactile reminder of the hours spent in this relentless pursuit. The taste of coffee lingered stale on his tongue, a bitter testament to the night's exertions. And then, without ceremony or intent, his body capitulated, sinking into the cushions of the couch that had become an impromptu bed among the disarray of his case files.

In the clutches of sleep, the realm of logic and reason gave way to the abstract theater of dreams. Here, the subconscious reigned, painting surreal vignettes across the canvas of his mind. Finn found himself drifting through a fog-laden corridor, each step echoing with an ominous weight. Shadowy figures emerged from the mist, their faces obscured, but their hands brandishing signet rings that glinted with sinister import.

The rings bore crests of power and heritage, symbols that held sway over life and death. They moved about him in a silent procession, a macabre dance that left traces of cold dread in its wake. In the dream, Finn reached out, driven by a compulsion to uncover the faces behind the rings, to reveal the truth that lay behind their gilded veneer. But as his fingers brushed against the cold metal, the figures dissolved into the ether, leaving him grasping at the void.

Finn's breaths came in shallow gasps, his body ensnared in the paradox of a sleep that offered no respite. The darkness of the room converged upon him, the unyielding silence punctuated only by the soft ticking of the clock—a relentless metronome counting down the moments of peace before the storm of reality would crash upon him once again.

The shrill siren of the telephone cleaved through the silent shroud covering Finn's flat. His heart punched against his ribs as he lurched from the couch, a slew of case files cascading to the floor in his wake. The room spun for a moment, reality snapping back into focus as Finn's hand grappled blindly for the receiver.

"Winters?" His voice was gravel, heavy with the remnants of sleep and the burden of unspoken dread.

"Finn, we've got another one," Amelia's words fell like leaden weights in the darkened room. Each syllable seemed to steal the very air from his lungs. "He's killed again."

CHAPTER THIRTEEN

The dark morning air was acrid, a mix of iron and disinfectant as Finn stepped over the threshold into Jillian Bruce's apartment. It was gut-wrenching in its familiarity; the same grotesque tapestry they'd seen unfurled at two other scenes. Except here, it was Jillian, a pale wraith amidst the crimson chaos, her eyes forever closed to the melody she'd never play again.

"Christ," he muttered under his breath.

Amelia studied him with an unreadable expression before turning back to survey the room. "At least she didn't die alone," she quipped dryly, nodding towards the stuffed armchair occupied by a stoic teddy bear, its glassy gaze fixed on the tragedy before it.

"Small mercies," Finn replied, the corner of his mouth twitching despite the grimness of the situation. He crouched beside Jillian's body, noting the precision of the cuts, the deliberate placement of her limbs. The killer had moved beyond murder; this was choreography.

"A similar M.O.," Amelia observed from across the room, her voice steady. "But not exactly. The body positions are all slightly different."

She pointed to a shattered vase, its flowers strewn across the floor like mourners at a graveside. "He leaves something every time. A signature?"

"Or a tantrum," Finn suggested, rising to his feet. He began a slow circuit of the area, his gaze roving meticulously over each surface, hunting for the telltale anomalies that marked the predator's passage. "but everything looks staged again. If we link this to a play, what significance do the flowers have?"

"Look at this," Amelia called out, beckoning him over to the wall where a series of photos hung. Finn approached, his eyes scanning the images of Jillian, violin in hand, lost in the rapture of performance. The images showed several performances in elegant halls and packed venues. She had clearly been a musician of some repute.

"Notice anything?" Amelia's finger hovered over the corner of one frame where a faint smudge marred the glass. Finn leaned closer, the gears in his mind churning. It was a partial print, left incomplete.

"It could be the killer, but it could equally just be Jillian's," he said. "We should notify the forensics team."

The air in Jillian's apartment was tainted with the metallic scent of blood as Finn crouched near her lifeless form. His eyes, sharp and unerring, swept over the polished wooden floorboards, tracing the chaotic splatter that told a silent story of struggle and death. It was there, amidst the crimson chaos, that something caught his attention—a tiny scrap, nearly hidden by her arm.

"Amelia," he called out, his voice a low murmur to avoid disturbing the crime scene's grim stillness. "Bring me the tweezers and evidence bags."

As she approached, Finn pointed to the fragments of parchment, their edges jagged and soaked with blood. The delicate fibers looked aged, the script upon them faded and barely legible. Amelia handed him the tools with a nod, knowing better than to ask questions when Finn was in full analytical mode.

"Old parchment again," he observed aloud. "This is the third time we've found it at the scene."

"There's no doubt then that the killer thinks this is his calling card," Amelia quipped, though her eyes were somber. "I wonder what the writing means this time, and if it's all from the one source text?"

"Let's find out," Finn replied, carefully collecting the pieces. He held one up to the light, squinting as he tried to decipher the ancient text. Each fragment seemed to be torn from a different page, each bearing words that spoke of history long past.

"De Bruce," Finn murmured, his mind racing through the implications. "That's dangerously to Jillian's last name."

"Wait," Amelia said. "The only De Bruce I can think of is the Bruce."

"Must be important if he's the only Bruce," Finn quipped.

"No, silly," she said. "Robert the Bruce was King of Scotland hundreds of years ago. He fought an extensive war against English rule and set in motion Scotland's independence, which lasted until the early 1700s. He was sometimes referred to as De Bruce."

"A king?" Finn rubbed his chin. He turned and looked at Jillian's still body on the floor. A theory was bubbling away. Amelia could clearly see it.

"You've got something, don't you?" Amelia asked.

"A severe case of the handsomes," Finn said, excitedly, "but also a theory. Rebecca Hanover, we know she was related to royalty and nearly gave up her birthright. Dominique Plantagenet, we thought their connection was working in the theater, but we did mention the royal connection… Didn't you say that Plantagenet was the name of a king?"

"That's right," Amelia nodded. "They originated on the continent, but they were essentially the royal family in England from the 1100s until the 1400s. Come to think of it, Richard the third was a Plantagenet I think."

"And Robert De Bruce was king of Scotland!" Finn said with verve. "Hanover. Plantagenet. Bruce. All kings or queens. Our killer has a theme." He stood slowly, his body tense with the realization. "The death of monarchs. It's not just random royals. Hanover, Plantagenet, now Bruce—names steeped in history, tied to thrones and power."

"Talk about having a type," Amelia said, half-joking. But Finn was not smiling. This was the work of someone obsessed, someone whose vision was painted in shades of blood and glory.

"Means and opportunity aside," Finn pondered aloud, "I wonder if the murders mimic the deaths of royal kings. Is the killer recreating what happened in the past with their descendants!?"

"Guess we'll have to catch our history buff to find out," Amelia said, her voice edged with determination.

"It feels as if the killer was disturbed this time," Finn mused. "He hasn't set the scene as carefully. He's left quite a mess from the struggle."

"Maybe he heard someone nearby and thought he'd be seen," Amelia answered.

Jillian Bruce's body lay silent, her final notes left unplayed. Finn felt a surge of anger and pity. Did all three women die simply because of their last names?

Finn's eyes flickered across the room, pausing at the spatters of blood that painted the walls—a gruesome fresco that told a story of violence and terror. He felt the familiar tightening of his jaw, the burning need for answers that always came with threads like this—threads that, when pulled, would unravel the tapestry of a killer's mind.

His attention was then snared by something out-of-place amid the chaos—an incongruous object on the otherwise pristine table by the door. It was a ticket, abandoned carelessly on the surface, its edges barely stained with the faintest touch of red. The name 'Jillian Bruce' emblazoned across its face, alongside the title of a concerto meant for that evening. She was to be the violinist; the star now fallen to darkness.

"Damn," he murmured, picking up the ticket between two fingers, examining it under the light. Details mattered. They were the lifeblood of an investigation like this—the difference between catching a ghost and letting him slip through the cracks.

"Playing tonight," Finn said more to himself than to Amelia, who had returned. "She never made it to the stage."

"Another performer misses her final curtain call," Amelia added quietly. Her words, though spoken lightly, carried the sorrow of the unfulfilled destiny that lay before them. "That is a thought, you know. Two actresses are dead, now a violinist. Perhaps someone in the theater or entertainment world is connected to this."

"Exactly," he agreed, pocketing the ticket. It was a lead, albeit a cold one, but it was all they had. "Let's see if there's anything else around here that might help," Finn suggested, moving toward her belongings, his mind whirring with the possibilities. The ticket had been an oversight, but it was their oversight now, and he intended to make the most of it.

Finn stood motionless for a moment, the chaos of Jillian's apartment sinking into his bones. The place was meant to be a sanctuary for creativity, not a tomb. His hands brushed over letters and envelopes, and then he paused, feeling the familiar texture of paper used centuries ago. The script was elaborate, archaic, Old English twisting like thorny vines upon the page. He recognized the style—it bore an eerie resemblance to Professor Hemingway's academic hand, yet they'd all but ruled him out. Finn's brow knitted together as he examined the threatening content, words weaving dark promises and echoes of historic grudges.

"Take a look at this," Finn said, his voice steady despite the chill that clawed up his spine. Amelia leaned over, her detective's curiosity replacing any revulsion at the grim backdrop.

"Another dialect of ancient English. I can't read this one, but no doubt it's old threats in an older tongue," she observed, her fingers deftly capturing images of the letters with her phone. "We should get it analyzed. Jillian knew someone hated her. If she had been receiving threats, maybe she wrote about it somewhere in a diary or journal?"

Finn looked around at the cluttered table. There was no sign of a diary, but there was an address book, its pages filled with names and notes. One name snagged his attention, penned sharply, almost violently: Margaret Thompson. Beside it, a scrawled comment: "hateful woman."

"Why would you write down someone's address you hate?" Amelia thought out loud.

"Just because you dislike someone," Finn said, "that doesn't mean you don't want to keep tabs on them. Maybe they didn't start out as enemies."

"I suppose..." Amelia said, sounding unconvinced.

"Do we know of anyone connected to Rebecca and Dominique by the name of Margaret Thompson?" Finn asked, showing Amelia the entry.

"Margaret Thompson... That name rings a bell," Amelia mused aloud as she tapped at her phone, the glow illuminating her determined face. "Yes, I thought so. She's a published author. She's written extensively against the crown, advocating for stripping wealth from royal descendants."

"The sort of stuff James Blackwood would read?"

"Yes," Amelia answered. "But I don't know much more about her."

For a moment, he considered a conspiracy; that Professor Hemingway, James Blackwood, and now this Margaret Thompson could all be in on it somehow. But the suspicion faded as quickly as it had arrived.

"Let's do a quick survey before finding where this Margaret Thompson lives," Finn suggested.

It wasn't long before he found something. As went to leave Jillian Bruce's bedroom, and the haunting remnants of Jillian's life behind, Finn's eyes fell upon a small newspaper clipping tucked away in a scrap book—a protest at one of her concerts. And there, in black and white, was the name again: Margaret Thompson, her dissent loudly proclaimed beneath the headline. It wasn't just scholarly theories now; Thompson had actively opposed Jillian no doubt because of her connection to royalty.

"Amelia," he said, holding the clipping out to her, "Margaret's been out there, in the flesh, at the very stages our victim graced."

"I wonder..." Amelia said, looking at her phone. "Yes! Here's a review of one of Dominique Plantagenet's performances - interrupted by none other than Margaret Thompson."

Finn grinned.

"Hmm," Amelia then said. "But her registered address is hours from here."

"Then we need to figure out where she might... Be..." Finn smiled again at a thought.

"What do you have going on in there?" Amelia asked.

"Care to take in a concert tonight?" he suggested.

"Why would she go there if she knows Jillian isn't going to attend... Unless someone else there could be under threat?"

"It couldn't hurt to check out the venue and speak with people there," Finn said.

"True," answered Amelia. "It's possible someone there knows more about this than us. Besides, some culture might rub off on you."

"After you, Madame," Finn said, cordially.

"Then let's not keep Ms. Thompson waiting," Amelia replied, her voice laced with urgency. They left the apartment, every step away from the crime scene a step closer to the elusive killer lurking somewhere beyond the bloodstained walls.

CHAPTER FOURTEEN

The late afternoon sky, a brooding canvas of grays, loomed over the Royal Albert Hall as Finn Wright and his partner Amelia Winters approached the iconic venue. Its Victorian Gothic architecture rose like an ancient sentinel amid the sleek glass and metal towers that pierced London's skyline. To Finn, the contrast felt like stepping into a chiaroscuro painting, the past and present clashing in the heart of the city.

"I always dreamed of being famous when I was a kid and singing here," Amelia muttered, her voice barely audible above the murmur of traffic and the distant echo of the Thames.

"If I ask them, maybe they'll let you," Finn replied with a smile, the quip doing little to lighten the sense of foreboding that had settled over him since their arrival.

They crossed the threshold, and the bustling sounds of the city fell away, replaced by the hush of reverence that always seemed to accompany such grandeur. The ornate interior, with its lavish frescoes and gilded accents, was breathtaking, but it did little to distract from the grim task at hand.

A man, whose posture bore the burden of recent events, approached them. He was the manager, his face drawn tight with concern. His eyes flitted to Finn and Amelia, clear indicators of nervous energy.

"Inspector Winters, Mr. Wright," he greeted, his voice a tremulous note that resonated oddly in the silence of the hall. "Thank you phoning ahead... And for coming so quickly."

"Of course," Amelia responded. "We understand this is a difficult time."

"Jillian was... she was one of our finest violinists," the manager said, leading them through the maze of corridors behind the stage. His hands wrung themselves compulsively, an unconscious gesture betraying his inner turmoil. "If there's anything we can do to bring the perpetrator to justice, we will do it."

"Her music filled these halls," he continued, his tone wistful, almost forgetting the detectives' presence. "Now, there's just this dreadful emptiness."

Finn stayed quiet, observing the man. He wondered if someone who worked with Jillian might know something important. Whether they wanted to hide that something or not, that was a different matter altogether.

"Was there anything unusual before the—before her death?" Finn asked, his question cutting through the somber air like a scalpel.

"Nothing out of the ordinary," the manager replied, shaking his head. "She was rehearsing for a concert up until yesterday, seemed in good spirits."

"Appearances can be deceiving," Amelia chimed in, her voice steady, hinting at untold stories lurking beneath the surface of routine.

"Yeah," Finn agreed, his mind racing through the possibilities, trying to piece together the fragments of Jillian's last days within these walls.

"Could you show us to Jillian's dressing room?" Finn asked.

"Dressing room?" the man said uncomfortably. "We are still trying to rehearse for tonight's concert."

"And I don't want any of your other musicians to share Jillian's fate," Finn said abruptly. "Please lead the way."

"Of course. But I still don't understand what can be gleaned from rummaging through the poor dead girl's things."

"We believe Jillian was receiving threats before she died," Amelia explained. "It's possible she received some of them here at her place of work. Please, lead on."

The manager nodded.

As they moved deeper into the labyrinthine backstage, the echoes of their footsteps seemed to press closer, eager whispers from the past clinging to the edges of Finn's perception. He could feel the history of the place, every performance and every secret it held, now marred by the stain of violence.

"Here we are," the manager finally announced, halting before a door marked with a brass plaque, 'Jillian Bruce'. The name stood as a solemn marker, the once bright star of a talented violinist snuffed out too soon.

"Thank you," Finn said, his tone gentle, acknowledging the manager's grief while trying to appease his curiosity for what lay beyond that door.

Finn stepped into the dressing room, the scent of resin and wood polish mingling with a chill that seemed to seep from the walls. The place was untouched since Jillian's last performance, her presence hanging in the air like the final note of an unfinished symphony. Amelia followed close behind, her steps measured and respectful as if entering sacred ground.

His gaze fell upon the violin resting on the makeup table—a Stradivarius by the looks of it, its varnished surface reflecting the dim lighting with a sorrowful gleam. It lay silent, its strings taut, as though poised to resonate with the touch of its master who would never return. Finn's fingers hovered over it, a surge of reverence stopping him short of contact. He wondered about the melodies it held captive, the joys and heartbreaks it had voiced under Jillian's deft touch.

"Beautiful, isn't it?" Amelia's voice cut through the silence, tinged with a hint of melancholy.

"More than that," Finn replied, his words soft. "I used to believe that musical instruments take a piece of the performer with them. It's a piece of her soul left behind."

"Why, Finn?" Amelia said, sounding surprised. "That was almost poetic."

"I do write, you know."

"I said almost," she said with a grin. "Don't get carried away with yourself.

They moved through the room, the air thick with the echo of rustling sheets of music and the ghostly applause of audiences past. Finn opened drawers and rifled through personal effects—lipsticks, scores, handwritten notes—all the mundane artifacts of a life interrupted. Amelia scanned the vanity, her reflection staring back at her amidst a clutter of brushes and powders.

"Over here," she called out, her tone shifting to one of urgency.

Finn joined her, his eyes narrowing on the letters spread across the tabletop. The ink was faded, but the script was unmistakable, each letter meticulously formed with an almost obsessive precision. He recognized the style; it was similar to the threats they'd found in Jillian's flat.

"Another message from our scribe," Finn muttered, his mind churning. "At least this is in a form of English I can understand. 'Thou shalt pay for thy lineage's sins.' or something to that effect."

"Someone's taking their history quite seriously." Amelia picked up a letter, studying it with a frown. "Or someone wants us to think they are."

"Either way," Finn said, tracing the loops and flourishes with his fingertip, "it's a direct link to the other victims. All part of the theater, all with ties to royalty. We can be certain the three deaths are part of a spree now."

"Seems like our killer wants us to understand why he's doing what he's doing," Amelia quipped, even as her eyes stayed locked on the threatening prose. "I think that's why he's leaving these notes."

"He keeps varying some of the crime scene details," Finn muttered. "He wants to keep us confused enough to wonder if we're missing something."

Taking out an evidence bag, Finn carefully pocketed the note for later analysis.

From somewhere nearby, a violin began to play.

"Can you hear that or am I going insane?" Finn asked.

"Yes," Amelia said. "Though I was tempted to say no and gaslight you."

"They must be doing a sound check," Finn said. "For a moment, I thought..." The ghostly echo of a violin's lament had barely faded when the discordant shatter of props in the distance jolted Finn from his reverie. Violence was afoot, and it was near. He exchanged a glance with Amelia, her eyes reflecting the same flicker of urgency that sparked within him. Without a word, they slipped into the shadows that clung to the walls of Royal Albert Hall like an ancient tapestry.

"Backstage," Finn mouthed, his hand instinctively reaching for the sidearm he no longer carried. They moved as one, their footsteps a muted symphony on the plush carpet, passing through the labyrinthine hallways that hummed with the whispers of performances past. Here, history bled into the present—a murder most foul in a setting steeped in grandeur.

Finn's gut tightened as they approached the commotion, the scent of sawdust and paint lingering in the air. His eyes searched the dimly lit corridor, catching the briefest glint of movement—a shadow darting between the colossal silhouettes of stage props. "There!" he hissed, pointing towards the fleeing figure, a stark blot against the otherwise meticulously organized backstage area.

Amelia nodded, already in motion. Finn followed, his legs pumping, heart racing, the chase igniting a fire that had often been dormant since his suspension. They weaved through the maze of corridors, dodging haphazardly placed costumes and sets that told stories of a thousand different worlds.

He could hear the ragged breaths of the suspect ahead, the clattering of disturbed objects marking their desperate attempt at escape. The adrenaline surged through Finn's veins, sharpening his focus. Each corner turned was a gamble, each doorway crossed a chance encounter with the unknown.

"Split up?" Amelia suggested her voice a terse whisper as they neared another fork in the backstage labyrinth.

"Left," he decided, veering down the hallway where the sounds of pursuit seemed loudest. She nodded again, peeling off to the right with a determined set to her jaw. Finn pushed harder, the suspect's silhouette now coming into clearer view with each stride.

Finally, they reached a cul-de-sac of dressing rooms, the suspect cornered. Props loomed like silent sentinels, bearing witness to the impending confrontation. Finn skidded to a halt, his pulse thrumming in his ears. There was nowhere left to run. The suspect turned, their back pressed against a door adorned with fading stars, their chest heaving with panicked breaths.

"End of the line," Finn said, the words slipping out in a cold, even tone, though his insides churned with a mix of triumph and dread. He could feel Amelia's presence behind him, a reassuring solidity in a world of shadows and doubt.

The suspect eyed them both, the whites of their eyes glaring in the half-light, calculating the odds, weighing the chances. But Finn knew the game was up. This was it—the moment before the mask was ripped away, revealing the face of the puppeteer who'd orchestrated this deadly dance.

Finn's muscles tensed as the suspect lunged forward, a blur of desperation and fear. With reflexes honed from years in the field, Finn intercepted, grappling with the shadowy figure whose breath came in ragged gasps against his ear. Fabric strained and tore as they twisted in a violent dance, each seeking to overpower the other. The suspect's elbow jabbed into Finn's side, eliciting a grunt of pain that echoed off the nearby props—a cacophony of distress in the otherwise silent backstage.

"Persistent, aren't you?" Finn spat out through gritted teeth, his grip tightening like a vice. He could feel the sinew and bone beneath the suspect's clothing, the frantic pounding of a heart racing to escape its inevitable conclusion. The scent of sweat and fear mingled in the air, pungent and acrid, as if the very walls absorbed the essence of their struggle.

In the midst of the fray, he sensed rather than saw Amelia move—a swift shadow converging on their position. Her arrival was a jolt of electricity, spurring him onward. Their assailant thrashed wildly, a cornered animal with nothing to lose. Amelia's hand found the crook of the suspect's arm, her fingers steel traps, and together they forced the flailing limbs behind a back that arched in resistance.

The suspect groaned and shouted "get off me!"

"Easy there," Finn murmured, though his voice bore an edge sharper than any blade. His former life as a Special Agent had prepared him for this—the close-quarters combat where every decision could be your last. Yet it was the first time since his suspension that he felt wholly alive, his past failures fueling his resolve rather than hindering it.

Amelia grunted as she avoided a stray kick, her tenacity a beacon in the dimly lit corridor.

The suspect's struggling waned, their energy spent, as the reality of capture set in. Finn's heart hammered in his chest, not just from the exertion but from the knowledge that each piece of this macabre puzzle brought them closer to a truth that seemed to lurk just beyond reach.

"Looks like we've got our own private performance," Finn quipped, even as his hands remained unyielding. Amelia's response was a stifled chuckle, incongruent with the gravity of their situation, yet somehow perfect.

"I'd have preferred a box seat and a glass of rose."

Together, they stood, the suspect subdued and pulled to their feet.

As the suspect's struggles subsided into defeated whimpers, Finn caught a glint of metal against their skin. His eyes narrowed, focusing on the object—a ring, ornate and imposing. With deliberate care, he twisted the ring free from the suspect's finger, holding it up to the light. A chill ran down his spine as he recognized the emblem etched onto the surface: Robert the Bruce's emblem, an unmistakable symbol of Scottish royalty and power.

"Margaret Thompson," Finn said, the name rolling off his tongue with disbelief as he eyed the ring in his palm. It was a piece of the puzzle they hadn't anticipated, a link that tied the historian's controversial views directly to their case.

"You have the right to remain silent…" Amelia began.

Amelia's voice was steady as she read Margaret her rights, the metallic click of the handcuffs punctuating each word. As Finn watched Margaret's face, he saw defiance there, but also fear. Fear of what came next, fear of the truth being unearthed.

CHAPTER FIFTEEN

Finn Wright's gaze locked onto the figure before him, a juxtaposition of scholarly intellect, criminal suspicion, and a lean physical strength that could only come from diligent training. Shackled wrists rested on the metal table in the observation room, the cuffs glinting under the harsh fluorescent lights. Margaret Thompson, historian and now suspect number three, bore her restraints with a kind of regal disdain. The air was thick with tension, a silent battle of wills set against the sterile backdrop of Hertfordshire Constabulary.

"Miss Thompson," Finn began, his voice steady, echoing slightly in the sparse chamber, "we've got a few questions about your interactions with Jillian Bruce."

Margaret's lips curved into a sardonic smile, her eyes sharp behind the lenses of her glasses. "Interactions? Is that what we're calling civil protest now?"

"Let's not dance around the subject," Amelia chimed in, sliding a notebook across the table towards the suspect. "I'm assuming you know she's been murdered. Your name was found at Jillian Bruce's home, labeled as a 'hateful woman.' Why would she write that?"

"Because I disagreed with her choice in music." Margaret's defiance rose like a shield. "Some of those pieces glorify an institution built on the backs of the suffering masses—the monarchy."

"Opposing viewpoints don't usually end in murder," Finn pointed out, leaning forward, elbows on the table. His mind was alight with details, digging for inconsistencies, for the slip that would unravel the truth.

"Of course not," Margaret replied coolly, her voice dripping with condescension. "But I suspect you know that already, Mr. Wright. You're just trying to connect dots that aren't there."

Amelia's fingers tapped a staccato rhythm on the tabletop, the sound a counterpoint to the tension. Finn could almost see the cogs turning in her head, the same relentless pursuit of good that drove them both. Their partnership, though forged in the fire of this investigation, had become his anchor, their mutual respect and dark humor a salve against the grimness of their task.

"Murder is no trivial matter, Miss Thompson," Amelia said, her tone sharpening like a blade. "And your protests seem more... personal than political."

"Personal?" Margaret leaned back in her chair, her laugh devoid of humor. "If opposing the celebration of a bloody history is personal, then yes, I suppose it is."

"Seems to me," Finn interjected, "that there's more to this story. So why don't you start from the beginning—why did Jillian Bruce hate you?"

"Because I spoke the truth," Margaret answered, her voice unwavering. "And truth, Mr. Wright, is often inconvenient. Indeed, it can be painful."

In that cold room, beneath the buzz of the overhead lights, Finn felt the weight of every unsolved case pressing upon him. He studied Margaret's face, searching for the crack in her armor, but found only the hardened resolve of someone accustomed to standing alone against the tide.

"Perhaps," he mused aloud, a faint smile playing on his lips, "but truth also has a way of coming out, one way or another."

As the interrogation stretched on, each question parried with practiced ease, Finn's admiration for Amelia's tenacity grew. Together they pressed, probed, tested every angle—but Margaret Thompson was an enigma, a fortress with walls too high to breach. And as much as Finn hated to admit it, his gut told him they were barking up the wrong tree. She was hiding something, yes, but was it murder?

Finn shifted his chair slightly, the metal legs scraping against the concrete floor with an abrasive echo that filled the sparse room. He leaned forward, resting his elbows on the cold steel table separating them from Margaret Thompson. The fluorescent lights above hummed a monotonous tune, casting an artificial glow over the scene. Finn felt the familiar flicker of adrenaline as he prepared to pivot the interrogation.

Margaret's gaze remained unwavering as Finn and Amelia delved deeper into their questioning. The stark room felt like a battleground, with words as weapons and silence thickening the air between them.

"Miss Thompson," Finn began, his voice cutting through the tension like a blade, "we're not just here about Jillian Bruce. What can you tell us about Dominique Plantagenet and Rebecca Hanover?"

A flicker of surprise danced across Margaret's features before she composed herself, her posture regal even in the face of suspicion. "I may have disagreed with their privileged lineage, but I am not a murderer," she retorted, her tone laced with defiance.

Amelia leaned in slightly, her eyes sharp with scrutiny. "Your views on monarchy are well known, but these murders seem to carry a vengeful touch, much in line with your writings. How do you explain that?"

Margaret's lips curled into a disdainful smile. "Vengeful touch? I may despise what royalty represents, but I am no executioner. My weapon is my pen, not a blade."

Finn studied her reaction closely, searching for any hint of deception in her words. "Yet each victim had ties to royal ancestry," he pointed out, his voice probing yet controlled.

"Coincidence," Margaret dismissed with a wave of her hand. "Their bloodline does not make them innocent or untouchable in the eyes of history. Besides, I think you've been too involved in recent serial killer cases, Mr Wright. Oh yes, I know you from the press. Perhaps it is you who sees something personal in these murders. Didn't America abandon the monarchy? All I want is the same for us."

Amelia's gaze bore into Margaret's own, unyielding. "And what of the notes left at each crime scene? The meticulous planning that mirrors historical deaths—does that align with your activism or your writing?"

"They certainly have an author's flair," Finn added.

Margaret's facade faltered for a moment before she regained her composure. "I may challenge the monarchy's legacy, but I would never resort to such barbarism. My fight is waged through discourse and debate, not bloodshed."

Finn observed the subtle nuances in Margaret's demeanor—the slight tremor in her hands, the fleeting glint of uncertainty in her eyes—as he pushed further. "Your convictions are clear, Miss Thompson, but we need more than words to rule out your involvement in these murders."

Margaret's gaze remained steady, her demeanor unwavering as Finn and Amelia pressed on with their questioning. The stark room felt suffocating, the weight of suspicion hanging heavy in the air.

"Miss Thompson," Finn's voice cut through the tension like a sharpened blade, "can you account for your whereabouts on the nights of Rebecca Hanover and Dominique Plantagenet's deaths?"

Margaret's lips curved into a cool smile, her eyes meeting Finn's with calculated composure. "I'm afraid those particular evenings escape me," she replied smoothly. "But I can assure you that my pursuits did not involve royalty or bloodshed."

Amelia leaned forward slightly, her gaze sharp and probing. "And what about the night Jillian Bruce was murdered? Can you provide an alibi for that night?"

A flicker of something unreadable passed through Margaret's eyes before she spoke. "Ah yes, that night," she began, her tone taking on a hint of intrigue. "I was in the company of a gentleman named Albert Marling." She reached into her pocket and produced a receipt from a quaint Italian bistro in Soho, dated the evening of Jillian Bruce's death. "We had dinner at La Luna Rossa that night."

Finn took the receipt, studying it intently. The details seemed to align with Margaret's claim. He glanced at Amelia, who nodded subtly in agreement.

"It seems you have an alibi for the night Jillian Bruce was killed," Finn acknowledged, his voice neutral but probing.

Finn observed her closely, searching for any sign of deceit or evasion in her words. The room fell silent for a moment, tension crackling between them like electricity.

Amelia spoke next, her voice sharp and direct. "Your association with these victims is undeniable due to your beliefs and writings," she pointed out. "But we will need more than just an alibi to clear you of any involvement in these murders."

As Margaret met their scrutiny head-on, Finn couldn't shake off the lingering doubt that lingered like a shadow over their interrogation—a doubt that whispered there was more beneath the surface than met the eye.

"An alibi is enough," Margaret said pointedly.

Finn nodded. "We'll see. Stay right here. A constable will be with you in a moment."

As Finn and Amelia exited the interrogation room, the weight of their conversation with Margaret Thompson lingered like a heavy fog around them. The bright hallway offered a brief respite from the suffocating tension within, but Finn's mind was already racing ahead to the next steps in their investigation.

Before they could exchange a word, Chief Constable Rob Collins appeared at the end of the corridor, his presence commanding attention. "Chief," Amelia acknowledged with a nod, turning to Finn. "I'll pass on the details about Margaret Thompson's alibi to one of our constables to follow up." She then faced Rob and added, "We're making progress on the case, Chief. Finn and I are onto something significant."

Finn felt that was stretching the truth.

Rob gave Amelia a playful grin as she turned to leave, his tone light despite the gravity of their investigation. "Don't go causing too much trouble out there, Inspector. I can't have Finn getting into more hot water on my watch."

Amelia shot back with a smirk, her eyes glinting mischievously. "Oh, don't worry, Chief. I'll make sure Finn behaves... as much as he can."

Their banter provided a momentary relief from the intensity of their work, a brief glimpse of camaraderie amidst the shadows of suspicion and doubt that loomed over them.

"I'll be back in a minute," Amelia said, excusing herself.

As Amelia headed down the corridor, Rob's chuckle followed her like a reassuring echo, a reminder that even in the darkest of times, a spark of humor could still shine through.

Alone now with Rob, Finn couldn't help but notice the gravity etched into his friend's features. "Where have you been, Rob?" Finn inquired, noting that Rob had been more absent than usual.

Rob's expression darkened as he spoke in hushed tones. "There's been a murder in Newcastle," he began, his words heavy with implication. "And we suspect it might be linked to Max Vilne."

Finn felt a jolt of adrenaline surge through him at the mention of Max Vilne—the elusive serial killer who had haunted him for so long. "I need to go up North and investigate," Finn stated firmly, his eyes reflecting determination.

Rob placed a hand on Finn's shoulder, his gaze somber. "Finish this case first," Rob urged quietly. "We need closure for those victims before pursuing another lead. I promise I'll keep both eyes on this. If we verify that it was Vilne, you'll be the first to know."

"I hate that he's still out there," Finn said with a sigh.

"We'll get him soon," Rob offered.

"Watch your back, Rob," Finn said. "He threatened you and Amelia to get at me. He follows through on his threats."

"I know," Rob said. "I am being very careful."

Reluctantly nodding in understanding, Finn knew that duty called for him to see this through to its conclusion. "Keep me posted," he requested as Rob turned to leave.

"I will," Rob said, patting Finn gently on the arm before disappearing down a hallway.

Left standing alone in the hallway, torn between two pressing investigations—Jillian Bruce, Rebecca Hanover, Dominique Plantagenet's murders or the looming threat of Max Vilne—Finn felt the weight of responsibility settle heavily on his shoulders. Each case demanded peace and resolution, yet time was a merciless adversary ticking away relentlessly, and with each strike of the clock, Finn knew in his soul that bad times lay ahead.

CHAPTER SIXTEEN

The city was a convulsing organism, its veins clogged with the midday rush as Finn navigated the unmarked police car through London's gridlocked arteries. Beside him, Amelia's posture mirrored the tension that had enveloped them since the interview had gone badly with Margaret Thompson.

"Margaret Thompson's alibi is solid," Amelia said, her voice slicing through the hum of idling engines as she glanced down at the text message on her phone screen. "Constable Amid spoke with the man she mentioned, and he vouched for her."

"Doesn't mean she's not involved," Finn replied, his eyes never leaving the road, reflecting a mosaic of brake lights and shopfronts. "Could be more than one person behind this." His mind whirred with possibilities, each one casting longer shadows over the case.

"Still, it's back to square one," Amelia sighed, the frustration evident in her tone.

"Never liked squares much," Finn quipped, offering a lopsided grin that failed to mask his underlying concern. "Was always more of a circle man.

"When we finish this case," Amelia said, "I'll get you a box of crayons and you can draw all the circles you want."

They arrived at the Bruce family home nestled within a quiet crescent, a strange contrast to the pandemonium they had just left behind. The modest two-story Victorian terrace stood dignified with its brick facade and white-trimmed windows adorned with lace curtains. A small garden, now bereft of color from winter's touch, held the promise of spring life within its sleeping bulbs.

As Amelia and Finn approached the Bruce family home, the air seemed to thicken with sorrow, weighing down on them like a shroud of grief. With each step towards the door, Finn's heartbeat quickened, anticipation mingling with dread in his chest. He raised his hand to knock, the sound echoing through the quiet crescent.

The door creaked open slowly, revealing Jillian's mother standing there, tears glistening in her eyes. Her face was etched with pain, lines of worry etching deeper into her features. Before Amelia could utter a word identifying them as police officers, Jillian's mother spoke in a voice heavy with sorrow.

"We know... Please come in," she said softly, stepping back to allow them entry. Her words hung heavy in the air, a poignant reminder of the tragedy that had befallen their family.

Amelia and Finn exchanged a brief glance before following Jillian's mother inside. The hallway was adorned with family photos capturing moments frozen in time—smiles frozen on faces now marred by loss. The scent of fresh flowers mingled with an undercurrent of sadness that permeated the atmosphere.

Jillian's mother led them into the living room where remnants of her daughter's life lingered—a violin resting against an armchair, sheet music scattered on a coffee table. The room felt suspended in time, caught between memories of joy and the harsh reality of loss.

"Hello," a man with gray hair said, sitting in an armchair. He looked as pale as a ghost. Finn instinctively knew he was Jillian's father.

Seated on a worn sofa, Jillian's mother composed herself before speaking again. "Thank you for coming," she began, her voice trembling but resolute. "I know why you're here... I just can't believe she's gone."

Finn felt a lump form in his throat at her words, the weight of grief settling heavily upon him. Amelia placed a comforting hand on Jillian's mother's shoulder as she spoke gently, "We are here to help and to find justice for Jillian."

Silence enveloped them like a suffocating blanket as they sat together in shared mourning for what had been taken from them—a daughter lost to senseless violence. In that moment of profound loss and unspoken understanding, Finn knew that their pursuit for truth would be fueled by more than duty—it would be driven by the need to bring closure to those left behind by tragedy.

"Someone from Albert Hall called us earlier," Mrs. Bruce uttered, her voice brittle with grief, cutting through the pleasantries that seemed so hollow under the circumstances.

Finn felt the discomfort tighten around his chest; he believed such news should always come from those trained to deliver it, to manage the fallout. Yet he kept his face composed, a mask of professional stoicism, though his insides churned with empathy for the family's premature plunge into mourning.

Amelia leaned forward, her elbows resting on her knees as she bridged the gap between official inquiry and personal concern. "Mr. and Mrs. Bruce," she began, her tone gentle, "was there anything recently that struck you as odd about Jillian's behavior? Anything at all?"

Finn observed the couple from his position, noting the flickers of recollection in their moistened eyes. He could almost see them rifling through the catalog of recent memories, searching for anomalies.

"Jillian," Mr. Bruce started, his voice heavy, "she was more anxious lately. About her performances." His thumb rubbed against the armrest, a rhythmic motion betraying his own anxiety.

"More than usual?" Finn interjected, watching closely for any sign of evasion or uncertainty.

"Yes," Mrs. Bruce chimed in, nodding slowly, her hands clasped tightly in her lap. "She always cared deeply about her music, but this was different. There was a...a tremor in her voice when she spoke of the future."

"Did she mention why?" Finn pressed, his gaze lingering on their faces, searching for the unsaid words that often lingered in the silences.

"We don't know," Mr. Bruce admitted, shaking his head, a gesture of defeat. "But we felt it—something was amiss. She seemed...haunted."

Finn exchanged a glance with Amelia, noticing the slight narrowing of her eyes—a silent signal that she too sensed the undercurrents of something larger at play. He appreciated this nonverbal shorthand they'd developed; even amidst the grimness of their work, their camaraderie offered a semblance of reprieve.

"Mrs. Bruce," Amelia continued, her voice soothing like a balm, "Jillian was a musician. Did she ever cross paths with Rebecca Hanover or Dominique Plantagenet? They were both involved in the arts as well."

"Rebecca and Dominique?" Mrs. Bruce repeated, the names seeming to trigger a distant connection. "It's possible. The arts community is close-knit. And Jillian... She played at various venues over the years."

"Could you think of any particular theater where their paths might have crossed?" Amelia probed further, her pen poised above her notebook, ready to document any sliver of information.

"Several theaters," Mrs. Bruce said after a moment, furrowing her brow in concentration. "The Lyceum, the Royal Opera House... But I can't say for certain if she knew them personally."

"Thank you," Amelia replied warmly, offering a comforting smile. "Every detail helps."

As Amelia scribbled notes, Finn sat back, his mind churning with possibilities. The connections were tenuous, but they were there, woven into the fabric of the victims' lives like an intricate tapestry waiting to be unraveled. It was in these threads that he hoped to find the pattern that would lead them to the killer.

Finn felt the tension in the room tighten like a bowstring as he broached the subject. "Did Jillian ever stay here with you?" he asked, his voice steady but infused with an undercurrent of urgency.

"Of course," Mrs. Bruce murmured, her eyes glistening with unshed tears. "Her room is just as she left it. She would come by often to escape the pressures of her performances. In fact, she often liked to keep some of her things here, so it would always feel like her own space."

"May we see it?" Finn pressed, sensing a reluctance from Mr. Bruce, whose mouth had set into a firm line of resistance.

"I don't know..." Mr. Bruce began the protective instincts of a father warring with the necessity of the investigation. "It feels wrong to let strangers roam through her most private space."

His wife reached across, placing a hand over his. "Love, it could help them find who did this to our Jillian." Her voice was soft yet carried the weight of conviction. "We need to do everything we can."

After a moment that hung suspended like a dissonant note, Mr. Bruce relented with a sigh that seemed to carry all his grief. "Alright," he conceded, rising stiffly from his armchair. "This way."

They ascended the stairs, each step creaking underfoot, speaking to the age of the house—a comforting sound in less dire times. Jillian's room lay at the end of the hallway, her name still painted on the door in elegant script, a poignant reminder of happier days.

The space was a capsule of Jillian's life, untouched and hauntingly personal. Sheets of music lay scattered across a polished mahogany desk, the intricate notes spiraling like the thoughts of their absent composer. Finn's gaze was drawn to a leather-bound notebook lying open; its pages were filled with annotations for a new piece—something grand and emotive about Robert the Bruce.

"Another royal connection," Finn muttered to himself, tracing a finger over the sketched image of a signet ring nestled between the staves. It was meticulously detailed, featuring the emblem of the Bruce lineage.

"Did Jillian display her royal heritage? A ring like this?" Amelia asked, her question piercing the heavy air of the room.

"That is an emblem of the Bruce family, yes, but we've never owned such a ring," Mrs. Bruce responded, her brow furrowing in consternation. "She must've seen it somewhere else."

"Or someone showed it to her," Finn added thoughtfully, the implications of this detail spreading through his mind like ink in water. He exchanged a look with Amelia—another piece of the puzzle, albeit one shrouded in mystery.

As they left the room, Finn felt the presence of Jillian Bruce lingering in the quiet hum of displaced air, in the resonance of unsung melodies. The clue of the signet ring lay heavy in his thoughts, a silent whisper from the victim leading them closer to the shadow that had extinguished her light.

"I don't feel too well," Mr Bruce said.

His wife took his arm. "It's okay, Love." Mrs Bruce turned to Amelia. "We'll be downstairs."

Amelia nodded as they left the room.

"Breaks your heart," Finn said. "We have to find this guy before anyone else has to grieve their daughters."

Finn thumbed through several pages of Jillian Bruce's diary, hoping for a glimpse into the mind of a woman whose life had been cruelly cut short. Each page was a tapestry of thoughts and events—a concert here, a rehearsal there—but nothing that screamed sinister or unusual. He could feel Amelia's presence behind him, her silence a shared frustration.

"Seems like she kept detailed records of her day-to-day, but it's all... ordinary," Finn said, closing the diary with a sigh. The room, once an incubator for Jillian's creative energy, now felt like a mausoleum preserving the mundane aspects of her existence. "She must have really still felt at home here to leave her diary."

"Maybe she had two," Amelia mused.

"That diary tells me she never quite left home," Finn said, sadly.

Amelia leaned over his shoulder, peering at a photo pinned to a corkboard—Jillian beaming on stage, violin in hand. "She lived for music. It's all here, every part of her life, except for the one we need."

"Unfortunately, killers don't tend to RSVP," Finn quipped, running a hand through his hair. A coping mechanism they both relied on, humor in the face of despair, a way to keep their heads above the dark waters they waded through daily.

They scoured the rest of the room, under beds, inside closets, beneath stacks of sheet music, each nook holding the potential key to unlocking the identity of a murderer. But as time went on, the promising leads dwindled, leaving them with a collection of dead ends.

"Nothing," Amelia declared, a hint of defeat edging into her tone. She perched on the edge of Jillian's bed, fingers idly tracing the floral bedspread. "We're missing something; it's like chasing shadows."

"Shadows have to come from somewhere," Finn mused aloud, though even his own optimism was beginning to wear thin. He glanced at the clock—time slipping away with nothing to show for it.

As they prepared to leave, Finn's mobile vibrated sharply against his thigh. He fished it out, the screen lighting up with Rob Collins' name. "Rob?" he answered, the Chief's voice crackling through the speaker.

"Finally, a break," came Rob's urgent reply. "The killer has made contact with us."

Amelia gave Finn a worried look, a gaze that said the world and their investigation was about to be turned upside down.

CHAPTER SEVENTEEN

Finn's gaze was locked onto the parchment sprawled across the conference room table, its edges curling like withered leaves. The low hum of the Hertfordshire Constabulary headquarters faded into a distant murmur as he leaned in, his eyes darting between the Old English script and the arcane symbols that looked more like relics from a forgotten age than pieces of a message.

"Are we certain this is from our killer?" Amelia's question pierced the thick air of concentration. Her voice held a measured calm, betraying none of the urgency that had brought them to this emergency meeting.

Rob Collins, 'Rob,' to Finn since their college days but 'Chief' to everyone else in the room, didn't miss a beat. "The details match up—things about the murders we've kept from the press. And Dr. Carter confirmed it's the same type of parchment left at each scene."

Finn's mind raced as he scrutinized the cryptic communication. The killer's choice to weave archaic language with these symbols was no random act—it was intentional, taunting. It spoke of someone not just living in the past, but obsessed with it.

"Symbols now, instead of plain text. Why?" Amelia mused aloud, her brow creasing in thought.

Finn straightened slightly, letting out a slow breath. "We need to understand what they represent," he said, his voice steady despite the cacophony of questions thundering through his head. Each symbol seemed to be a piece of a larger puzzle—a puzzle that could crack open the twisted mind behind these killings. "I do wonder, about old Professor Hemingway. Didn't he say that he studied cryptography as well as having an extensive knowledge of Old English and other periods?"

Amelia nodded. "He did. But we'd need something to go on. We can't arrest someone just because they're smart. Let's keep looking."

A shiver of anticipation trailed down Finn's spine. He was part excited, part worried about the killer's change in notes. It may have been because they were getting close and the killer now wanted to put them off, but Finn worried that if the killer was going through some sort of psychological change, that this could lead to escalation and more deaths.

Amelia caught his eye, a glimmer of shared resolve passing between them. Even in the face of darkness, they found solace in their camaraderie, exchanging a wry grin that served as a silent acknowledgment of the grim humor that kept them grounded.

As they poured over the parchment, the symbols began to whisper secrets, hinting at an obsession with history, lineage, perhaps even ritual. Finn's analytical mind pieced together fragments of knowledge, drawing from old texts and cases long since buried in the archives of his experience.

Finn's gaze lingered on the parchment, the symbols etched into its fiber as if mocking their efforts to decipher them. The room was a cavern of thought, where shadows of past crimes played across the walls in the dim light of the computer screens. Amelia leaned back in her chair, her eyes clouded with frustration and fatigue. It was then that Rob, standing with an aura of quiet authority, broke the silence that had settled over them.

"Look," he began, his voice measured, "we're running circles around these words and getting nowhere. Let's shift gears for a moment—focus on what we know about the materials our killer favors: antique parchments, archaic symbols. There has to be a reason for this specific choice."

Amelia straightened up, considering the Chief's angle, while Finn felt a tinge of respect for Rob's ability to see through the fog of dead ends. They were indeed at a standstill, and the suggestion pricked at his detective senses. He nodded slightly, the motion almost imperceptible.

"Right, Rob," Finn agreed.

They turned to the databases, hungry for any scrap of knowledge that might connect the dots. Digital archives sprawled before them, vast and unyielding, but they persisted, driven by the urgency that the killer's next move could be imminent. Finn's fingers flew over the keyboard, summoning records of antiquities dealers, museum acquisitions, and obscure collectors who dabbled in the macabre trade of historical relics.

"Anything that looks out of place," Amelia said, her voice a soft hum against the click-clack of keys. Her sharp mind was a beacon in the murkiness of conjecture. Finn appreciated her intuition as much as he did her quick wit, which often cut through the tension when it threatened to overwhelm them.

"Here," Finn pointed to a list that appeared on his screen, each entry a whisper from the past. "Dealers who specialize in medieval artifacts. Could be our killer is sourcing his materials from one of these."

"Or knows someone who does," Amelia chimed in, leaning closer to scan the list. Their heads nearly touched, two detectives united in purpose and determination.

Hour after hour, they sifted through transactions and correspondences, every so often exchanging glances that spoke volumes—each look a mix of hope and weariness. The symbols from the notes became their silent companions, hovering at the edges of their vision as they combed through data, hoping to unearth a connection that would lead them to the shadow that had cast such a pall over Hertfordshire.

As time wore on, Finn felt the threads of the case twisting, intertwining with the fibers of the ancient parchment, as if history itself was a labyrinth they needed to navigate. Yet neither he nor Amelia would allow themselves to fall prey to despair; instead, they fortified themselves with shared resolve and the occasional dry quip that only they could appreciate amidst the gravitas of their hunt.

The glare of the computer screen had long since ceased to be a nuisance, fading into Finn's mental periphery as he and Amelia continued their digital excavation. He felt the muscles in his neck protest from the hours of tension, and he rolled his shoulders in an attempt to dispel the discomfort. Amelia, ever observant, caught the small gesture.

"Hit a wall?" she asked, her tone light but her eyes keen with concern.

"Feels like it," Finn admitted, rubbing at his eyes before refocusing on the task at hand. "But walls are meant to be scaled, or broken through."

"Or to hide treasures behind them," Amelia added, her lips curving into a wry smile.

Finn couldn't help but smirk in return; it was their way—their silent pact to keep spirits buoyed in the face of adversity. He turned back to the symbols, tracing one with a fingertip on the screen. That's when he saw it—a connection, a semblance of familiarity that tugged at his memory.

"Amelia, look at this," he called out, his voice low but urgent. She was immediately at his side, her presence a comforting solidity.

He pointed to a symbol, intricate and ancient looking. "Doesn't that symbol match up with a couple on the parchment?"

Her eyes narrowed as she studied it. "You might be onto something. It does bear a resemblance to—"

"The Temple of the Silver Sun," Finn read out loud, looking at info online.

"What else does it say?" Amelia asked.

"Long thought extinct," Finn mused, his mind racing through the implications. The Temple of the Silver Sun—a subculture entwined with mysticism and British history, its members shrouded in secrecy and bound by allegiance to a forgotten creed. "Most historians believe the society crumbled long ago, but some suggest such a group could still exist across the British Isles."

"Could our killer be a modern-day disciple?" Amelia pondered aloud, turning to Finn with a speculative gleam in her eye.

"Or obsessed with their teachings, using their symbolism to communicate," Finn suggested, feeling a flicker of excitement amidst the ominous undercurrent of their case. "Either way, we've got a new angle to pursue."

Amelia was already steps ahead, her gaze locked onto the screen as she began searching for more information. "If this is a language he's speaking, then we need a translator. Someone who can decode the intricacies of this subculture."

"An expert in esoteric societies, perhaps?" Finn raised an eyebrow, impressed with Amelia's quick thinking.

"Exactly." Amelia straightened, her resolve hardening into determination. "I'll reach out to the university archives first thing tomorrow. Oldbridge is one of the oldest universities in the world, if they don't have a specialist in ancient cults and forgotten societies, they must know someone who is."

Finn nodded, feeling a surge of hope amidst the fatigue that clung to his bones. This was progress, however slight, and in their line of work, every bit counted. The Temple of the Silver Sun—an arcane piece of the past that could very well illuminate their path to catching a murderer who seemed as much a specter as the victims he left behind.

CHAPTER EIGHTEEN

The hushed sanctum of a long-forgotten wing within the venerable London library was where the killer found solace, surrounded by the silent scrutiny of history's elite. The musty scent of antique tomes mingled with the faint musk of varnished wood, providing an oddly comforting aroma to the Killer as he traced his gloved fingers over the gilded frames that housed the stoic faces of kings and queens long deceased.

A singular bulb hung precariously overhead, casting a sallow glow upon the portraits that watched him from every wall. Its light flickered, as if even electricity hesitated to disturb this solemn chamber. And there among the oil-painted eyes, some bore the mark of his triumph—a red X slashed across canvas and wood with surgical precision, marring the visages of those who had become unwitting participants in his lethal legacy.

He moved through the room with reverence, each footfall muted by the thick carpet underfoot. Here, among echoes of past grandeur, he imagined himself a curator of fate, the arbiter of life and death. This quiet corner of the world belonged only to him and to the memories of his conquests.

As he approached the mahogany shelf that cradled his most prized possessions, the Killer's pulse quickened. His collection of mementos, each a testament to his work, lay before him—a symphony of silent screams and unspoken stories. His hands, steady and sure, reached out to the newest addition: a rare porcelain doll, meticulously crafted with delicate features and soft, curling locks of hair that mirrored Jillian Bruce's own.

This doll, unlike the other crude tokens, was special. It spoke of an intimacy, a connection with his victim that transcended the mere act of murder. He positioned it on the shelf with care, ensuring it stood prominently among the lesser souvenirs. It was more than a trophy; it was a symbol of his evolution, a reflection of the growing complexity of his desires.

With a tenderness that belied his cruel nature, the Killer caressed the fine lines of the doll's face, admiring the artistry of its creation. The way its glassy eyes seemed to hold a glimmer of life, the way its small porcelain hands were poised as if caught in a moment of grace, it was almost too perfect an effigy of the woman whose last breath he had claimed.

For a moment, he allowed himself the indulgence of recollection—the memory of Jillian's fear, the sound of her plea, the resistance fading from her delicate body as he took from her what was never his to claim. He relished these memories, for they were all that remained of his victims once their flames were extinguished, and he stood alone in the darkness of his lair, shrouded in the omnipotence of his acts.

The air in the secluded chamber was thick with dust and silence, a crypt for the forgotten wing of an ancient library where history whispered through the decrepit shelves. Shadows clung to the walls like specters, but one area stood bathed in the light of a single, stark bulb, illuminating the Killer's private exhibition. With the meticulous care of a curator crafting his final showcase, he retreated a few steps from the shelf that cradled his latest acquisition—the porcelain doll, a chilling likeness of Jillian Bruce.

His eyes roamed over the collection, each piece a sinister echo of a life he had snuffed out. There was Rebecca Hanover's silver comb, its once-shiny teeth now stained and dull, discarded in the aftermath of her death. Dominique Plantagenet's antique brooch lay next to it, a jewel missing from its ornate setting, much like how her life had been so abruptly cut from the fabric of existence.

No mere murderer, he fashioned himself an artist, and these were his masterpieces. The memories surged forward unbidden: Rebecca's apartment, where he relished the shock that crossed her face when she recognized the inevitable; Thornheart House, where Dominique's blood had flowed as freely as the wine at the banquet she'd never leave. And then there was Jillian, her apartment a silent stage for their final, deadly dance. Each recollection brought with it a resurgence of the thrill—the chase, the plan, the execution—all woven into a tapestry of power and control that only he could appreciate.

Among the scattered mementos, a new token caught his eye, distinct in its simplicity—a violin string, coiled around a small figurine. This was not a part of his usual ritualistic trophies. It was something more—something personal. He reached out, fingers tracing the cold, smooth texture of the string. The tactile sensation conjured the vivid image of Jillian's horror-stricken visage, eyes wide with the dawning realization of her fate, her pleas dissolving into the final, silent plea for mercy that would never come.

The Killer allowed himself a moment to savor the memory, the dominance he had exerted in snatching away her future. Then, his attention was drawn to a photograph placed deliberately amongst the chaos. Clara Tudor smiled back at him, her eyes alight with vivacity, her lips curved in an expression of joy so pure it was almost painful to behold.

He leaned in closer, studying her features with an intensity that bordered on reverence. In that smile, he saw not just a challenge, but a promise—a promise of the continuation of his grand design. Clara Tudor, unaware and alive, was yet another chapter waiting to be written, another life ready to be woven into the dark tapestry of his making. Her bright demeanor mocked him from the photo, seemingly impervious to the shadows that crept ever closer. But he knew better. He understood the fragility of life and the ease with which it could be extinguished.

The killer's breath formed misty halos in the cold air of his hidden sanctum, each exhale a silent whisper amidst the thick tomes and dust-covered relics of his private chamber. The dim glow of a single bulb cast shadows that danced across walls lined with royal histories, their spines cracked and worn from years of obsessive study. He moved with a predator's grace, every motion deliberate as he circled his collection, the artifacts of his conquests.

His gaze lingered on the porcelain likeness of Jillian Bruce, whose addition had been the latest triumph in his series of calculated retributions. The doll, with its hauntingly accurate representation, was more than just another trophy; it was a symbol of his meticulous craft, an embodiment of the lives he'd claimed with such precision. He adjusted the violin string that adorned the small figure, ensuring its prominence amongst the other mementos.

Then he turned, drawn as if by magnetic force, to the photograph that had captivated his attention since its placement. Clara Tudor's image beamed up at him, her smile exuding a warmth that seemed to radiate through the grainy picture. But beneath her veneer of happiness, he saw the potential for his next masterpiece—a canvas yet untouched by his dark artistry.

As the seconds ticked by, the urge within him swelled like a tide, pulling him closer to the edge of action. His fingers twitched with eagerness, itching to orchestrate the demise that would not only silence

Clara Tudor's bright smile but also serve as a crescendo to his sinister symphony. The game beckoned him forward—unrelenting, irresistible.

He traced the outline of her face, his touch ghosting over the photograph as though he could reach through time and space to touch the very life he yearned to extinguish. Anticipation coiled tightly within him, a spring ready to uncoil at the opportune moment. He imagined her eyes wide with the realization of her fate, the moment when she would understand that she was nothing more than a pawn in his grand scheme.

Clara Tudor, the enigma that pulled at his thoughts, was destined to be the next note in his deadly composition. The thought of claiming her filled him with a fervor that bordered on ecstasy. In the quiet of the library, surrounded by the ghosts of monarchies past, he made his silent vow.

CHAPTER NINETEEN

Finn leaned back in the train seat, watching as Amelia's gaze lingered on the passing landscape, her eyes tracing the blur of colors that swept by. The compartment was quiet except for the steady cadence of the wheels, a lulling soundtrack to their introspection. Breaking the silence, he spoke, his voice a soft rumble amidst the train's rhythm.

"The trains are so different here."

"How so?" Amelia asked.

"The size, mainly," Finn explained. "It's funny, even after a year of being in the UK, I still see things that take me by surprise."

"You must miss home, Finn," Amelia said, gently. "Do you never want to go back and visit family?"

"Most of my family are gone," Finn said, trying to hide the pain of it. "Estranged or otherwise."

"What about the town you mentioned where you grew up, no friends still there?"

"Yeah, there are," Finn said, "But it's tricky revisiting your past."

"That's true," Amelia answered. "What was it like when you were a kid?"

"Growing up in Florida wasn't easy," Finn confessed, tilting his head to catch Amelia's attention. "A poor town where everyone knew your name and business. They all thought I'd end up just another trouble-making statistic."

Amelia turned to face him, her expression open, inviting him to continue. He hesitated, unaccustomed to sharing personal tales, but something about the trust between them urged him on.

"Did you just leave?" asked Amelia.

"Yeah," Finn said. "But things were difficult. No one trusted me."

The train clattered slightly on the tracks.

"Then one day, everything changed," he said, his voice dipped lower with the weight of the memory. "A girl from my town nearly got hit by a car. I managed to pull her out of the way. After that, people started seeing me differently."

He paused, reflecting on the pivotal moment. "That's when I realized I wanted—needed—to help others. It wasn't long before that path led me to the FBI." His past, once a shadowy backdrop to his life, now seemed like the prologue to his purpose.

Amelia nodded, her eyes reflecting an understanding that went deeper than words. Just as she opened her mouth to respond, Finn seized the opportunity to shift the focus onto her.

He felt a need to lean in and kiss her. But he respected her boundaries. Then, one question he had wanted answered bubbled to the top of his mind.

"Have you seen anyone since your fiance passed?" he asked gently, aware of the delicate ground he trod upon.

"No," she replied, her voice steady yet distant, as if the question pulled her back through time.

Finn leaned in closer, moved by their shared vulnerability. "It's okay if you don't want to talk about it."

"It's hard Finn," she said, softly. "You imagine your world with a man, then that world takes him away for good. You think you'll never feel that way again. Then... A chance encounter..."

"A chance encounter," Finn nodded, repeating the phrase quietly.

They stared into each other's eyes before Finn finally plucked up the courage and said: "Amelia, would you ever like to..."

"Tickets, please," a conductor with rosey cheeks asked, suddenly from the aisle.

Finn ruffled through his pockets. "Um."

"Don't tell me you lost them?" Amelia said.

"No," Finn answered. "I had them in my hand, and I went to the toilet and... Oh dear."

"Two returns to Wendsley, please," Amelia laughed, paying the conductor.

The conductor handed over the tickets, nodded, and then walked along the aisle.

"I'll hold on to them for now," Amelia said, pocketing them.

Finn nodded, feeling the moment was gone. His courage certainly was diminished for the time being. Outside, the cityscape gradually gave way to the rolling countryside, signaling the end of their temporary respite. As if on cue, they both straightened up, the familiar mantle of duty reasserting itself. They were detectives first, everything else came after. The task at hand was grim, but necessary. There would be time for personal matters later—if at all.

The train carried them further from the city's chaos, towards the answers they hoped lay with the eccentric historian awaiting them far from London on the West coast.

***

The tires of their unmarked police car crunched over the gravel as Finn steered it up the serpentine drive that led to Thaddeus Trumble's home. The building stood secluded amid a grove of ancient trees, their bare branches clawing at the gray skies above like desperate fingers seeking salvation from the coming storm.

"You would think the local police department could have given us something a little easier to drive," Finn grimaced as he navigated the winding path.

"You get what you get," Amelia smiled, her eyes scanning the impressive façade of the historian's residence. "Besides, I'm sure Mr. Trumble will make it worth our while."

Finn raised an eyebrow at her comment but said nothing as he killed the engine. They stepped out into the crisp air, tinged with the metallic scent of impending rain, and approached the front door. It loomed before them, heavy wood carved with intricate scenes that seemed to tell tales of glory and tragedy long forgotten by the world beyond this threshold.

Before they could knock, the door swung open, revealing a man who seemed to embody the perfect blend of intellect and charm. Thaddeus Trumble, despite his young age of thirty, exuded an air of confidence and knowledge that belied his years. His chiseled features were framed by a mane of dark hair, artfully tousled as if he'd just stepped out of a university lecture hall. His eyes, a striking shade of green, sparkled with a mix of curiosity and mischief behind his stylish glasses.

"Detectives," he greeted, his voice smooth as silk. "I've been expecting you."

Amelia seemed momentarily taken aback by the historian's appearance, a faint blush coloring her cheeks. Finn felt a pang of jealousy as he watched her compose herself, extending a hand to Thaddeuss.

"Mr. Trumble," she began, her tone professional yet warm. "Thank you for seeing us on such short notice."

"Please, call me Thaddeus," he replied, his smile dazzling as he shook her hand. "And it's my pleasure. Anything to assist the law enforcement in their noble pursuits."

As Thaddeus led them into his study, Finn couldn't help but notice the way Amelia's gaze lingered on the historian's broad shoulders and lean frame. The room itself was a testament to Thaddeuss's passion for history—books lined every inch of wall space, maps dotted with countless colored pins covered the remaining gaps, and ancient artifacts were displayed with reverent care.

"Please, sit," Thaddeuss offered, gesturing to a pair of plush armchairs that faced his impressive oak desk. As they settled in, he leaned against the edge of the desk, his posture casual yet commanding. "So, what brings two of Hertfordshire's finest to my humble abode?"

Finn cleared his throat, determined to prove his own worth in the face of this charismatic scholar. "We're investigating a series of murders that seem to have a connection to an ancient secret society known as the Temple of the Silver Sun. We were hoping you might be able to shed some light on their history and practices."

Thaddeuss's eyes lit up at the mention of the obscure group. "Ah, the Temple of the Silver Sun. A fascinating bunch, shrouded in mystery and whispers of revolution. I've come across a few references to them in my research, but hard facts are scarce."

As Thaddeuss delved into the lore surrounding the society, Finn found himself struggling to keep up with the rapid-fire barrage of historical tidbits and academic jargon. He glanced at Amelia, who seemed entirely engrossed in the historian's words, her pen flying across her notebook as she jotted down key points.

Feeling a bit out of his depth, Finn attempted to interject with a question of his own. "So, this 'Secret Hand' figure—could it be more than just a title within the society? Could it be a role passed down through generations, even after the Temple itself disbanded?"

Thaddeus paused, considering the idea. "It's certainly possible. Many secret societies have hereditary positions, ensuring the continuation of their traditions and beliefs. The Secret Hand could very well be a mantle carried forward through time, even if the Temple itself has faded into obscurity."

Finn nodded, a small surge of pride welling up in his chest at having contributed something valuable to the discussion. However, his moment of triumph was short-lived as he reached for a leather-bound tome on Thaddeuss's desk, intent on examining it more closely. In his eagerness, he misjudged the distance and knocked over a precariously balanced stack of papers, sending them fluttering to the floor in a chaotic whirlwind.

"Oh, damn—I'm so sorry," Finn stammered, his face flushing with embarrassment as he scrambled to gather the scattered documents. Amelia and Thaddeus moved to help, their hands brushing against each other's as they worked to restore order to the historian's desk.

"No worries at all," Thaddeus assured them, his smile genuine and kind. "Accidents happen, especially when one is caught up in the thrill of intellectual pursuit."

As they finished tidying up, Amelia glanced at her watch. "We should probably get going," she said, a hint of reluctance in her voice. "Thank you so much for your time and insights, Thaddeuss. You've given us a lot to think about."

"It was my pleasure," Thaddeus replied, his gaze lingering on Amelia a moment longer than necessary. "If there's anything else I can do to assist in your investigation, please don't hesitate to reach out."

As they made their way back to the car, Amelia couldn't help but tease Finn. "You seemed a little intimidated in there," she said, a playful smirk tugging at her lips. "I never thought I'd see the day when the great Finn Wright was tongue-tied by a handsome academic."

Finn scoffed, feigning indignation. "Intimidated? Please. I could rock a tweed jacket and bow tie way better than any stuffy professor. In fact, I might just start wearing them to crime scenes. You know, to add a touch of class to the proceedings."

Amelia burst out laughing, the sound echoing through the misty air. "Oh, I would pay good money to see that. Detective Finn Wright, the sartorial savant of the Hertfordshire Constabulary."

Finn grinned, enjoying the easy banter that had become a hallmark of their partnership. "Hey, don't knock it until you've tried it. I bet I could solve cases twice as fast if I had a pipe and a monocle to go with the ensemble. And you know, if that sort of thing does it for you..."

Amelia's phone buzzed sharply, demanding their attention.

Her expression grew somber as she listened to the voice on the other end, and Finn felt a familiar sense of dread settling in his gut. When she ended the call, her eyes met his, the gravity of the situation etched into her features.

"There's been another murder," she said, her voice tight with a mix of frustration and determination. "Same M.O. as the others."

Finn nodded grimly, the weight of their responsibility pressing down on his shoulders. As they climbed into the car and set off towards the latest crime scene, he couldn't shake the feeling that they were racing against an invisible clock, the hands of fate spinning ever faster towards an inevitable conclusion.

Finn knew they were now dealing with an assassin, and the problem with assassins was that you never knew when or where they would strike next.

CHAPTER TWENTY

The air was thick with an unsettling stillness as Finn Wright stepped over the threshold into Clara Tudor's apartment. The luxurious trappings of her life were in disarray, a morbid tableau set amidst velvet and gold. The grandeur of the place did little to mask the tragedy that had unfolded within these walls. He exchanged a grave look with Amelia Winters, who gave a slight nod before they began to divide the expansive space between them, each setting out on a silent quest for truth amidst the chaos.

Finn's gaze traced the ostentatious contours of the room, his mind laboring to piece together the narrative of the crime. The killer's brazen act had left an eerie echo of regal demise; it wasn't lost on him that Clara Tudor had met an end reminiscent of her distant ancestor. Each detail seemed to pulse with significance, as though history itself bled into the present, painting a foreboding picture of a murderer draped in the cloak of the past.

"Another royal connection," Amelia murmured from across the room, her voice low but carrying the weight of their shared realization. "The Tudors were the royal family for over a hundred years back in the sixteenth century."

"Seems like the killer's not shy about sending a message," Finn replied.

Clara Tudor's body lay sprawled on the floor, a macabre centerpiece in her opulent apartment. Her once-elegant gown was now a twisted shroud around her, the fabric stained with the crimson mark of violence. Finn's eyes lingered on the stillness of her form, noting the haunting resemblance to historical tragedies that echoed through time.

"I'll speak with the forensics team in the other room," Amelia said. "This flat is huge. Have a look around and see if the killer has been tidying and organizing here like some of the other scenes, would you?"

"Your wish is my command," Finn smiled.

As Amelia excused herself to confer with the forensics team in another room, Finn remained alone with Clara's lifeless figure, a silent witness to the chilling artistry of death that had visited this place. The weight of their task pressed down on him as he stood amidst the grandeur turned grim play, a lone sentinel in a realm where shadows danced with secrets untold.

Moving through the rooms with methodical care, Finn's thoughts churned around The Secret Hand assassin theory. If true, he understood the implications—the killer would relentlessly pursue some linked to the crown, a shadow cast long by ancient lineage, and offer the sacrifice up to their mysterious god. As he sifted through the remnants of Clara's life, the sight of a framed photograph drew his attention. Clara Tudor, resplendent in evening attire, was captured mid-laughter at a fundraiser for The Noble Stage. His eyes narrowed, recognizing the pattern that wove through the victims: a thread spun from stages and performance, a motif repeating with chilling regularity.

In the hushed corner of Clara Tudor's apartment, where the cacophony of the outside world seemed like a distant murmur, Finn crouched low. His eyes combed over the space, every fiber attuned to the subtleties that lay beyond the obvious disarray. The plush carpet, once a canvas for elegant furnishings, now framed a lone piece of parchment, its edges curled like the leaves of an ancient tome weathered by time.

Finn reached out, his fingers grazing the rough texture before lifting the paper with a delicacy reserved for sacred relics. The script was a dance of archaic English, flourishes and loops crafting words that spoke of forgotten eras. Beside the note rested an emblem, etched into metal - the distinct imprint of a signet ring. It was chilling in its familiarity; the killer's signature left behind as though it were a calling card at a high society soiree.

"Amelia," Finn called softly, knowing that even within the breadth of the apartment, she would hear him. "Found something."

Amelia soon entered the room where Finn now stood.

"What is it?"

"A note and the imprint of a signet ring."

The note held secrets he could feel but not yet decipher, whispers of a motive entwined with historical threads that wove through the present crime. He photographed the evidence meticulously, storing images that would soon be pored over with fervent scrutiny back at the precinct.

As he stood, a shiver ran through him, not from foreboding, but from a tangible cold that seeped into the room. He glanced around, senses heightened, until he detected the source—a stream of air that sent a nearby curtain fluttering like a ghostly specter.

Stepping closer, Finn drew back the fabric to reveal an open window, night air invading the space like an unwelcome intruder. He examined the latch, or rather, where the latch should have been. Broken, its jagged edges bore silent witness to forceful entry—or a hasty retreat.

"Window's unlatched," he announced, directing the statement to Amelia, wherever she might be in the labyrinth of rooms. This wasn't just a break-in; it was an escape route, perhaps still warm from the killer's touch.

His gaze shifted to the street below, searching the darkness for any sign of movement, any hint of the shadow that had struck down Clara Tudor. But the night held its secrets close, revealing nothing to his probing eyes. Finn memorized the scene—the position of the window, the angle of descent, the potential paths of flight. This breach was another piece of the puzzle, silent testimony to a murderer's boldness and cunning.

"Amelia, better check the other windows too," Finn said, voice steady despite the racing thoughts. "Our guest might've left prints."

Finn's fingers traced the cold, metallic remnants of the latch before he leaned forward, his head breaching the apartment's threshold into the open air. The chill of the night caressed his face, a stark contrast to the stifling silence within the apartment walls. He squinted, attempting to pierce the veil of darkness that shrouded the upscale neighborhood below. His breath fogged in front of him, the moisture glinting in the moonlight as if mocking his efforts to find clarity.

A sound—a mere rustle—barely perceptible over the distant hum of city life, tickled his ears. Instinctively, he craned his neck, peering down along the ornate facade of the building. The street was deserted, save for the occasional car that slid past, its headlights casting long, spectral shadows that danced across the pavement.

"Anything?" called out Amelia from somewhere inside the apartment, her voice laced with the tension of their grim task.

"Quiet as the grave," Finn murmured under his breath, unaware that he was about to experience just how deceptive silence could be. As he withdrew his head, preparing to report back to Amelia, a blur of motion flickered at the periphery of his vision.

In an instant, a hand shot up, gripping his collar with startling strength. Finn's instincts screamed danger, but it was too late. His body jolted forward, and his temple collided with the jagged edge of the window frame. Pain exploded behind his eyes, white-hot and blinding. And then, the world went dark.

***

Consciousness returned to Finn in trickles, like water seeping through cracks in his mind. A dull throbbing engulfed his head, each pulse dragging him further from the abyss. Groaning, he tried to piece together the fractured moments before the blackness had claimed him.

"Easy, Finn." Amelia's voice was steady, a beacon in the fog that clouded his thoughts. Her hands were on his shoulders, grounding him as he blinked against the harsh light of the room.

"Killer..." The word stumbled out of his mouth, thick and sluggish.

Amelia's brow furrowed, her eyes hardening with resolve. "You saw him?"

"No," Finn managed, his voice gaining strength as the pieces fell into place. "But he was here. He must have been watching us."

The realization sent a shiver down his spine. They had been under surveillance, their every move possibly cataloged by the very predator they sought to cage. The brazenness of it—the sheer audacity—was chilling.

Amelia turned to the window, her gaze sweeping the emptiness beyond. "Gone now," she concluded. Without hesitation, she reached for her radio, alerting the constable positioned outside to sweep the area. Their chances were slim; their quarry was a phantom, slipping away into the night with ease.

"Could've been anyone," Finn muttered, pushing himself to his feet, his body protesting with sharp stabs of pain. "But it wasn't. It was him."

"Let's hope our constables are quick on their feet," Amelia replied, though her tone betrayed the understanding that they were grasping at straws.

Finn straightened his jacket, setting his jaw with determination. The encounter had been brief, but it was a connection, however tenuous, to the shadow that had haunted them since the first murder. The game was escalating, and so too must their resolve.

Through the haze of his recent strike to the head, Finn's thoughts sharpened as he weaved between the ostentatious furnishings of Clara Tudor's apartment. The ambient light cast long, dancing shadows on the walls, a macabre performance to match the gravity of their situation. Amelia paced nearby, her silhouette framed by the backdrop of opulence turned mausoleum.

"Play it back for me, Finn," she said, her voice a calm command amid the disquiet. "Why linger? Why let us get so close?"

He rubbed at the tender spot on his skull, feeling the narrative unfurl like a scroll within his mind. "Recognition," he muttered, his gaze drifting to the now silent grand piano, its black lacquer reflecting distorted images of their investigation. "The clues, the notes to the constabulary... It's all breadcrumbs."

Amelia paused, her eyes narrowing. "But why?"

"Because," Finn began, stepping closer to her, "he wants to be seen. The thrill isn't just in the hunt or the kill—it's in the chase. He's taunting us, hovering just out of reach. He wants the spotlight, but not the handcuffs."

A hushed moment passed between them, and then Finn reached into his jacket, extracting the photograph of Clara Tudor he had found earlier. He handed it to Amelia, who studied the image—the victim alive, smiling at a fundraiser for The Noble Stage.

"Look at this," he urged, pointing to the details that now screamed significance. "Another tie to the theater And if our killer revels in the dramatic..."

"Then they might be an actor!" Amelia finished, her voice steady but with a hint of incredulity. "It would fit. The flair, the staged scenes..."

"Exactly," Finn agreed, his thoughts aligning like actors taking their marks upon the stage. "This isn't just about ancestry or revenge; it's theater, Amelia. Deadly theater."

She handed the photograph back to him, her expression contemplative, yet tinged with a steeliness he'd come to admire. "So, we're looking for someone who can blend into any role. Someone who understands timing, spectacle..."

The constable's entrance was as abrupt as the message he carried, a disruption in the stillness of Clara Tudor's apartment where death lingered like an unwelcome guest. He held out a piece of parchment, its edges worn as if it had traveled through time to deliver its silent testimony. Finn accepted the offering with a practiced hand, his gaze locking onto the symbols inked into the paper—arcane, enigmatic.

"Two notes this time. Symbols again," Finn murmured, the cryptic script twisting beneath his scrutiny.

Amelia leaned over his shoulder, her presence a steady force. "We should take these to Thaddeuss; he might make sense of it."

Finn shook his head, a flicker of frustration igniting within him. "No. We've been dancing to the killer's tune long enough." He straightened, the resolve hardening in his eyes. "It's time for us now to direct the play." Amelia's lips twitched in a semblance of a smile, her way of acknowledging the layered metaphor that was both their coping mechanism and unspoken understanding.

He withdrew his phone, its screen a cold glow against the dim backdrop of opulence and tragedy. Dialing with deft fingers, he waited for the familiar voice on the other end. "Rob, it's Finn. Listen, I need a rundown of local archivists dealing with ancient texts."

"Archivists?" Rob's voice crackled through the line, tinged with both curiosity and urgency. "What's the angle?"

"Cross-reference them with anyone who's been an actor at some point. It's a hunch," Finn said, his mind piecing together the shadows of a profile. "Our killer might be playing the most dangerous role of their life."

"Got it. I'll get back to you as soon as I have something," Rob replied, the undercurrent of his words a reflection of the trust forged between old college friends turned colleagues.

"Thanks," Finn said before ending the call. He pocketed the phone and glanced at Amelia. "Our killer's not just staging murders; they're curating a performance. And if we're right about the theater connection, they won't be able to resist an encore. "

"Why do I get a feeling you have a plan and that it will be more dangerous than necessary?" Amelia smiled.

"You know me too well, Winters," Finn said. "If our theory holds, the killer is both an actor and an archivist of some description. Someone who has access to those old parchments. He is also the last in line of The Temple of the Silver Sun. He is combining his connection to the theater with his connection to that cult that wanted to wipe out royalty."

Finn's phone rang. "Hello?"

"Finn, it's Rob," the Chief Constable said. "You were right on the money. The second we searched for an archivist and an actor, we got a single hit in the London area. A man named Victor Hastings. He once played Oliver Cromwell in the West End, but in recent years he's been a freelance archivist. He spends most of his time though working at Milton Library. And get this, he has been previously arrested for vehemently protesting against the monarchy. He got a little violent and spent a year in prison."

"My God," Amelia said, listening in. "This could be him... Didn't we speak with a Hastings back at the University library? Professor Hemingway's assistant?"

Finn clenched his fist. "Yes... Under our noses... Can you get us an address?" Finn asked.

"Him playing Cromwell in a play, too..." Amelia said. "A famous anti-monarchist."

"And Doctor Carter said that the fragments," Finn shook his head. "That the ink fragments on the notes used iron gall, something only someone who is passionate about history would use. Like an archivist!"

"Not to mention the use of Old English and even older English dialects on the notes," Amelia said, sounding aggravated.

"Someone who is an archivist would also know a lot about history, emblems, and cryptography," Finn replied, a gleam in his eyes. "It all fits. So let's get him!"

"But Finn, there's something else," Rob said, his voice grim.

Finn could feel the bad news on the horizon.

"What is it?" he asked, nervous.

"A woman by the name of Sarah Beaufort was attacked near your location ten minutes ago," Rob explained. "She was dragged from her home and taken away."

"That's terrible," Finn said. "But the killer was here about twenty minutes ago…"

"Be that as it may," Rob said. "Sarah Beaufort was taken in a hurry. Witnesses spotted a man with black hair and sharp features drag her away from the house. We have constables scouring the area."

"Chief," Amelia said loudly so she could be heard on the line. "What connection does this have to our killer?"

"Sarah Beaufort is a distant cousin of the King's," he said. "This can't be a coincidence."

"Agreed," Amelia said. "If you are scouring the area, we'll head to this Victor Hastings. We might get lucky."

"No," Rob said. "I already have someone closer. You two, go to the library where Hastings works, we've had a possible sighting of him there, and it's closer to your current location."

"Be safe," Rob said. "The man is clearly a maniac."

"Come on, Amelia," Finn said. "Let's be done with this once and for all."

The curtain was rising on a new act, one where he and Amelia weren't merely players, but playwrights scripting the final scenes of a murderer's macabre production.

CHAPTER TWENTY ONE

The ancient timbers of the door to Milton Library groaned a reluctant welcome as Finn Wright pushed against its weathered surface, his mind churning with the incriminating threads that were now inexorably weaving together. Amelia Winters stepped in beside him, her sharp gaze sweeping across the expanse as if to seize upon any shadow that dared to dance out of place.

"Here we are," Finn murmured, more to himself than to Amelia. The air was thick with the musk of knowledge, and there was something about the sheer volume of history contained within these walls that anchored him to the moment, despite the chaos of the case swirling around them.

The hum of silence that filled the library was punctured only by their footsteps, the sound amplified by the cavernous space. He could sense Amelia's presence—a steadfast force at his side—as they ventured deeper into the labyrinth of literature. The dim lighting cast long, monstrous shadows between the aisles, creating an ominous tapestry that seemed to cloak their approach.

With each step, the carpet swallowed the sound of their advance, lending a predatory stealth to their movements. Finn's eyes traced along the spines of countless tomes, some leather-bound, others threadbare from the touch of time. They spoke silently of forgotten tales and concealed wisdom, and amongst their volumes, he felt the whisper of answers drawing near.

"Feels like stepping back in time," Amelia said, her voice low but carrying in the stillness. Finn glanced at her, the briefest flicker of a smile crossing his lips in shared jest. Even now, amidst the grim hunt for a killer, their camaraderie found a way to assert itself.

"Let's hope it leads us to Hastings." Finn's hand brushed against the grain of a shelf as they passed, feeling the etchings of age. He considered the suspect—Victor Hastings—his mind connecting dots that once seemed disparate. An actor, archivist, and anti-monarchist, Hastings' life was steeped in the past, perhaps too deeply.

"Check this out," Amelia gestured towards a section where the books appeared older, the leather cracked and titles faded. Finn leaned closer, the scent of decaying paper and ink tugging at the edges of his consciousness. It was the smell of antiquity, of secrets bound in hide and pulp, and it resonated with a haunting familiarity.

"Antique parchments, historical narratives... it fits," Finn whispered, and he could feel the dark pulse of the case throbbing beneath the surface. The connection to theater, his access to ancient documents—it all culminated here, in the lair of knowledge that Hastings curated. "I wonder if he was consulting Professor Hemingway for his expertise as well. Maybe the old man unwittingly helped him put together the notes."

"It fits almost too well," Amelia added, her eyes reflecting the gravity of their situation. She traced a finger along the dusty cover of a book on British monarchies, and Finn saw the implication in her gesture. Their killer didn't just live in the past; he was using it as a weapon.

As they moved through the rows, the weight of their findings pressed invisibly upon them, each revelation adding momentum to their search. Victor Hastings had crafted a stage from death and history, and now, ensconced within the heart of his domain, Finn could feel the curtains drawing back, ready to reveal the final act.

Finn's hand brushed against the spines of ancient tomes, his eyes scanning for the entrance to Victor Hastings' personal study. The air was thick with the musk of old leather and the silent whispers of centuries past. Amelia moved ahead, her flashlight cutting through the dimness, casting elongated shadows between the bookshelves that seemed to stretch on indefinitely.

"Over here," she murmured, pausing before an almost hidden door, its edges well-blended with the mahogany wall paneling. Finn nodded, stepping forward to push it open, the hinges releasing a faint groan that echoed like a prelude to darker revelations. They stepped inside, their presence disrupting the stillness of the secluded room.

The study was a sanctuary of the past; maps unfurled across the walls like tapestries of exploration, depicting realms whose boundaries had long since shifted. Family trees branched out in intricate detail, the bloodlines of British royalty traced with painstaking precision. And there, in a glass cabinet, lay an assortment of signet rings, each one a symbol of lineage and power—silent witnesses to the heritage that Hastings both revered and despised.

Amelia pointed towards a crest similar to the one they had found at Rebecca Hanover's home. "These aren't just collector's items," she said, her voice laced with grim understanding, "they're trophies."

"Obsession turned deadly," Finn agreed, his gaze lingering on the collection that seemed to echo the killer's twisted justification for each life taken—an attempt to sever the roots of a history that had wronged him so deeply.

The heart of the lair presented itself as a large oak desk, a bastion amid the relics. A chair, slightly askew, hinted at recent occupation. Papers were strewn about, notes scrawled in a script that mimicked the annals of old English, meticulous sketches of royal emblems interspersed among them. It was clear that Hastings had immersed himself into a bygone era, blurring the lines between his identity and the persona of the avenger he had conjured from the depths of his resentment.

"Look at these," Amelia said, holding up a sheet adorned with a family crest they'd seen marked in blood at the crime scenes. "He's been planning this, studying his victims' lineages like a genealogist plotting a course through history."

"Except his endgame is murder," Finn added, the disgust rising within him like bile. He could almost picture Hastings sitting there, cold and calculating, choosing his next victim with the same detached curiosity of a scholar selecting a book from a shelf. This desk, this room, it wasn't just where Hastings researched; it was where the Secret Hand orchestrated his grim campaign against the descendants of those he deemed culpable for his family's downfall.

"Let's see what else we can find," Finn said, determination setting his jaw. Together, they sifted through the papers, searching for any clue that might lead them to Sarah Beaufort before it was too late.

Finn's heart hammered against his rib cage as he stepped into the chilling embrace of Victor Hastings' study. The air was dense, heavy with the musk of ancient tomes and the metallic tang of fear that seemed to seep from the walls themselves. Amelia moved with a silent grace beside him, her eyes scanning the room with an alertness that matched his own.

"Victor Hastings," Finn muttered under his breath, the name now synonymous with the faceless terror they had been chasing. It was no longer a question of if; the evidence sprawled out before them left no room for doubt. But the gnawing pit in his stomach twisted tighter as he considered the more pressing concerns: Where was Hastings now? And what of Sarah Beaufort?

"Alive or another trophy in this grotesque collection?" Amelia's voice cut through his thoughts, low and steady, yet Finn could detect the edge of urgency beneath her calm exterior.

"Let's find out," he replied, pushing the dread to the back of his mind where it simmered like a storm waiting to break.

They began to comb through the chaos of reports, maps, and diagrams that cluttered the oak desk, each document a glimpse into the mind of a scholar turned executioner. Amelia sifted through the stacks with practiced hands, while Finn's gaze was drawn to an open journal resting amongst the disarray. He approached it, a cold shiver slithering up his spine.

The pages were filled with entries penned in a meticulous hand, detailing the murders with a chilling sense of pride and precision. Finn felt the blood chill in his veins as he read descriptions of how each victim was chosen, the calculated planning, the cold deliberation of their final moments. This wasn't just a journal; it was a manifesto of madness, a road map of ruin inked in the blood of innocents.

"Amelia, look at this." His voice was a whisper, barely audible over the distant hum of London outside the library walls. He couldn't tear his eyes away from the page, from the stark reality of their killer's psyche laid bare.

She joined him, her expression tight as she read over his shoulder. "God, he's savored every moment," she said, her voice laced with revulsion. "We have to find him before he kills Sarah Beaufort!"

"Every detail is here," Finn added, flipping through the pages with a growing sense of horror. But as much as he wanted to slam the book shut and erase its existence, he knew that within these entries might lie the key to saving Sarah Beaufort—if only they weren't too late.

Finn's hands trembled as he turned to the final entry of the journal, his fingers grazing the edge of the paper as if it were made of glass. The words sprawled across the page in Victor Hastings' meticulous handwriting froze him to his core. "The finale approaches," it read, "the last act for Sarah Beaufort." There was no specific location, no address or landmark to pinpoint her fate. Only a phrase that echoed with an ominous tone— "where land meets sea."

"Amelia, this is it," Finn said, his voice steady despite the hammering in his chest. "He's planning to end it at the coast."

"Which coast, though?" Amelia replied, concern etched into her features. "This island's rimmed with shoreline."

"Details about tides… timings…" Finn muttered, scanning the text for more clues. "He's thorough, has to be something we're missing."

They poured over the journal once more, their eyes racing across the entries, until a pattern emerged—a fixation on history, lineage, and the cleansing power of water. The coast wouldn't just be any stretch of beach or cliffside; it would be symbolic, a place where Hastings could feel the weight of history bearing down upon his final act.

"Got it!" Amelia exclaimed, tapping a finger against a margin note referencing the execution of a royal during the medieval period. "Historic beheadings by the sea—Hastings must be taking her to Fortune's Coast! It's the area where an ancient Anglo-Saxon queen was executed by the French Normans during an uprising nearly a thousand years ago!"

"It's a big slice of coast," Finn said. "Well, need help."

"Let's call it in," Amelia suggested, already pulling out her phone.

With a deep breath, Finn stepped away from the desk, feeling the urgency of every passing second. He watched Amelia speak rapidly into her receiver, requesting immediate backup and a trace on Hastings. Her face was set, her determination clear even as she cracked a wry joke to the operator to keep the tension at bay.

"Scotland Yard's deploying units to the coast and they're pinging Hastings' financials for recent transactions," she reported, slipping her phone back into her pocket.

"Good. Let's move." Finn felt the gears shift within him, a relentless drive taking over. They had a direction, a slim thread to follow, but it was enough. Enough to fuel the hope that they might yet save Sarah Beaufort and stop Hastings before another life was claimed.

Together, they hastened from the library, the silence of the stacked volumes replaced by the urgency of their mission. As they exited into the cool air of the evening, the surrounding city seemed oblivious to the sinister drama unfolding. But not for long. With every step toward their car, with every mile they put between themselves and the library, Finn felt the unseen hand of the clock ticking down, each tick a thunderous beat in the quiet symphony of the impending night.

The coastal line loomed ahead, a vast expanse where land met the relentless churn of the sea. It was there, somewhere along that jagged edge, that Sarah might be held captive, her fate uncertain. Finn pressed his foot harder against the accelerator, willing the car to devour the miles faster.

Closing in on the coast, the urgency of their mission crystallized into a visceral need to act. Every fiber of Finn's being was attuned to the task at hand. The scenery outside blurred into streaks of color as they raced against the dying light, the glare of the headlights a beacon of hope piercing the encroaching darkness.

Amelia's hand found his on the gearshift, squeezing it briefly—a gesture of solidarity that fortified his resolve. Their hearts beat a furious rhythm, twin drums heralding the approach of what they both knew would be a final confrontation. With each passing second, the promise of resolution drew closer, their minds sharpened by the pressing need to end Victor Hastings' reign of terror and save Sarah Beaufort's life.

CHAPTER TWENTY TWO

The coastal line loomed ahead, a vast expanse where land met the relentless churn of the sea. It was there, somewhere along that jagged edge, that Sarah might be held captive, her fate uncertain. Finn pressed his foot harder against the accelerator, willing the car to devour the miles faster.

Closing in on Fortune's Coast, a bay on the coast of England known for its turbulent waters and rugged cliffs, the weather took a turn for the worse. Dark clouds gathered ominously overhead, casting a shadow over the landscape below. The wind howled like a banshee, whipping at their coats and sending salty spray from crashing waves into the air.

Amelia pointed towards a cluster of police vehicles parked near the shoreline, their lights flashing in sync with the raging storm. "There," she said above the din of nature's fury. "They're searching along this stretch."

Finn scanned the area with a critical eye, his instincts honed by years in law enforcement. "Hastings won't choose just any spot for his grand finale," he remarked, squinting through the rain-splattered windshield. "He craves drama, spectacle. Somewhere with history."

As they rounded a bend in the road, Finn's gaze locked onto a distant silhouette rising above the tumultuous sea—a lighthouse standing tall and proud amidst the tempest. His gut twisted with certainty as he realized its significance.

"That's it," Finn declared firmly, his voice cutting through the roar of wind and waves. "Hastings will want a stage for his final act. Not somewhere dreary like this beach on a January day. He'll choose that lighthouse as his backdrop, it's the only point of interest here.."

Amelia followed his gaze to the looming structure perched on a cliff overlooking Fortune's Coast. Its beacon flickered defiantly against nature's onslaught, beckoning ships home but now serving as an unwitting accomplice to impending tragedy.

Without another word spoken between them, Finn steered their car towards that solitary sentinel of light and shadow. As they drew closer to their destination, each passing moment heightened their awareness of what awaited them—the culmination of months of pursuit and investigation condensed into this pivotal juncture.

The lighthouse loomed larger with every heartbeat, its solid form etched against a sky painted by storm clouds and fading daylight. Finn felt an electric charge in the air as they approached—part anticipation, part dread—as if destiny itself awaited them at that windswept precipice.

The sky brooded over the heaving sea as Finn's gaze locked onto the figure of Victor Hastings disappearing into the lighthouse. The structure loomed, an ancient sentinel on the jagged coastline, its weathered stones clutching secrets in their gritty embrace. Finn's hand remained steady on the wheel as Amelia, beside him, jotted down Victor's inventory—a catalog of items betraying his intent to stay hidden.

"Looks like he's settling in for the long haul," Amelia remarked, her voice a low hum against the thrumming wind outside.

"Or he's making sure Sarah doesn't starve before we can make our move," Finn replied, eyes never leaving the beacon that now housed a viper within its walls.

They stood momentarily a discreet distance away, gravel crunching under their feet like a whispered warning. As they continued on, the briny scent of the ocean mingled with the tang of seaweed, wrapping around Finn like a shroud. His heart prowled in his chest, a caged animal awaiting release.

"I'll call in backup, but we need to act. Ready?" Amelia asked.

How Finn wished either of them was armed. But they had to act, time was of the essence. Backup would have to wait.

"Since yesterday," Finn muttered as they moved forward, their shadows elongating across the rocky terrain like dark omens trailing behind them.

Finn felt the absence of his gun through his jacket as they approached the lighthouse, a beacon that no longer promised guidance but threatened peril. He could hear the distant call of gulls, their cries oddly mournful under the cloak of night. The sea clashed with the rocks below, an endless battle that churned the water into froth.

"Feels like another world, this place, doesn't it?" Amelia quipped, her attempt at levity not quite reaching her eyes.

"As long as we don't end up staying here permanently," Finn said, his gaze scanning their surroundings for any sign of movement. Every sense was heightened, attuned to the danger that awaited within the spiraling tower.

"You mean like ghosts of the coast? A least we'd have each other for company," she whispered back, and despite the gravity of the situation, a smirk tugged at the corner of Finn's mouth.

Their steps were muffled by the damp grass, but each one echoed in Finn's ears, the sound amplified by the anticipation and dread that twisted in his gut.

The lighthouse door groaned open at Finn's touch, revealing a dimly lit spiral staircase that coiled upwards like a serpent ready to strike. He stepped inside, the musty smell of disuse and decay assaulting his nostrils. As they ascended, the staircase creaked beneath their weight, the sounds a discordant symphony punctuating the tense silence.

"Watch your step," Finn warned softly, noticing the uneven wear on the steps. "Wouldn't want to give him a heads-up with a grand entrance."

"Right, because I'm known for my grace and poise," Amelia shot back, her voice barely above a whisper.

With each rise of the staircase, the air grew thicker, as if charged with the imminence of what was to come. Finn counted the steps, a silent rhythm that kept time with his racing pulse. At mid-level, a sliver of light beckoned from beneath a door, the only barrier between them and their quarry.

"Showtime," Amelia breathed, and Finn nodded, his hand resting on the doorknob, waiting for the moment to strike.

Finn's hand lingered on the cool brass of the doorknob, delaying the inevitable for a heartbeat. The thin light seeping from the gap beneath the door painted a pale yellow line across the floor, bisecting the darkness that clung to them. He glanced at Amelia, her features drawn tight not with fear but with the gravity of their situation. She nodded once, sharp and quick. It was time.

He twisted the knob, easing the door open with calculated slowness. The hinges protested with a faint squeal, the sound grating in the oppressive silence. They stepped into the room, eyes scanning, muscles tensed for any hint of movement.

"Looks like we've found the actor's back stage," Finn murmured, taking in the stark space.

"Minus the cast, though. Or perhaps it's a small part?" Amelia quipped beside him, her gaze never leaving the shadows that clung to the walls.

The room was a relic of another era, with peeling wallpaper and a porthole window that offered a glimpse of the restless sea beyond. A single bulb dangled from the ceiling, casting more shadows than light. Finn felt the weightlessness of being so high up, the lighthouse like a needle piercing the sky.

"Careful now," he said.

They checked behind the sparse furniture—a rickety table, a couple of chairs that had seen better days. No sign of Hastings or his captive. But there was another door, slightly ajar, on the far side of the room. Finn approached it, every sense alert, aware of Amelia covering his back.

Finn pointed to it. Amelia nodded.

Finn pushed the door open, and as it swung inward, they were met with another staircase.

Inside, they cautiously ascend the winding staircase, each creaking step amplifying their anticipation of what awaits.

Finn's hand hovered near where his service weapon used to have been, an old habit from his days as a Special Agent. The spiral stairs twisted upwards like a helix, and with every step, the sea's roar grew fainter, replaced by the sinister symphony of groaning metal and his own thudding heartbeat. His eyes, meanwhile, traced the graffiti-laden walls, reading them like tea leaves for any hint of danger. Amelia, just behind him, moved with equal care, her presence a silent reassurance at his back.

"Ever feel like we're in one of those classic Gothic novels?" she whispered, her breath warm on his ear despite the chill that clung to the air.

"More like a trashy paperback," he replied without looking back. "One where the protagonists make questionable life choices."

"Like climbing a lighthouse after a madman?"

"Exactly."

They shared a smirk, but Finn could see the tightness around her eyes. It wasn't fear—he doubted anything could truly scare Amelia—it was focus, the kind that honed her instincts to a fine point.

As they neared the top, the staircase narrowed, forcing them to move even more carefully. Finn paused, listening. There was movement above: soft but deliberate. He signaled to Amelia, two fingers pointing upwards, and received a nod in response.

"Time to crash the party," he murmured. They ascended the last few steps in silence, every muscle tensed for the confrontation ahead.

At the top level, Finn breathed a sigh of relief.

Amelia rushed over to the unconscious Sarah Beaufort tied to a chair, her face pale but unharmed.

Then, something stirred from the shadows. Stepping forward, a tall, powerfully built man with piercing eyes and sharp features came, a cold smile playing on his lips.

"Looks like Sleeping Beauty's had a rough night," Finn quipped quietly, though his gaze never left Hastings.

The room was sparse, stripped down to bare wood and echoes. Sarah Beaufort, the missing cousin of the king, slumped in a wooden chair, her head lolling to one side. The ropes binding her were almost delicate, a mockery of restraint against the violence that had brought her here.

"Except our prince charming is more of a toad," Amelia added, her voice steady as she assessed the situation.

Hastings stood a few paces away, a silhouette framed by the weak light filtering from the stairwell. His posture was relaxed, too relaxed for someone with nowhere left to run. The smile on his face wasn't one of happiness; it was the one people wore when they believed they held all the cards.

"Detectives Wright and Winters, nice to see you again," Hastings said, his voice holding an edge of theatrical flair. "I very much enjoyed bumping into you the other day at the library. How lovely of you to join us for tonight's performance."

"Wouldn't miss it for the world," Finn replied, keeping his tone even. "Especially since you've been leaving such heartfelt invitations."

"Indeed," Hastings said, his eyes flickering with something dark. "History is being written tonight."

"By a librarian with delusions of grandeur," Amelia retorted.

"History often favors the bold," Hastings shot back, his cold smile unwavering.

"Sure," Finn said, stepping forward slowly, trying to gauge Hastings's intent. "But how does history treat the delusional?"

A tense standoff ensued between the detectives and Victor Hastings. His gaze flickering from Finn to Amelia, showing no signs of fear or remorse.

"Let's not pretend this will end well for you," Finn said, his voice calm but firm as he locked eyes with Hastings. "You took something precious from these families. And you might have kept going as The Secret Hand, if you hadn't had that need to be seen. A need for flair and dramatics. A flair that only an actor could possess. That was your undoing."

"Ah, but you see," Hastings replied coolly, "I've already walked so far. What's a few more steps?"

"You're cornered, Hastings," Amelia chimed in, her voice betraying none of the tension that Finn knew she felt. "Downstairs, the coast is swarming with constables. You're going to prison. This isn't a stage—you don't get to bow out after the final act."

"Life is a stage, my dear detective," Hastings said, his gaze sharp as flint. "And I am merely playing my part, a part to rid our society of this royal scum, to offer her up to the great elder one. He will be pleased."

"Problem is," Finn said, shifting his weight slightly, ready for any sudden moves, "the audience didn't much care for your performance. Reviews are in, and it turns out, you shouldn't have quit your day job."

"Bravo," Hastings said mockingly. "Always time for one last joke, right?"

"Jesus, you are melodramatic," Finn said. "I hope you're a better librarian than you are an actor."

That last quip seemed to sting Hastings.

Finn kept his gaze locked on Victor, reading the micro-expressions that flitted across his face, the slight twitch of muscle that betrayed his calm demeanor. This was a man who had steeped himself in history, who had let the bitterness of the past ferment into a toxic resolve.

"Let her go, Victor," Finn said firmly, his fingers itching for action but his mind acutely aware of the delicacy of the situation. "This ends now."

Victor's eyes, darkened by more than just the shadowed room, fixed on Finn with an intensity that spoke of deep-seated rage, a fire that had been smoldering for years, waiting for the perfect moment to burst forth.

"Ends?" Victor's tone was mocking. "Oh, detective, you must realize by now—this is merely the opening act."

Victor shifted his weight, a predator adjusting for a better vantage. The dim light glinted off the signet ring in his hand, casting elongated shadows that danced across the cracked walls of the lighthouse.

Amelia's hand rested by her sides, her eyes darting between Sarah and our quarry.

"You wear a royal ring?" Finn asked.

"It is not a royal ring, but the insignia of The Temple of the Silver Sun," he sniped.

"I hate all of this animosity. Let's talk, Victor," Finn said, keeping his tone steady. "We both know how this goes. Hostages, demands... But what is it you're really after?"

His eyes narrowed, flickering momentarily with something that might have been amusement—or madness. "You think you understand, Detective Wright? You think you can psychoanalyze me? I am the last of a line going back a thousand years. Why should this royal poison continue while my line ends?"

"Retribution against the crown? You're aware they won't even notice your little crusade," Finn prodded, careful to keep his voice calm, despite the pulse pounding in his ears. "But innocent lives, Victor? That's a heavy price to pay for a personal vendetta. And you've only targeted distant royals. Ones you could get close to. Not much of an assassin, are you?"

He paused then, and in that hesitation, Finn saw an opportunity. He continued, weaving a web of words meant to ensnare his attention. "The royals, they live in their palaces, insulated from the likes of us. But people like Sarah," Finn nodded toward the unconscious woman, "they're just trying to make their way in the world, same as you once did, despite their relations."

Victor's gaze wavered, darting to Sarah before snapping back to Finn. His jaw clenched, the muscles working beneath the skin. "She represents everything I despise—privilege, power, an unearned place in this world..."

"Yet here we are, giving her the stage," Finn added quickly, seizing the momentary crack in his composure. "The question is, Victor, do you want to be the villain of this piece, or is there more to your story? An anti-hero perhaps?"

Behind Victor, Amelia had begun inching closer to Sarah, her movements deliberate and silent. Finn knew she was counting on him to keep Victor's focus locked onto our verbal duel, which had become as palpable as the salt-laden breeze that slipped through the gaps in the aged wood.

"More to my story?" he echoed, the corner of his mouth twitching upwards. "Detective Wright, you have no idea. But perhaps you're right about one thing..."

As he trailed off, Finn sensed the shift in his attention—the internal struggle between his desire to explain himself and his need to maintain control. It was the distraction Amelia needed.

"Perhaps," Finn pushed, holding his gaze, "it's time to turn the page, Victor. Time to decide how history will remember you."

Amelia was almost at Sarah's side now, her fingers deftly working at the knots that held her captive. Finn kept talking, kept his focus on Victor, knowing that every second mattered, that every word could tip the balance.

The air in the lighthouse was thick with tension, a stifling cloak that seemed to muffle even the sound of the waves crashing against the rocks far below. Victor's silhouette loomed in the dim light, his shadow merging with the rusted gears and crumbling brick like a specter from the past.

"This is revolution, and I am the tip of the spear!" Victor shouted dramatically.

"Revolutionary hero?" Finn scoffed, his words calculated to provoke. "Seems to me you're nothing but a poor actor on a stage too grand for your talents."

Victor's eyes darkened, the muscles in his jaw twitching with a cocktail of anger and hurt pride. For a moment, he faltered, the facade of the cold, calculating assassin slipping to reveal the wounded man underneath.

"An actor?" His voice was a hiss, a leaking tire before the blowout. "I am the hand of retribution, the—"

"Hand of retribution?" Finn interrupted, allowing a smirk to play on my lips despite the danger. "More like a puppet, dancing on strings of misguided vengeance. Vanity. Melodramatics. Just plain maniac who will leave nothing behind but a footnote in a newspaper. I'll be the one giving the interviews while you rot in prison, anonymous, having achieved nothing, spending your days as a hack."

That did it. Victor's controlled exterior shattered like glass under a hammer's weight. With a guttural cry, he lunged at Finn, the hidden blade in his hand glinting briefly as it caught the faint light from the stairwell.

Adrenaline surged through Finn's veins, a primal response that had nothing to do with thought and everything to do with survival. Finn sidestepped, narrowly avoiding the cold blade that whispered death. The close call sent shivers up his spine, the kind that warned of how close he had come to a permanent end.

"Amelia!" Finn shouted, his voice echoing off the walls. In the periphery of his vision, Finn saw her spring into action, her own training kicking in with seamless precision.

Victor's eyes blazed with a fervor that bordered on madness as he turned and lunged at Finn, the blade flashing dangerously in the dim light of the lighthouse. With a swift sidestep, Finn thought he had narrowly avoided the lethal arc of the weapon again, but then he felt a searing pain erupt in his side as Victor's strike had opened a wound in him. He was losing blood. Fast.

Amelia's scream pierced the tense air as she lunged towards Victor, her strikes filled with a fierce determination. But Victor, fueled by his twisted mission, overpowered her with a brutal efficiency that sent shock waves through Finn. She wouldn't hold out long under those fierce punches.

As Finn felt his strength wane and darkness encroach on his vision, a primal instinct surged within him. Ignoring the searing agony in his side, he mustered every ounce of willpower and pushed himself upright. With a guttural roar, he launched himself at Victor, their bodies colliding with a violent force that shattered through the nearest window.

The world outside rushed past them in a blur of motion as they plummeted towards the unforgiving rocks below. In a desperate bid to save Amelia and end this deadly dance, Finn grappled with Victor even as gravity pulled them inexorably downwards.

With one final push, Finn managed to seize hold of the crumbling edge while Victor slipped from his grasp, hurtling down into the abyss below. As Finn dangled precariously above the churning sea, consciousness slipping away like sand through his fingers, he heard frantic voices calling out to him.

Through a haze of pain and fading awareness, Finn felt strong, faithful pulling him up to safety. The faces of Amelia and Sarah swam into view, their expressions etched with relief and concern.

"Finn..." Amelia said.

Weakly managing a smile through gritted teeth, Finn said: "Looks like Victor exited stage left."

Amelia smiled. "I'm smiling because I've stopped the bleeding, not because of the joke."

"Don't lie," Finn said.

Amelia smiled and kissed him on the forehead. "Let's get you an ambulance."

EPILOGUE

The pale morning light filtered through the high windows of Hertfordshire Constabulary headquarters, casting a serene glow over the bustling office space. Finn Wright stood slightly aloof from the crowd, a mug of steaming coffee in hand, his gaze lingering on the lively throng of detectives exchanging hushed stories of last week's take down Amelia was beside him, her sharp green eyes catching every detail around them, despite the casual tilt of her head as she listened to the muted celebrations.

"Never thought I'd see the day when a librarian would out fight Finn," Amelia quipped, nudging Finn on the arm with an elbow that held years of shared toils and triumphs. Her smile, often reserved, now played freely on her lips.

"It's because I have overdue books," Finn said. "I'd have rather put him in cuffs, though."

"He won't hurt anyone else now," Amelia said.

Their banter was cut short as Rob Collins approached, his posture relaxed yet carrying the authority befitting his role. His eyes met Finn's with an unspoken camaraderie that only old college mates could share, while he addressed Amelia with the respectful nod due to a trusted colleague.

"Good work, both of you," Rob said, his voice carrying a genuine warmth that filled the space between the words. "The Home Office is singing your praises. Commendations are in order for solving the case and apprehending Hastings. Even the King apparently will send a letter of thanks."

"Thank you, Chief," Amelia responded, her tone serious once more, though her eyes still reflected the embers of their earlier humor.

Finn stood in the midst of a gentle buzz that filled the Hertfordshire Constabulary headquarters, his gaze sweeping over the familiar terrain of desks cluttered with files and walls adorned with maps and whiteboards scrawled with case details. Morning sunlight filtered through the windows, dust motes dancing in the beams like tiny specters of the night's chaos now put to rest.

He leaned against a desk, arms folded, a small smile playing on his lips as he observed this world that had once seemed so foreign. Underneath the hum of conversation and the clatter of keyboards, there was an undercurrent of camaraderie, of shared purpose. It was a far cry from the cold scrutiny he'd once endured in the sterile halls of the FBI.

His eyes caught a fleeting reflection in the glass—a man with haunted eyes and a resolute jaw. Finn barely recognized himself; he was no longer just the outcast agent grappling with shadows of suspicion. Here, he was Detective Wright, cloaked in the respect and trust he'd earned from his peers.

Yet, despite the lightness in the air, he couldn't shake off the sense of unfinished business that gnawed at him. Max Vilne, the man who was more phantom than flesh, still eluded their grasp. He was a name whispered in dark corners, a ghost story for criminals, always one step ahead. And there was the looming court date back in the States, a specter of Finn's past that still demanded a reckoning.

"Lost in thought?"

The voice, tinged with warmth and a hint of mischief, drew Finn from his reverie. Amelia stood before him, her usual stoicism softened by a glow of pride. Her presence was a grounding force, an anchor in the tumultuous sea that was his life these days.

"Sometimes I wonder if you ever stop working, even in your head," she continued, the slight tilt of her head inviting him into a reprieve from the weight that burdened his thoughts.

"Old habits," Finn replied with a wry smile, recognizing the truth in her words. He noticed the way her eyes crinkled when she smiled, another reason to love her. He'd add it to the list.

"Considering we've stared down death together and came out on top..." Amelia paused, her gaze locking onto his with an intensity that sent a ripple through the calm surface of the morning. "The case is done. Isn't it about time you asked me out on a date?"

Finn blinked, momentarily taken aback. The invitation hung between them, bold and unexpected—just like Amelia herself. He could see the challenge in her eyes, but also a warmth that spoke of more than just the adrenaline-fueled bond they'd forged in the fires of their investigation.

"Amelia, I would be—"

His response was cut short as the door to the squad room burst open with an urgency that immediately set Finn's nerves on edge. A young constable, chest heaving with the sprint from the communications room, skidded to a halt before them, his eyes wide with a blend of excitement and apprehension.

"Sir, ma'am," he gasped out, "Max Vilne's been spotted. Great Amwell, not five minutes from where you're staying, Detective Wright."

The air in the room seemed to constrict, the celebratory atmosphere sucked away in an instant. Finn's mind bristled as the name Max Vilne clawed through his thoughts, the specter of the cunning killer eclipsing the momentary lightness.

"Can't even let us have this one moment, can he?" Amelia sighed, the stoicism in her voice unable to mask the undercurrent of frustration. Her features were etched with resignation, the familiar mask of the investigator sliding back into place over her earlier softness.

"Life never pans out the way you want," Finn said. "This is the third time I'll be chasing Vilne. We can't fail again."

NOW AVAILABLE!

WHEN YOU'RE GONE
(A Finn Wright FBI Suspense Thriller—Book Seven)

When a killer in London strikes using Victorian-era weaponry, FBI Agent Finn Wright plunges into eerie murder scenes of a bygone age. With only cryptic poetry as his clue, will Finn stop the murderer—or face his own gruesome end?

"A masterpiece of thriller and mystery."
—Books and Movie Reviews, Roberto Mattos (re Once Gone)

WHEN YOU'RE GONE is book #7 in a long-anticipated new series by #1 bestseller and USA Today bestselling author Blake Pierce, whose bestseller Once Gone (a free download) has received over 7,000 five star ratings and reviews. The series begins with WHEN YOU'RE MINE (book #1).

Recently put on leave and divorced after he caught his wife cheating on him, Finn needs a fresh start in life. He thought a visit to an old friend in a tranquil small town in England would be a good step—until his friend needs his expertise with a series of murders in spectacular estates. With the local police chief impressed, Finn is asked to stay on, as they need his help.

As Finn's eyes are opened to a world of storied wealth, history and privacy, he realizes that he has much to learn—but that killers are universal….

A page-turning crime thriller featuring a brilliant and tortured FBI agent, the Finn Wright series is a riveting mystery, packed with non-stop action, suspense, twists and turns, revelations, and driven by a breakneck pace that will keep you flipping pages late into the night. Fans of Rachel Caine, Teresa Driscoll and Robert Dugoni are sure to fall in love.

Future books in the series are also available!

"An edge of your seat thriller in a new series that keeps you turning pages! ...So many twists, turns and red herrings... I can't wait to see what happens next."
—Reader review (Her Last Wish)

"A strong, complex story about two FBI agents trying to stop a serial killer. If you want an author to capture your attention and have you guessing, yet trying to put the pieces together, Pierce is your author!"
—Reader review (Her Last Wish)

"A typical Blake Pierce twisting, turning, roller coaster ride suspense thriller. Will have you turning the pages to the last sentence of the last chapter!!!"
—Reader review (City of Prey)

"Right from the start we have an unusual protagonist that I haven't seen done in this genre before. The action is nonstop... A very atmospheric novel that will keep you turning pages well into the wee hours."
—Reader review (City of Prey)

"Everything that I look for in a book... a great plot, interesting characters, and grabs your interest right away. The book moves along at a breakneck pace and stays that way until the end. Now on go I to book two!"
—Reader review (Girl, Alone)

"Exciting, heart pounding, edge of your seat book... a must read for mystery and suspense readers!"
—Reader review (Girl, Alone)

Blake Pierce

Blake Pierce is the USA Today bestselling author of the RILEY PAGE mystery series, which includes seventeen books. Blake Pierce is also the author of the MACKENZIE WHITE mystery series, comprising fourteen books; of the AVERY BLACK mystery series, comprising six books; of the KERI LOCKE mystery series, comprising five books; of the MAKING OF RILEY PAIGE mystery series, comprising six books; of the KATE WISE mystery series, comprising seven books; of the CHLOE FINE psychological suspense mystery, comprising six books; of the JESSIE HUNT psychological suspense thriller series, comprising thirty-five books (and counting); of the AU PAIR psychological suspense thriller series, comprising three books; of the ZOE PRIME mystery series, comprising six books; of the ADELE SHARP mystery series, comprising sixteen books, of the EUROPEAN VOYAGE cozy mystery series, comprising six books; of the LAURA FROST FBI suspense thriller, comprising eleven books; of the ELLA DARK FBI suspense thriller, comprising twenty-one books (and counting); of the A YEAR IN EUROPE cozy mystery series, comprising nine books, of the AVA GOLD mystery series, comprising six books; of the RACHEL GIFT mystery series, comprising thirteen books (and counting); of the VALERIE LAW mystery series, comprising nine books; of the PAIGE KING mystery series, comprising eight books; of the MAY MOORE mystery series, comprising eleven books; of the CORA SHIELDS mystery series, comprising eight books; of the NICKY LYONS mystery series, comprising eight books, of the CAMI LARK mystery series, comprising ten books; of the AMBER YOUNG mystery series, comprising seven books (and counting); of the DAISY FORTUNE mystery series, comprising five books; of the FIONA RED mystery series, comprising eleven books (and counting); of the FAITH BOLD mystery series, comprising eleven books (and counting); of the JULIETTE HART mystery series, comprising five books (and counting); of the MORGAN CROSS mystery series, comprising nine books (and counting); of the FINN WRIGHT mystery series, comprising five books (and counting); of the new SHEILA STONE suspense thriller series, comprising five books (and counting); and of the new RACHEL BLACKWOOD suspense thriller series, comprising five books (and counting).

An avid reader and lifelong fan of the mystery and thriller genres, Blake loves to hear from you, so please feel free to visit www.blakepierceauthor.com to learn more and stay in touch.

BOOKS BY BLAKE PIERCE

RACHEL BLACKWOOD SUSPENSE THRILLER
NOT THIS WAY (Book #1)
NOT THIS TIME (Book #2)
NOT THIS CLOSE (Book #3)
NOT THIS ROAD (Book #4)
NOT THIS LATE (Book #5)

SHEILA STONE SUSPENSE THRILLER
SILENT GIRL (Book #1)
SILENT TRAIL (Book #2)
SILENT NIGHT (Book #3)
SILENT HOUSE (Book #4)
SILENT SCREAM (Book #5)

FINN WRIGHT MYSTERY SERIES
WHEN YOU'RE MINE (Book #1)
WHEN YOU'RE SAFE (Book #2)
WHEN YOU'RE CLOSE (Book #3)
WHEN YOU'RE SLEEPING (Book #4)
WHEN YOU'RE SANE (Book #5)

MORGAN CROSS MYSTERY SERIES
FOR YOU (Book #1)
FOR RAGE (Book #2)
FOR LUST (Book #3)
FOR WRATH (Book #4)
FOREVER (Book #5)
FOR US (Book #6)
FOR NOW (Book #7)
FOR ONCE (Book #8)
FOR ETERNITY (Book #9)

JULIETTE HART MYSTERY SERIES
NOTHING TO FEAR (Book #1)
NOTHING THERE (Book #2)

NOTHING WATCHING (Book #3)
NOTHING HIDING (Book #4)
NOTHING LEFT (Book #5)

FAITH BOLD MYSTERY SERIES
SO LONG (Book #1)
SO COLD (Book #2)
SO SCARED (Book #3)
SO NORMAL (Book #4)
SO FAR GONE (Book #5)
SO LOST (Book #6)
SO ALONE (Book #7)
SO FORGOTTEN (Book #8)
SO INSANE (Book #9)
SO SMITTEN (Book #10)
SO SIMPLE (Book #11)

FIONA RED MYSTERY SERIES
LET HER GO (Book #1)
LET HER BE (Book #2)
LET HER HOPE (Book #3)
LET HER WISH (Book #4)
LET HER LIVE (Book #5)
LET HER RUN (Book #6)
LET HER HIDE (Book #7)
LET HER BELIEVE (Book #8)
LET HER FORGET (Book #9)
LET HER TRY (Book #10)
LET HER PLAY (Book #11)

DAISY FORTUNE MYSTERY SERIES
NEED YOU (Book #1)
CLAIM YOU (Book #2)
CRAVE YOU (Book #3)
CHOOSE YOU (Book #4)
CHASE YOU (Book #5)

AMBER YOUNG MYSTERY SERIES
ABSENT PITY (Book #1)
ABSENT REMORSE (Book #2)

ABSENT FEELING (Book #3)
ABSENT MERCY (Book #4)
ABSENT REASON (Book #5)
ABSENT SANITY (Book #6)
ABSENT LIFE (Book #7)

CAMI LARK MYSTERY SERIES
JUST ME (Book #1)
JUST OUTSIDE (Book #2)
JUST RIGHT (Book #3)
JUST FORGET (Book #4)
JUST ONCE (Book #5)
JUST HIDE (Book #6)
JUST NOW (Book #7)
JUST HOPE (Book #8)
JUST LEAVE (Book #9)
JUST TONIGHT (Book #10)

NICKY LYONS MYSTERY SERIES
ALL MINE (Book #1)
ALL HIS (Book #2)
ALL HE SEES (Book #3)
ALL ALONE (Book #4)
ALL FOR ONE (Book #5)
ALL HE TAKES (Book #6)
ALL FOR ME (Book #7)
ALL IN (Book #8)

CORA SHIELDS MYSTERY SERIES
UNDONE (Book #1)
UNWANTED (Book #2)
UNHINGED (Book #3)
UNSAID (Book #4)
UNGLUED (Book #5)
UNSTABLE (Book #6)
UNKNOWN (Book #7)
UNAWARE (Book #8)

MAY MOORE SUSPENSE THRILLER
NEVER RUN (Book #1)

NEVER TELL (Book #2)
NEVER LIVE (Book #3)
NEVER HIDE (Book #4)
NEVER FORGIVE (Book #5)
NEVER AGAIN (Book #6)
NEVER LOOK BACK (Book #7)
NEVER FORGET (Book #8)
NEVER LET GO (Book #9)
NEVER PRETEND (Book #10)
NEVER HESITATE (Book #11)

PAIGE KING MYSTERY SERIES
THE GIRL HE PINED (Book #1)
THE GIRL HE CHOSE (Book #2)
THE GIRL HE TOOK (Book #3)
THE GIRL HE WISHED (Book #4)
THE GIRL HE CROWNED (Book #5)
THE GIRL HE WATCHED (Book #6)
THE GIRL HE WANTED (Book #7)
THE GIRL HE CLAIMED (Book #8)

VALERIE LAW MYSTERY SERIES
NO MERCY (Book #1)
NO PITY (Book #2)
NO FEAR (Book #3)
NO SLEEP (Book #4)
NO QUARTER (Book #5)
NO CHANCE (Book #6)
NO REFUGE (Book #7)
NO GRACE (Book #8)
NO ESCAPE (Book #9)

RACHEL GIFT MYSTERY SERIES
HER LAST WISH (Book #1)
HER LAST CHANCE (Book #2)
HER LAST HOPE (Book #3)
HER LAST FEAR (Book #4)
HER LAST CHOICE (Book #5)
HER LAST BREATH (Book #6)
HER LAST MISTAKE (Book #7)

HER LAST DESIRE (Book #8)
HER LAST REGRET (Book #9)
HER LAST HOUR (Book #10)
HER LAST SHOT (Book #11)
HER LAST PRAYER (Book #12)
HER LAST LIE (Book #13)

AVA GOLD MYSTERY SERIES
CITY OF PREY (Book #1)
CITY OF FEAR (Book #2)
CITY OF BONES (Book #3)
CITY OF GHOSTS (Book #4)
CITY OF DEATH (Book #5)
CITY OF VICE (Book #6)

A YEAR IN EUROPE
A MURDER IN PARIS (Book #1)
DEATH IN FLORENCE (Book #2)
VENGEANCE IN VIENNA (Book #3)
A FATALITY IN SPAIN (Book #4)

ELLA DARK FBI SUSPENSE THRILLER
GIRL, ALONE (Book #1)
GIRL, TAKEN (Book #2)
GIRL, HUNTED (Book #3)
GIRL, SILENCED (Book #4)
GIRL, VANISHED (Book 5)
GIRL ERASED (Book #6)
GIRL, FORSAKEN (Book #7)
GIRL, TRAPPED (Book #8)
GIRL, EXPENDABLE (Book #9)
GIRL, ESCAPED (Book #10)
GIRL, HIS (Book #11)
GIRL, LURED (Book #12)
GIRL, MISSING (Book #13)
GIRL, UNKNOWN (Book #14)
GIRL, DECEIVED (Book #15)
GIRL, FORLORN (Book #16)
GIRL, REMADE (Book #17)
GIRL, BETRAYED (Book #18)

GIRL, BOUND (Book #19)
GIRL, REFORMED (Book #20)
GIRL, REBORN (Book #21)

LAURA FROST FBI SUSPENSE THRILLER
ALREADY GONE (Book #1)
ALREADY SEEN (Book #2)
ALREADY TRAPPED (Book #3)
ALREADY MISSING (Book #4)
ALREADY DEAD (Book #5)
ALREADY TAKEN (Book #6)
ALREADY CHOSEN (Book #7)
ALREADY LOST (Book #8)
ALREADY HIS (Book #9)
ALREADY LURED (Book #10)
ALREADY COLD (Book #11)

EUROPEAN VOYAGE COZY MYSTERY SERIES
MURDER (AND BAKLAVA) (Book #1)
DEATH (AND APPLE STRUDEL) (Book #2)
CRIME (AND LAGER) (Book #3)
MISFORTUNE (AND GOUDA) (Book #4)
CALAMITY (AND A DANISH) (Book #5)
MAYHEM (AND HERRING) (Book #6)

ADELE SHARP MYSTERY SERIES
LEFT TO DIE (Book #1)
LEFT TO RUN (Book #2)
LEFT TO HIDE (Book #3)
LEFT TO KILL (Book #4)
LEFT TO MURDER (Book #5)
LEFT TO ENVY (Book #6)
LEFT TO LAPSE (Book #7)
LEFT TO VANISH (Book #8)
LEFT TO HUNT (Book #9)
LEFT TO FEAR (Book #10)
LEFT TO PREY (Book #11)
LEFT TO LURE (Book #12)
LEFT TO CRAVE (Book #13)
LEFT TO LOATHE (Book #14)

LEFT TO HARM (Book #15)
LEFT TO RUIN (Book #16)

THE AU PAIR SERIES
ALMOST GONE (Book#1)
ALMOST LOST (Book #2)
ALMOST DEAD (Book #3)

ZOE PRIME MYSTERY SERIES
FACE OF DEATH (Book#1)
FACE OF MURDER (Book #2)
FACE OF FEAR (Book #3)
FACE OF MADNESS (Book #4)
FACE OF FURY (Book #5)
FACE OF DARKNESS (Book #6)

A JESSIE HUNT PSYCHOLOGICAL SUSPENSE SERIES
THE PERFECT WIFE (Book #1)
THE PERFECT BLOCK (Book #2)
THE PERFECT HOUSE (Book #3)
THE PERFECT SMILE (Book #4)
THE PERFECT LIE (Book #5)
THE PERFECT LOOK (Book #6)
THE PERFECT AFFAIR (Book #7)
THE PERFECT ALIBI (Book #8)
THE PERFECT NEIGHBOR (Book #9)
THE PERFECT DISGUISE (Book #10)
THE PERFECT SECRET (Book #11)
THE PERFECT FAÇADE (Book #12)
THE PERFECT IMPRESSION (Book #13)
THE PERFECT DECEIT (Book #14)
THE PERFECT MISTRESS (Book #15)
THE PERFECT IMAGE (Book #16)
THE PERFECT VEIL (Book #17)
THE PERFECT INDISCRETION (Book #18)
THE PERFECT RUMOR (Book #19)
THE PERFECT COUPLE (Book #20)
THE PERFECT MURDER (Book #21)
THE PERFECT HUSBAND (Book #22)
THE PERFECT SCANDAL (Book #23)

THE PERFECT MASK (Book #24)
THE PERFECT RUSE (Book #25)
THE PERFECT VENEER (Book #26)
THE PERFECT PEOPLE (Book #27)
THE PERFECT WITNESS (Book #28)
THE PERFECT APPEARANCE (Book #29)
THE PERFECT TRAP (Book #30)
THE PERFECT EXPRESSION (Book #31)
THE PERFECT ACCOMPLICE (Book #32)
THE PERFECT SHOW (Book #33)
THE PERFECT POISE (Book #34)
THE PERFECT CROWD (Book #35)

CHLOE FINE PSYCHOLOGICAL SUSPENSE SERIES
NEXT DOOR (Book #1)
A NEIGHBOR'S LIE (Book #2)
CUL DE SAC (Book #3)
SILENT NEIGHBOR (Book #4)
HOMECOMING (Book #5)
TINTED WINDOWS (Book #6)

KATE WISE MYSTERY SERIES
IF SHE KNEW (Book #1)
IF SHE SAW (Book #2)
IF SHE RAN (Book #3)
IF SHE HID (Book #4)
IF SHE FLED (Book #5)
IF SHE FEARED (Book #6)
IF SHE HEARD (Book #7)

THE MAKING OF RILEY PAIGE SERIES
WATCHING (Book #1)
WAITING (Book #2)
LURING (Book #3)
TAKING (Book #4)
STALKING (Book #5)
KILLING (Book #6)

RILEY PAIGE MYSTERY SERIES
ONCE GONE (Book #1)

ONCE TAKEN (Book #2)
ONCE CRAVED (Book #3)
ONCE LURED (Book #4)
ONCE HUNTED (Book #5)
ONCE PINED (Book #6)
ONCE FORSAKEN (Book #7)
ONCE COLD (Book #8)
ONCE STALKED (Book #9)
ONCE LOST (Book #10)
ONCE BURIED (Book #11)
ONCE BOUND (Book #12)
ONCE TRAPPED (Book #13)
ONCE DORMANT (Book #14)
ONCE SHUNNED (Book #15)
ONCE MISSED (Book #16)
ONCE CHOSEN (Book #17)

MACKENZIE WHITE MYSTERY SERIES
BEFORE HE KILLS (Book #1)
BEFORE HE SEES (Book #2)
BEFORE HE COVETS (Book #3)
BEFORE HE TAKES (Book #4)
BEFORE HE NEEDS (Book #5)
BEFORE HE FEELS (Book #6)
BEFORE HE SINS (Book #7)
BEFORE HE HUNTS (Book #8)
BEFORE HE PREYS (Book #9)
BEFORE HE LONGS (Book #10)
BEFORE HE LAPSES (Book #11)
BEFORE HE ENVIES (Book #12)
BEFORE HE STALKS (Book #13)
BEFORE HE HARMS (Book #14)

AVERY BLACK MYSTERY SERIES
CAUSE TO KILL (Book #1)
CAUSE TO RUN (Book #2)
CAUSE TO HIDE (Book #3)
CAUSE TO FEAR (Book #4)
CAUSE TO SAVE (Book #5)
CAUSE TO DREAD (Book #6)

KERI LOCKE MYSTERY SERIES
A TRACE OF DEATH (Book #1)
A TRACE OF MURDER (Book #2)
A TRACE OF VICE (Book #3)
A TRACE OF CRIME (Book #4)
A TRACE OF HOPE (Book #5)

Made in United States
North Haven, CT
07 January 2025

64051498R00112